Love of  From First Sight to Forever.

Vidya Iyer

Copyright © 2025 Vidya Iyer
all rights reserved.

Disclaimer *"This is a work of fiction. Names, characters, businesses, places, events, locales, and incidents are either the products of the author's imagination or used in a fictitious manner. Any resemblance to actual persons, living or dead, or actual events is purely coincidental."*

Table of Contents

Chapter One: When Fate Calls 1

Chapter Two: The Unexpected Feeling 5

Chapter Three: A Walk Toward Destiny 10

Chapter Four: A Silent Connection........................... 16

Chapter Five: When Eyes Meet Hearts...................... 19

Chapter Six: Moments That Matters......................... 23

Chapter Seven: A Love In Between.......................... 27

Chapter Eight: Silent Signals, Loud Hearts 32

Chapter Nine: Love's Quiet Revolution..................... 37

Chapter Ten: A Moment To Forever 42

Chapter Eleven: Love On The Fast Lane................... 45

Chapter Twelve: Breaking The Shell......................... 50

Chapter Thirteen: First Kiss, Forever Memory 56

Chapter Fourteen: Passion's Silent War 60

Chapter Fifteen: Through Her Eyes, Through His Heart 63

Chapter Sixteen: When Love Knocks........................ 67

Chapter Seventeen: Held By The Clock 72

Chapter Eighteen: The Promise Of Soon................... 78

Chapter Nineteen: A Love That Crosses Miles 83

Chapter Twenty: Steps Into His World 87

Chapter Twenty-One: A Hug That Heals 92

Chapter Twenty-Two: Sana's Eventful Day 98

Chapter Twenty-Three: The Fire Between Us 103

Chapter Twenty-Four: A Weekend to Remember ... 108

Chapter Twenty-Five: Tides of Love 114

Chapter Twenty-Six: A Night of Love and Promises 119

Chapter Twenty-Seven: The Test of Tradition 126

Chapter Twenty-Eight: The Silent Struggle 131

Chapter Twenty-Nine: A Ray of Hope 136

Chapter Thirty: When Culture Collide 142

Chapter Thirty-One: Against All Odds 148

Chapter Thirty-Two: Hearts Against Caste 153

Chapter Thirty-Three: Bound By Fate 160

Chapter Thirty-Four: A Battle For Love 165

Chapter Thirty-Five: Shadows of Doubt, Lights of Hope 170

Chapter Thirty-Six: Transformation Of The Heart .. 176

Chapter Thirty-Seven: Destiny's Crossroads 182

Chapter Thirty-Eight: The Price Of Silence 190

Chapter Thirty-Nine: Love's Test 198

Chapter Forty: Silent Confessions 207

Chapter Forty-One: When Hearts Speak 214

Chapter Forty-Two: Written In The Stars 221

Chapter Forty-Three: A Union of Hearts And Cultures 231

Chapter Forty-Four: Sun And Moon Vows 240

Chapter Forty-Five: The Rhythm of Us 246

Chapter Forty-Six: A Path of Togetherness 252

Chapter Forty-Seven: Embracing Love 259

Chapter Forty-Eight: A Tapestry of Love 266

Chapter Forty-Nine: From Slumber To Celebration 273

Chapter Fifty: Serenade of Souls 280

Epilogue 284

Acknowledgment 292

Chapter One:
When Fate Calls

Sidesh Sharma gripped the steering wheel, his eyes flicking between the road ahead and the time on his watch. Ghaziabad's hot, humid air, honking horns, and slow-moving traffic made his daily drive to Noida feel like an eternity. Even in the frustration, there was a glimmer of positivity. *At least my office isn't in Delhi or Gurgaon*, he thought. That would mean hours on the road every day. This is better. The thought comforted him as he pushed through the gridlock, knowing he had just 45 minutes left to get to his meeting.

Finally, after what felt like an eternity, the traffic cleared. Sidesh accelerated, eager to reach the office on time. Punctuality was important to him; he had always believed in the principle that the want of punctuality is a want of virtue. It was a motto he had lived by for years, and he wasn't about to break it now. He parked his car and stepped out, determined to make the most of his time before the meeting. As he approached the entrance, he quickly glanced at his watch and smiled to himself; he had 20 minutes to prepare.

His thoughts, however, shifted the moment he entered the lobby. Sidesh had seen the receptionist, Mona, plenty of times, but today, someone else was with her. A woman whose presence caught him off guard in the most unexpected way. Sidesh froze for a moment. She had flawless glowing skin, long chocolate-brown hair that cascaded like a silk curtain, and a small mole on her left cheek that only added to her beauty. An innocence in her features made Sidesh's heart skip a beat.

Mona broke the silence, speaking to him with a friendly smile. "Good morning, Sir. This is Ms. Sanaya Iyer. She joined today to fill in for me while I'm on maternity leave."

Sanaya turned to face him, her smile warm and confident. "Hello, Sir, nice to meet you," she said in a smooth voice that seemed to seep into Sidesh's very soul.

Sidesh blinked, still dazed, but responded, "Welcome to VS Corporations, Ms. Sanaya. I look forward to working with you." He smiled though his heart was still racing. As he walked towards his office, he couldn't help but glance back at her, feeling as though his world had been shifted slightly off balance. What just happened? Sidesh thought. He had never believed in love at first sight. It sounded silly, something out of a movie. But now, for the first time in his life, he was beginning to understand why people spoke of it so highly.

He sank into his office chair, running a hand through his hair as he tried to steady his thoughts. *Focus, Sid*. He reminded himself sharply that you've got a meeting to prep for, flipping open his laptop. Yet the harder he tried to bury himself in charts and figures, the more his mind betrayed him, circling back to her. Sanaya. Her name was almost magnetic, drawing him into a reverie he couldn't quite shake. He couldn't lose himself over fleeting distractions—especially not during work. But this wasn't fleeting. It wasn't just her smile; it was something deeper that left him both restless and strangely alive.

The meeting felt like a blur, a dance of numbers, strategies, and sharp negotiations that Sidesh moved through with the precision of someone who had done it a thousand times. He led the conversation effortlessly, guiding each discussion to a conclusion with the quiet confidence he was known for. When they wrapped things up after three long hours and secured the deal, a familiar rush of accomplishment surged through him. Yet, as he exchanged firm handshakes and polite smiles with the clients, something lingered- a gnawing thought, a pull in his chest, maybe she is my lucky charm. *What's wrong with me?* He wondered, his brow furrowing as he walked back to his office. *Since when I started believing in signs, in odd superstitions!* He tried to push it away, but her image lingered gently in his mind, like a soft melody he couldn't quite forget. It wasn't unsettling but rather a quiet presence woven into his thoughts in a way that felt both calming and inevitable.

He shook his head, a soft chuckle escaping his lips, but the feeling persisted, a quiet ache beneath the surface. Sanaya, her name drifted through his thoughts like a song, and with it came a rush of lightness, as if the world's weight had momentarily lifted. How could one person do that? He didn't understand it. He only knew that thinking of her made everything easier, brighter, and more alive. Her pull over him unsettled him, yet he couldn't deny the truth. She was changing something inside him, and he wasn't sure and he didn't wanted it to stop.

Sidesh couldn't resist the urge to take a glance at the lobby as he passed by on his way back to his office. There she was again, Sanaya, sitting at the reception desk in a simple pink churidar, talking intently with Mona. The sight made him pause. He wanted to stop, to sit and just watch her, but he knew better than to appear like a fool. Still, the temptation to get to know her was overwhelming. What is it about her? he wondered, his heart racing again.

Later that day, Sidesh called Raj, his personal assistant, and asked him to bring in Mr. Gupta, the HR manager. As they sat together in Sidesh's office, discussing Mona's upcoming maternity leave and her replacement, Sidesh curiously asked about the new hire. He also asked Mr. Gupta to share her resume, which he shared immediately.

"Is there a reason she's temporary?" Sidesh asked, glancing through her resume.

Mr. Gupta explained, "She's a recent graduate from Delhi University, Sir. This is her first job, and we want to ensure she can adapt to our fast-paced environment before we make her permanent."

Sidesh nodded thoughtfully. Age 21... he read in his head, trying to reason with himself. She's too young. Way too young for me. But why do I feel so... connected? He couldn't understand it. It was like a magnetic pull that he couldn't escape.

After the meeting with Mr. Gupta, he typed out emails, but his thoughts kept drifting back to Sanaya. He wondered about her life, her dreams. *What's she really like?* he thought. But then, in a moment of self-awareness, he paused. *I'm being ridiculous, get a grip, Sid.*

He sat there, staring at his phone, his mind racing. He couldn't call Mom or his sister Kajal; they would only worry. Maybe he could reach out to Sumit, his best friend since childhood, but he knew that would only lead to a scene, a whole dramatic production. He sighed in frustration, feeling the weight of his uncertainty. *Who should I talk to?* he wondered desperately. He needed someone who would understand without overreacting. His gaze flicked back to the résumé on his desk, a bitter thought crossing his mind. *Since when did you become a detective, Sid?*

Phone in hand, he dialed the company reception. A soft, musical voice hit his ear.

"Hello, you've reached VS Corporations. This is Sanaya. How can I help you?"

For a moment, Sidesh's mind went completely blank. The words he wanted to say escaped him, lost in the sudden rush of emotion that washed over him. Her soft and gentle voice seemed to echo in his mind, confirming everything he had been feeling but couldn't quite put into words. He leaned back, the weight of realization settling heavily on his chest. *This is it*, he thought, a quiet certainty blooming inside him. He had fallen for her. Completely. The call ended abruptly, but the warmth of her voice lingered, wrapping around him like a secret he was finally ready to accept. He had never believed in love at first sight until now.

Chapter Two:
The Unexpected Feeling

Removing her sandals at the entrance of her flat, Sanaya stormed inside, shouting, "Amma ji, Appa ji."

"We are here," came Mom's voice from the kitchen.

Sanaya rushed inside, excitement bubbling as she hugged her mom and then her dad, who was chopping vegetables. "What's cooking? Hmmm, it smells so good," she said, inhaling deeply and kissing her mom's cheek before peeking into the pan.

"Sana, go and wash your hands, freshen up. I'm making chai with bread pakoda. We will have Idly and Sambhar for dinner," said her mom, patting her cheek.

"Wow, super! I will have bread pakoda for dinner as well. Make extra, okay? No Idly for me," complained Sanaya, heading to the bathroom to freshen up.

By the time she returned, her dad had questions ready. "How was your first day at work? Did you like the environment? How is your manager, and did you make any friends?"

Sanaya, already munching on a bread pakoda with ketchup, answered with a bright smile. "I liked it, Appa. The best part is that Mona, the previous receptionist, will train me for a week. She's so patient. She's pregnant and going on maternity leave, and I'm replacing her. I got a company tour and was introduced to some higher officials and managers. You know, Appa, they even has a manufacturing factory behind the building! That was a surprise. They also have a big canteen, so I can eat there if I don't take lunch sometimes."

"Also, I checked on the transportation. They have a company bus that stops just outside our community gates. It's free, and starting tomorrow, it will pick me up at 7:15 am and drop me back at 6:00 pm," she added, sipping her chai.

Her dad smiled, ruffling her hair. "That's fantastic. At least we don't have to worry about your commute."

Everything seemed perfectly normal: her mom and dad chatting, the neighbors' voices drifting in from the courtyard, her mom exchanging words with Aunty on the ground floor. The familiar sounds of her home felt grounding, yet Sanaya's heart raced uncontrollably. Her thoughts, though, wandered elsewhere—towards him.

Mr. Sidesh Sharma, the company VP.

His name alone sent a thrill through her, but his presence had truly mesmerized her. Tall, dark, and undeniably handsome, Sidesh carried himself with an air of authority that made her stomach flutter. It wasn't just his good looks; it was the way he commanded attention without saying a word. She had never felt so drawn to someone before.

The moment his deep voice had called her name, it was as if the world had slowed down, every syllable lingering in the air. Butterflies had erupted in her stomach, a feeling that refused to go away. She constantly replayed it in her mind—his gaze, how he stood confidently, and every small detail.

Mona, who seemed to know everything about everyone in the office, had filled Sanaya in on Sidesh's impressive career achievements. But the tidbit Mona casually mentioned made Sanaya's cheeks flush with warmth; he was single.

The realization sent her heart racing again. Could it be? Could someone like him, so powerful and perfect, be available?

"Am I normal, or am I going crazy?" she wondered, her thoughts spiraling. She had never felt anything like this before. His deep, commanding voice echoed in her mind, and the way he said her name sent her a shiver. The memory consumed her—his confident stride, the way his perfectly tailored suit accentuated his presence, and the effortless way he carried himself. Every detail repeated in her head as if her mind refused to let go. Her heart raced, thundering in her chest, as she questioned whether this was an infatuation, or something else entirely.

"Kya hua, beta? Where are you lost? Are you tired? Go light the diya in the pooja room and take a walk. Maybe you can catch up with Payal," her mom suggested, breaking her reverie.

"Okay, Amma," she said, eager to escape before her mom noticed her blushing. Sanaya knew the best person to confide in was her next-door bestie, Payal Di. Payal had been her confidante since childhood, always guiding her with practical advice.

After lighting the diya, chanting her daily mantra, and applying vibuthi to her forehead, Sanaya slipped on her sandals and called Payal. "Di, chalo na, let's take a walk. I have so much to tell you about my first day."

Payal smiled, grabbing her chappals. "Coming! Mummy, I'm going out with Sana," she informed her mom before following Sanaya.

They lived in a close-knit community of 36 flats, where everyone knew each other. The cool evening breeze carried the scent of blooming jasmine as they walked around the park in front of their apartment. They greeted familiar faces with "Hi," "Hello," or "Namaste," the sounds of children playing and laughter creating a lively backdrop.

"Chal, bata, how was your first day?" Payal asked, her curiosity piqued.

"Arre di, it was great! But the best part? I saw a man who took my breath away for the first time in my life," Sanaya gushed, clutching Payal's hand tightly. Her eyes sparkled with excitement, and her cheeks were flushed a soft pink as if the memory alone could ignite her.

Payal's eyes widened in surprise, a grin tugging at her lips. "OMG, Sana! Finally! Who is he? Tell me everything!"

Sanaya's voice grew animated as she began to recount her encounter. "Di, he's like a Greek God. Tall, with broad shoulders and a perfectly tailored suit that made him look... I don't even have the words! And his presence—commanding, confident, like he owned the space. And those eyes! Piercing, intense, like they could see right through me." She shivered, hugging herself at the memory. "And his voice, di! Deep, smooth, and so powerful. He just said, 'Excuse me,' but I swear I forgot how to breathe."

Payal listened intently, her smile slowly fading as Sanaya added, "And guess what? He's the VP of my company!"

Payal gasped, her brow furrowing. "VP of your company? Are you sure about this, bacha? Attraction and office crushes are fine, but don't let it get too serious. These things can be tricky, especially in the workplace."

Sanaya's excitement faltered for a moment, and she looked thoughtful. "I know, di, but I can't help how I feel. He's... different."

Payal gave her a reassuring pat on the hand. "Just be careful, okay? Crushes can be fun, but they can also get complicated. Keep your head straight."

Sanaya nodded, though her heart still fluttered at the thought of him. Sanaya smiled at her and said, "You know, di, how I am. I never believed in love and love-at-first-sight things. In real life, you have to marry a guy your parents choose for you. But di, when I saw him today, I never felt this anxiousness before. It was real, my heartbeat, it won't lie, di. I know I have to be very careful before I dive into something and trust me, I will treat my emotions for him very carefully. I don't know anything about him. This is happening just by seeing him, and I shared this with you. I have not thought of eternity with him yet. But if he is written for me as a life partner, I would be the happiest."

Payal paused, her tone softening. "I know, Sana. I've always known you to be a sensible girl, but even sensible hearts can be fragile. Just keep your emotions in check, okay? And hey, enjoy the journey without rushing it."

Sanaya nodded, her expression thoughtful. "I know, Di. Thanks, you always know what to say."

They continued their walk, the rhythm of their footsteps matching the ebb and flow of their conversation. The stars above twinkled, and Sanaya felt excitement and apprehension for what lay ahead.

Chapter Three:
A Walk Toward Destiny

Sid didn't find his drive back home that frustrating today. In fact, his usual, uneventful commute felt unexpectedly pleasant. His mind was occupied by thoughts of her—the beautiful, adorable face he had glimpsed earlier that day. Her presence had injected his life with a dose of happiness he never saw coming. He thought, *Will it be possible to have a life with her? Just a day of her glimpse made me so happy. What will happen when she is sharing my life with me?* His heart fluttered as the radio played softly in the background, the familiar hum of the car almost drowned by his growing anticipation. Reaching his home, he parked the car and walked inside, still lost in his thoughts.

"Mom, Mom..." Sid's voice echoed as he entered the living room.

"Kya hain? Why are you shouting? I'm here only talking to Kajal," his mom responded, her voice laced with warmth and a hint of impatience. She was chatting on the phone with her daughter, who lived in Kanpur, a place that felt so far from Sid's life.

"Acha chal, I'll cut the call now. Let me see what Sid wants. Call me tomorrow, take care, and give my love to Abhi. Bye," she finished the call and noticed Sid approaching her, smiling in an uncharacteristic way for him.

"Kya baat hai, smiling and all? Did you get the project?" she asked, her eyes narrowing in curiosity.

Sid nodded, unable to hide his joy.

"Bless you, beta. May you have lots of success. Chalo, I'll make a good cup of chai. I was waiting for you only to have my second round of evening chai." With a flourish, she rose from the sofa and walked toward the kitchen, leaving Sid standing there, his mind still preoccupied with thoughts of Sana.

He opened his phone, fingers trembling slightly as he unlocked it. His heart skipped a beat as he saw her resume saved in his contacts, her number, her address, everything. He had everything but the courage to take the next step. Fidgeting, he entered her address into Google Maps. It was a short distance, a mere 20-minute walk or a 5-minute drive. *How could I never have crossed paths with her before?* Sid mused. He had grown up in this city, familiar with every corner, yet fate had kept them apart until now. Better now than never...

"How was your day today?" His mom's voice broke his reverie.

"It was good, very good, in fact," he replied, still smiling like a lovestruck teenager.

"Good. Something special happened today? You're smiling a lot," she said, narrowing her eyes with playful suspicion.

Sid let out a deep breath, trying to maintain his composure. "Haan, aisa hi hain kuch, samaj lo..." he said, showing all his teeth in an exaggerated grin.

"Share with me also the source of your Colgate smile," she teased, sipping her hot chai with biscuits, her voice dripping with playful affection.

"I will, Mom, but have patience. Who else will I share it with? I need to confirm myself before I can discuss it with you," Sid said, his voice filled with a mixture of excitement and uncertainty.

"Oh my God! Is this related to a girl? Aakhir Bhagavan ne meri sun li... Thank you so much, mere Prabhu," she said, her hands folded in prayer. Sid couldn't help but chuckle at her dramatic flair.

"Okay, I'm going to the restroom now, and then I will go for a walk. Aap apna serial dekho and call me if you need anything from the shop. I'm going to meet Rahul," Sid added, his mind already shifting towards his meeting with Rahul.

He quickly dialed Rahul's number, eager to catch up. "Abey saale, yaad aa gayi meri? Calling after a long time, Sid. How are you, and what's up, bro?" Rahul's excited voice echoed through the phone.

"Teek hoon, kamine. Kahan hai tu? Ghar main hain?" Sid asked, his tone casual but his mind still racing with thoughts of Sana.

"Yes, yes, I'm at home only. Come! When are you planning to come? Let's have dinner and some drinks with that. Neetu will be happy to see you," Rahul replied.

Sid paused, conflicted. "Nahin, dinner some other time. I'll take a rain check on that. Bhabi kaisi hain? And how is your daughter? Just come out, and we'll take a walk and catch up. I'm reaching your place in 10 minutes."

"Sure, man, I'll come down. All are good here. See you soon," Rahul said before disconnecting the call.

Sid quickly changed into blue shorts and a white T-shirt, his heart thumping with anticipation. He began his walk toward Rahul's community, his mind buzzing with excitement. *What if she sees me there? Will she think I'm following her and take it the wrong way?* He wondered, pacing quickly, trying to shake off the feeling.

As he reached Rahul's community, he saw his friend from a distance, standing near the entrance gate, looking casual in his jeans and T-shirt.

"What's up, bro? Seeing you after a long time," Rahul said, grinning as he hugged Sid tightly.

"All good, yaar. I hope I didn't disturb you on a Monday evening! Sorry if I did that," Sid said, apologizing but secretly relieved to be in the comfort of his friend's presence.

"Aree nahi, yaar. Tu kabhi bhi kar le disturb, saale. Tu kabse itna formal ho gaya?" Rahul teased, nudging him as they walked inside the community. But Sid wasn't listening. His heart had just begun to race again as he spotted her ahead, walking gracefully with a friend.

Her beauty was undeniable. Even from a distance, Sid could see how her hair flowed in the evening breeze, the soft waves catching the light. Her laughter was unrestrained, starkly contrasting to the quiet, composed woman he had seen that morning. She was radiant, without makeup, yet radiated an effortless charm that captivated him.

Rahul continued talking, but Sid's focus was solely on her. He couldn't take his eyes off the way her eyes lit up when she laughed, and her smile seemed to make the world around her brighter. He felt a sudden surge of emotion, the kind of connection he had never experienced before.

Suddenly, she turned as if she had sensed his gaze. Their eyes met, and the world seemed to pause for a brief moment. Sid felt a flutter in his chest, a connection that was too real to ignore. Was she feeling the same way? Did she sense the pull between them?

Rahul's voice broke the moment, but Sid barely registered the words. He turned to his friend, his heart still racing. "Kya hua tujhe, Sid? I'm talking, and you're just standing frozen. Sab teek hain? Do you know Sana?" Rahul asked, his voice filled with concern.

"Sana?" Sid echoed, still in a daze.

"Yes, Sana..." Rahul pointed to her.

Sid's mind raced, and he tried to keep his composure. Sana, the name felt like honey on his tongue. He had to speak to her.

"Yes, she joined my company today. I'm surprised to see her here," Sid said, trying to act casual, but inside, he was anything but calm.

"Hello, Sanya. What a surprise! It's nice to meet you here," he said, addressing her formally but with a soft smile.

"Hello, Sir. I'm very surprised to see you. Hello, Rahul Bhaiya. How are you?" she responded, her voice conveying nervousness, yet the way she looked at him made Sid wonder if she knew something he didn't.

"Hello, Sana. I'm good. Hello, Payal. I heard you joined Sid's company today. Congratulations!" Rahul chimed in, oblivious to the tension between Sid and Sana.

"Yes, Bhaiya. Thank you," Sana said, smiling shyly. Sid noticed her glance at him and then look away, her cheeks tinged with a soft blush. The expression on her face was unreadable, yet it made Sid's heart skip a beat.

"Do you live here in this community, Sana?" Sid asked, his voice suddenly more serious.

"Yes. And you, Sir?" she replied, a hint of curiosity in her voice.

"Call me Sid, Sana. No need to be formal. I live just 15 minutes away from here," he said, his voice warm as he tried to break their formality.

As they walked together, Sana introduced him to her friend, Payal Didi, who gave Sid a warm smile, though it seemed like she was privy to some unspoken connection between Sid and Sana.

"Sana..." a voice called from above, and she turned. "I have to go; my brother is calling. See you tomorrow, Sid. Bye, Rahul Bhaiya. Chalo, Di."

Sid stood frozen as she waved and ran toward her apartment, a whirlwind of emotions coursing through him. Was this the beginning of something? He wondered, a mix of hope and uncertainty swirling within him. He watched her disappear, a smile tugging at his lips, but his heart felt heavy with longing.

"Bye, Sana. Good night," he whispered to the air, knowing that this was only the beginning of a journey that would change both of their lives forever.

Chapter Four:
A Silent Connection

Sana ran towards her apartment holding Payal's hand, her heart pounding not just from the sprint but from the moment's thrill. She couldn't help but replay how he had smiled at her, wondering if it meant more than she dared to hope. She turned her face back one last time to see if he was still there. He waved at her with a soft smile that sent a shiver down her spine. Once they reached the base of the stairs in the corridor, hidden from prying eyes, Sana caught her breath and looked at Payal. She placed Payal's hand over her chest, right where her heart was racing.

"Can you feel this, Di?" she asked, her flushed cheeks glowing under the dim light, her eyes sparkling with a mix of excitement and nervous anticipation.

Payal nodded with a knowing smile. "Di, did you see him? He's the one I was talking about… What do you think? Why did he come here? Does he feel the same as I do? Otherwise, why would he appear here all of a sudden? Di, kuch toh bolo!" Sana's words spilled out in a rush, her excitement barely contained.

"Ruk ja, saans toh le le bache! Kitne sawaal puchegi?" Payal teased as they began strolling up the stairs. "Sana, he's so handsome! Like, seriously, what a personality. I didn't know a man could look so hot in just shorts and a T-shirt."

"Haina? I told you!" Sana's face lit up with joy.

"You know, Sana, I think he's fallen head over heels for you. I saw it in his face…" Payal said with a mischievous grin.

"What? Do you really think so? I mean, I don't know! We just met today," Sana said, her mind racing with conflicting emotions. A part of her wanted to believe Payal's words, but another part whispered insecurities, reminding her of the differences between their worlds. And besides, look at him, Di. He's so beautiful and successful, and he holds such a high place in society. Why would he like me? I'm just a simple plain Jane," Sana's excitement faltered, doubt creeping into her voice.

"Where is this coming from now?" Payal scolded gently. "Don't tell me you're letting all these insecurities build up. That's the last thing I expected from you! Besides, let's head home. Otherwise, Guru Anna is going to kill you or at least make you explain yourself."

"Hmm," was all Sana could muster, her thoughts swirling.

Guru, Sana's elder brother by four years, was the epitome of responsibility. He was the kind of person who always had a plan, whether it was for his career or family dinners. Despite his seriousness, there was an undeniable warmth in how he cared for his siblings. Hardworking and focused, he had carved out a successful career in IT. As they approached the door, Sana called out, "Anna! I'm here talking to Di. I'll come in five minutes."

He opened the door, raising an eyebrow. "How come you always have so much to say to her but only a few words for me? Come in and tell me about your first day. I'm eager to hear about it."

"It was fantastic, Anna... bas do minute. I'll be there in the blink of an eye, Sachi," she said, giving him a quick hug. He shook his head with a smile, retreating inside and closing the steel mesh door behind him.

Sana and Payal sat on the stairs. "Hayee, Di, do you really think he likes me?" Sana's voice was tinged with hope and vulnerability.

"I think so, yes. But you should answer that for yourself. Don't jump to conclusions, though. Be sure about your feelings and his. Take cautious steps, bacha. If you're going to commit emotionally, you need to know if he's the right one. Besides, you've just met him today. Give it time. Observe him, understand him, and see if you're truly compatible. There's so much to consider," Payal advised, her tone maternal yet firm. "Now stop overthinking. Go inside, relax, eat, and get some sleep. You have to wake up early for work tomorrow."

Sana hugged her bestie, bid her goodnight, and opened the mesh door. Before stepping inside, she peeked out one last time, hoping to catch a glimpse of him. To her surprise, he was there, walking back home alone. The faint glow of the streetlight cast soft shadows across his face, and his steps were slow and deliberate. As their eyes met, her breath caught, the unspoken connection between them feeling almost tangible. Their eyes met across the distance, exchanging a silent yet deep connection in that fleeting moment. With a heart full of unspoken emotions, Sana smiled, entered her home, and closed the door. All her doubts melted away like snow under the sun.

Dinner at Sana's house was always lively, with laughter and stories bouncing around the room. After her meal and a refreshing shower, Sana set her alarm for 6:00 AM. She slipped under the covers, her mind replaying the events of the day, a content smile gracing her lips as she drifted off to sleep, dreaming of what tomorrow might bring.

Chapter Five:
When Eyes Meet Hearts

Sid walked home with a soft smile playing on his face, a new and unfamiliar feeling blooming in his heart. This was unlike anything he had ever experienced. Always studious and career-driven, Sid had shouldered his family's responsibilities since his father's untimely death when Sid was only 19. His mother, a homemaker, and his younger sister, Kajal, relied on him entirely. Kajal was still in school, and her tuition classes barely covered their basic needs. Sid had no time for flings, parties, or the carefree luxuries his peers indulged in. Instead, he devoted himself to his education and worked tirelessly to build a stable life for his family. Though he had once dreamed of becoming a model, he set that passion aside without regret, choosing instead to ensure his family's happiness and security. Now, with his sister settled and his life in order, Sid felt content, or at least he thought he had been until he saw Sana.

Since the moment he first laid eyes on her, something inside him shifted. The idea of a family, of a life partner, had never stirred him before. Yet now, the thought of Sana filled him with an urgency and yearning he couldn't ignore. "A wife," he thought, almost in disbelief. The word felt foreign yet tantalizing. He hadn't even spoken to her properly, yet her presence alone seemed to awaken a part of him he hadn't known was dormant. Could someone truly have such an impact with just a glance?

The next morning, Sid awoke with an eagerness he hadn't felt in years. He arrived at the office well before usual, his eyes instinctively searching for her. She was at the reception desk, radiant in a white churidar, her long hair flowing freely, a small bindi sparkling on her forehead. She greeted him with a warm smile and a sweet, "Good morning, Sid... Sir."

Sid smiled back. "Good morning; please call me Sid. No need to be formal, Sana. Good morning, Mona. Hope you're doing well."

"Good morning, sir. I'm good, thank you," Mona replied, her tone tinged with surprise at the informal exchange between Sid and Sana.

Turning his attention back to Sana, Sid said, "It was nice to meet you yesterday evening. I want to discuss something with you. Can you please visit my cabin now?"

Sana's heart skipped a beat. "Sure," she managed to reply, her voice barely above a whisper. She nodded to Mona and followed Sid, her nerves tightening with every step. What could he possibly want to discuss?

Sid opened the door to his cabin, holding it for her as she walked in with her face lowered, her hands clasped in front of her. He noticed the faint blush on her cheeks and the delicate scent of rose and lily that seemed to trail behind her. She was petite, her burgundy-brown hair cascading below her waist, contrasting with his tall, muscular frame.

She turned to face him, offering a nervous smile that left him momentarily speechless. Her kohled eyes, sharp nose adorned with a tiny mole, and pink lips seemed to him like the perfect artistry of nature. Sid was captivated, utterly lost in her presence, until his phone ringing brought him back to reality.

He gestured for her to sit, answering the call quickly but keeping his eyes on her. Once the call ended, he leaned forward slightly, his voice soft yet unsteady. "Hi."

"Hi," she replied, her voice barely audible.

Sid took a deep breath. "I don't know how to say this, and I hope you don't mind... but I'll come straight to the point. Sana, I'm so attracted to you. I've never felt this way about anyone before. I want to get to know you and understand this feeling. Do you... do you feel the same?"

Sana's eyes widened in shock, her cheeks flushed. "I... I don't know what to say. This is so sudden," she stammered, her voice tinged with uncertainty. "I felt something, too. I won't deny that, but I don't know what it is. This is all so new to me. And you... you're so respectable, in such a great position, and I'm just a new hire."

Sensing her discomfort, Sid got up and knelt in front of her, gently asking, "May I?" before taking her hand in his. His large, rough hands enveloped her smaller, trembling ones, and the touch sparked through both of them.

"Did you feel that?" he asked, his voice barely above a whisper. She nodded, her breath quickening. "Say it, Sana. I need to hear it."

"I... I think I'm going to have a heart attack," she said, half-joking, clutching her chest. Sid chuckled, releasing her hand gently and handing her a glass of water.

"Relax," he said, his tone soothing. "I don't want to stress you out. I just needed to share my feelings with you, and I'm glad you feel something, too. I want to spend more time with you and get to know you better. Will you meet me outside of work?"

"No... I can't," Sana replied nervously. "I've never been on a date, and my family is very conservative. I hope you understand."

"I do," Sid said thoughtfully. "How do you commute to work?"

"I take the company bus," she replied. "I just enrolled for transportation yesterday."

"Perfect. After work, I'll drop you home. We can talk during the drive," he suggested. Seeing her hesitation, he added, "Don't worry. I'll handle everything. Just meet me in the parking lot after your shift."

After a moment of consideration, Sana nodded. "Okay," she said softly.

Their eyes met, and both blushed. Breaking the moment, Sana stood. "I should go. Mona might be looking for me."

"Of course," Sid said, wishing she could stay longer. "Though I won't lie, I don't want you to go."

With butterflies in their stomachs and newfound hope in their hearts, Sid and Sana counted the hours until their next meeting, each wondering what the evening would bring.

Chapter Six:
Moments That Matters

It was an adventurous day for Sana. She never thought when she woke in the morning that she would be experiencing something like this. The encounter with Sid was unprecedented, but it was a tantalizing one. It was her lunchtime. She was sitting with Mona in the canteen and having her food from the lunch box packed by her mom, but her mind was filled with Sid and his words. She didn't expect him to be this fast in approaching her; she knew she was attracted to him, and it was a relief to know that he, too, felt the same. But just in a day, getting their consent for their feelings felt very unusual to her.

"Do you know Sidesh sir before?" enquired Mona. "No, I just met him yesterday in the office, but he has a common friend in my community, and he came to meet him in the evening, and we saw each other when I was on a walk," she answered. "Oh, so you both live in the same city, that's good. He is a very good man, a gentleman, very helpful and thorough professional." Mona said. Sana smiled and blushed to hear praises of his man; she felt proud of him... wait... 'His Man' where did that come from... Sana, keep your emotions on hold, she told herself. But, somehow, she felt a connection with him, an instant attachment, especially when he held her hand and asked her for the drive back home. She could see his eagerness to spend time with her. She also wanted to know him better, but she could not understand if this was what everyone called 'Love.'

It was 5 pm, and she took her purse and lunch bag and walked towards the parking lot, feeling frenzy and thrilled. This is something she is doing for the first time, and she feels scared too... but excited; all her feelings are mixed. She had this doubt if she was doing it right, sitting in someone's car without informing her parents. "I hope I will not get caught by someone, hey Prabhu bacha

Lena," she blabbered to herself. She saw a blue Tata Safari coming towards her, but it stopped next to her, and she couldn't see anything through the tinted glasses. It had total black windows, which rolled down, and she saw smiling Sid in the driver's seat gesturing her to come inside.

She sat inside, and cool AC air hit her face. "Put on your seatbelt," Sid told her. She kept her bags on her feet and did as instructed. "Nice car, I love the color," she said. "Thanks. Do you want to go and grab a coffee somewhere, and we can talk there?" he asked. Nervously, she said, "No. No. I have to be at home by 6:15, that's when the bus drops us off. If I go late, then that amma appa will question me. What will I say that I didn't come home by bus… but my VP dropped me!" she was talking nonstop without a pause, making all dramatic faces, making Sid laugh and transfixed to her face.

"Aap has rahe hain, I am serious. My family is very strict; if my Anna even sees me talking to a boy, he will put an inquiry on me like... police waley type inquiry until it's a boy approved and investigated by him." She paused, realizing that they were still in the parking lot and he had not moved the car. *"Aap yahin kade rehenge? Chaliye na..."* "Hmm…" he could just say that to all the chatty Sana he is seeing.

Sana turned and looked at him and was awestruck; oh boy! He was something to drool on. The musk perfume, the black aviator glasses in the sharp nose, messy thick hair, and that jawline to die for. She moved down to his muscular arms, one holding the gear and one in the steering. She was engrossed in him when he said, "Like what you see?" with a chuckle and then that hypnotizing smile. She thought she was gone for real; there was no coming back.

"Hmmm… yes," she abruptly said, then realized what she said and shied away, looking out the window all red. "Happy to know that I am not the only one fascinated," he cracked up laughing, which filled her heart with contentment. Then silence filled up the car; Sid switched on the radio at low volume, which somehow helped her to control her rushing emotions. "Sana, you know right why I asked for your time with me?" he questioned her with a soft, mellow voice. She did not know what to say, so she bit her lower lip and looked at him. He glanced at her lips and looked at the other side, and the Adam's apple in his throat moved up and down. He was driving very slowly; she could see all the cars overtaking them.

"To know each other, I guess," she gently said. "Yes, tell me about yourself, your friends, family, school, and college. Anything," he asked. *"Okay, par bahut time lagega.. pehle hi bol dethi huin, then don't regret why I asked."* She lightened the mood, shifting her body towards him. She had this quality in her to make the environment light and jovial, quite opposite to Sid, who had always been serious and focused.

She had been an introverted and shy person in public or with new people, but with family and friends, she was just the opposite; she would be the center of attention, full of energy, cracking jokes and stories, and non-stop talking. She felt the same comfort with Sid; he didn't feel like a stranger to her. New feelings were creeping into her body. She was blushing a lot, her cheeks were hot, and she had a rapid heartbeat and sensations in her stomach when he was around her.

"Just kidding, long story short, my father, Mr. Balasubramaniam Iyer urf Bala Appa, is a bank officer, my mother, Seetha Lakshmi Iyer urf Seethu Amma is a housewife, my brother Guru Subramaniam Iyer aka Guru Anna who is 4 years elder to me and behaves like a Hitler, works in an IT firm in Delhi. A normal middle-class South Indian traditional family. We are from Chennai basically, but I have grown here in Ghaziabad from my fifth year and have been living in the same community since then." She said without taking a break from all actions, hand moving and dancing with a satisfying and proud smile.

"Interesting," Sid said absorbing all the information she said and admiring her beautiful antics simultaneously trying hard to not get distracted.

"What about you, Sid?" She asked, looking at him. "I live with my mother here; I have a sister who is married and settled in Kanpur. I lost my father when I was 19; he had a heart attack!" he sighed with sadness in his voice. Sana touched his arm and caressed it, giving him the strength he needed the most. "I am sorry for your loss, Sid," she genuinely said with a sad voice. "I miss him a lot, Sana. I never get emotional like this, but I can't hide my emotions in front of you! I don't know why! I had the responsibility of my mother and sister when I was least expecting…" he crackled. "I am not complaining; please don't take me wrong." He said, looking at her.

"No. No. Not at all, Sid. I am not. In fact, I am so proud of you. At that young age, I couldn't imagine collecting myself and taking on the family responsibilities, but I could imagine how efficiently you fulfilled them. I respect your dedication, and the sacrifices you have made are unimaginable," She said, assuring him. He nodded and took his glasses off; they were about to reach her community. How fast time had gone, he thought, which otherwise would have been a grueling drive back home.

Chapter Seven:
A Love In Between

He wanted to spend more time with her and asked, "We entered the city and still have some time to drop you, shall we just roam around? Maybe I will show you my home, just from outside, before we reach your home?"

"Hmm... okay, sure, but buses usually take more time as they take a different route to drop off other employees." She said, excited to hear that he would show her his home and treasure each moment spent with him. With a big smile, he turned the steering towards the highway. She was just admiring him and suddenly asked playfully, *"Aap hero ya model ban sakthe the aap ne kabhi socha nahi? You have a hero's physique and charm bilkul Akshay Kumar types... Dhole sholey... Tall, Dark, Handsome,"* swinging her arms.

Surprised and smiling, he replied, concentrating on the road, "I wanted to be a model myself. I'll show you my modeling photoshoots someday. I was a cricket player in my school and college days... that helped me keep my body fit. I still go to the gym and work out. I cannot compromise on that. By the way, thanks for the compliment, and I'm surprised too how you guessed what I wanted to do!"

She smiled and sighed, *"I hate doing any workout, gymming, shimming... arre baba, too much for me! The only thing I do is walk and gossip with my friends around the park, and I also love doing Bollywood dancing, full-on thumka and dhamal."* She is a piece, he thought, and said, *"Full nautanki hain re tu."*

"Who toh main huin," she said, raising one brow with pride.

"Mere saath rahoge toh aapko bhi bana dungi," she said. He looked into her eyes and said, "That's the plan, baby." She

blushed and looked outside, biting her lower lip. She eyed an ice cream shop.

"You want to have ice cream?" he asked, reading her mind.

She nodded. "Ya, sure."

"Which one?" he asked.

"Butterscotch," she replied.

He smiled, parked the car, and went out, leaving the car and A.C. on for her. She blushed again, thinking about him. His aura was so captivating, and 'Baby,' she thought. *"Ek din main Ms. Sanaya Iyer se Sana se Baby… kuch zyada advance main nahi jaa rahe!!"*

It was nothing different on Sid's side. He was mesmerized by her beauty, but now, talking with her, he felt relaxed and satisfied. He thought how beautiful and fun my life would be with this *'Nautanki.'* But there was something else running through his mind, something he wanted to clarify and ask her.

He entered the car and handed the ice cream to her. Eating, he asked very casually, "Do you know my age, Sana?"

She nodded. "Umm... No," she replied, hesitating.

"I am 34, and you are 21. We have an age difference of 13 years! Will that bother you in the future?" he asked, masking his worry, wondering what her answer would be. What if she won't accept him? What if she likes someone her own age? What if she rejects him? There were so many questions piling up, a turmoil of complexities building inside him, insecurities growing.

She was quiet, breathing in, turning her body to face him. She kept the ice cream in the cup holder and said, "Age is just a number, Sid. That will not bother me in the future. My parents have a 12-year age difference. My grandparents have a 25-year age difference, and they are in a blissful marriage. When you really love someone, age, weight, height, and miles are just numbers. Please don't have those insecurities in your mind. And by the way, you look so young. I would have never guessed it if you hadn't told me. If you stand near my anna, he will look old in front of you." She nonchalantly said, taking her ice cream back and devouring it.

He was shocked—pleasantly shocked by the words spoken by her. He breathed out a long sigh, which he was holding in unknowingly. "I am in awe, Sana. You don't know how much this was bothering me!" He grabbed her hand in his rough hands and said with excitement in his voice. Surprised, she blushed again, which she was doing a lot around him, and bit her lower lip. He touched her right cheek with his left hand and caressed it gently, taking the lip out of her teeth with his thumb, eyes not leaving hers, and said, "Thanks for making me realize this beautiful feeling that I have never experienced in my life. I know you have the same effect that I have for you, and don't bite your lip."

She moved away and made a distance slowly. She felt overwhelmed with unknown emotions. "I think we should leave. I don't want to get late and get questioned."

He felt embarrassed. He shouldn't have overstepped. This was their first meeting, and he felt ashamed to make her uncomfortable. *"I am sorry if you felt uncomfortable. I was just so happy, Sana, the bus just uss moment mein... you know what I'm saying, right? I didn't even realize that I overstepped!"* he said genuinely, driving fast.

"Nahi, please aap sorry kyun bol rahe hain? It's just that this is all new to me," she said sincerely in a very low voice, still blushing. He nodded, and then both were quiet again.

"I'll show you my house. It's this one here." He showed her his white, freshly painted house with grey gates, a modern design, and a beautiful yet simple two-story home.

"It's beautiful," she said. "I have never come to this side. You live so close to my place. I have come here walking, but always on the outer road, and never come inside this housing community. Why haven't I seen you before?"

"I had the same question when I saw your address and walked towards your community yesterday," he spit out.

"Oh! Then you planned your visit. Was it not a coincidence? I doubted that," she said, coming back from her shy shell to her chirpy self, giggling.

They reached the entrance gate of her community, both with a heavy heart that they had to part ways now. Sid said, looking at her, "Can I pick you up in the morning and also drop you in the evening, please? I want to spend time with you."

"You want to become my driver and leave your VP position?" she said, laughing, and kept her hands covering her mouth. Gathering her bags, she said, "I don't know, Sid. I am not comfortable lying to my family, and what if they find out from someone that I am climbing in and out of this car? It's a small city, and my parents are very strict."

"I understand and respect you for that. My admiration for you has gone tenfold, Sana. But I would suggest telling your family that instead of the bus, the company car is coming to pick you up and drop you off, and it won't be a lie. This car I've bought from the company loan and am still paying the EMI... what do you say?" His eagerness to not miss a single chance to be with her was evident on his face, and she couldn't say no to that face.

"Okay, but what about your timings? I would not like you to ignore your work and schedules," she said, concerned.

He smiled and said, "I'll take care of that. So, what time do you want this cab service at your door, ma'am?"

She laughed and replied, *"7:15 am, driver ji, 8:00 am my shift starts, so don't get late... time pe aa jaana, warna meri VP ke saath jaan pehchaan hain, and you will face the consequences."*

"Ji Madam," he laughed at her antics.

"Bye," she said and exited the car, walking towards her apartment.

Chapter Eight:
Silent Signals, Loud Hearts

He stood still in the car, dazzled, her fragrance lingering in the air, feeling lonely all of a sudden as he watched her walk away to her home. He didn't want to leave yet; he wanted to see her again—maybe just a glimpse, he wished! He drove the car into her community to see if there was any chance. But she had already gone inside, nowhere to be seen.

He took a round in the park, anticipating… and then she came out onto the balcony of her first-floor apartment, leaning and peeking toward the community entrance where he had dropped her. Perhaps she wanted to see if he was still there. Pouting with a frown when she didn't find the car, she looked straight ahead—and there it was, the same blue car driving very slowly toward her. She recognized him. A smile spread across her face.

He honked: Beep… Beep… Beep, Beep Beep, and steered away.

He was happy. Very, very happy to see her again, as if she had heard his unspoken heart's desire. The excitement of doing crazy things, things he would never have done otherwise, made him feel youthful again. He was elated with this new special feeling, something that filled him with joy! Being responsible, hardworking, and focused on earning for his family had been his entire life so far. But now, this was a new chapter, and he was loving every part of it. He was happy from the inside, and there was no going back. He loved Sana and wanted her in his life. He couldn't wait any longer to express his feelings to her.

She, on the other hand, was on cloud nine. She had never imagined it would be so fun and exciting to fall in love. Yes, she was in love with him. It was something she had always kept at bay, never allowing herself to feel that way. She had always kept a shield around her heart. Sana had been a good daughter, a good sister, a good student, and a good friend. Her parents had instilled in her the importance of their culture and religion, and she had loyally followed their guidance and valued their trust.

For her, love was serious—something for a lifetime. If she was in love, it would mean marrying that person and being loyally devoted for better or worse. She couldn't help it now; she couldn't stop herself from falling for him. It was as if he was a magnet made just for her. Her attraction to him came so naturally. If this was called soulmate magnetism, then she was feeling it and experiencing it herself.

"Where are you lost?" asked Guru Anna, flicking Sana's head as he sat next to her on the living room sofa, picking up the newspaper.

"Kya hai, Anna!" she yelled irritably, rubbing her head.

"I heard that from tomorrow, a car will come to pick you up. *Kya baat hai, Sana! I also go to work; nothing like this happens to me. Wah, maja hai! Special treatment and all,"* he smirked.

"Aisa kuch nahi hai!" she retorted. "It's just that the bus has to take a long route to pick me up, so they suggested a car pick-up, and I said yes. *Aur waise bhi, I have to be there by 8 a.m., and because of traffic, the bus gets delayed. So management decided this."*

She explained, thinking how true it was that "one lie leads to another." But all is fair in love and war, she thought, smiling. She understood this phrase better now, practically experiencing it.

"Hmm... but be careful. Give the driver's details to Amma and message her when you reach the office. We can't trust anyone, okay?"

"Okay," she replied. "Now, give me the entertainment page. I want to know the new gossip in town." She snatched the paper from him.

"*Kuch real news bhi padh le, moti! Jab dekho, hero-heroine ki khabar padhti rehti hai,*" he snapped.

"*Aap ho na, you read and tell me that. It's so boring—just like you! Aur, I am not moti! You are motey and ganjey… Kashandi!*" she teased, giggling. "See your hair in front. Hardly any hair left. Apply oil!"

Their banter continued even at the dinner table.

Later that night…

I'm sitting in the park with Rahul.

She received a message from an unknown number. But she knew who it was. She washed her hands and went to the balcony to confirm—and yes, it was him, sitting with Rahul Bhaiya. She typed:

Coming.

"*Amma, I'm going for a walk with Di,*" she informed her mother, not waiting for a response. She headed toward Payal Didi's flat.

"*Di, kya kar rahe ho? Chalo na, we'll take a walk. We missed our evening walk. Where were you in the evening?*" she asked, pulling her sister's hand and gesturing for her to get up.

"*Kaam tha kuch. Went to the market. Let's skip the walk now, bacha. Abhi khana khaya hai; my stomach is full. It's late, too.*"

"*Arre… it's not late—just 9:30! And besides, you can't skip the walk. If your stomach is that full, a slow walk is healthy. Chalo na, please!*" she pleaded, giving puppy eyes and pouting.

"Now, who can say no to that face," Di said, smiling. She got up, and they walked out together.

"What happened today? Walk ka bahana banake kya batana hai?" Di teased.

"Batana toh hai… par dikhana bhi hai aur dekhna bhi hai," Sana said mischievously, blushing.

Confused, Di asked, "What are you saying?"

"He's here. Sitting there on the bench with Rahul," she said, gesturing toward him, her eyes fixed on him.

"Oh my God, Sana! You both are gone! This is serious! And you're using me for your romance?" Di teased her.

"Who else will I use? You're the only one. Be ready to be used many more times—this is serious!" Sana replied confidently.

"Haan haan, karle use, mera bacha. I'm so happy you've found your love," Di said warmly.

As they strolled around the park, Sana stole glances at him, enjoying the moment. Visual flirting and just his presence were enough for her at that moment.

When she received a call, she had to go back to the flat, but she stayed on the balcony for a while.

You should go home; it's getting late. You don't want to be late tomorrow morning ☺

She sent him a message.

Yes, I was just leaving. By the way, thanks for coming. ☺

He hadn't asked her to come out but had only hoped for a glimpse. He was elated when she wrote "Coming." What else could he ask for?

She was now in another dilemma. "What name should I save his number as?" she thought. A girl's name? No. Hero? No, what if Mom asks who Hero is?

Idea! She saved it as SS 🚗.

As soon as she saved it, she saw his WhatsApp profile picture and couldn't help caressing it.

SS 🚗: Good night. See you tomorrow. By the way, nice profile pic. ✌

Sana: I was also seeing your profile pic. It's cool. Good night ❤

It had been an eventful day, both thought, as they drifted off to sleep, dreaming of what the next day might bring.

Chapter Nine:
Love's Quiet Revolution

SS🚗

I am here...

Sid messaged her while sitting in the car; he was early, he knew that, but he was too excited to meet her. This is insane; he thought I didn't know that I would be so crazy for someone. She was in his mind all evening, night, and morning!! He couldn't stop himself from walking towards her apartment in the evening yesterday, knowing that Rahul might doubt him and ask questions... he decided he would tell him everything if that is what is needed to meet her daily *'Pyaar kiya toh darna kya,'* he chuckled being filmy. As doubted, he asked when he saw his eyes glued on Sana's flat, and his doubt was even more confirmed when he saw Sana come out to walk and eyes on Sid all the time blushing.

Sid told his heart's condition and likeness towards Sana truthfully.

Rahul was happy for him; he said, "She is a very nice girl, Sid. I have known her since she came to this community; she is like my sister. She is very homely, respects elders, is helpful and is very lively. She will be a good life partner for you; it seems like you both are made for each other." He confirmed that with confidence. Rahul has always been a very mature and responsible man, unlike Sumit, his best friend. Sumit was a carefree and funny guy, opposite to Sid's personality, and maybe that's why he loved him. Patting Sid's shoulders Rahul said, "I will always be there for any help you need bro. Have you guys expressed your feelings to each other?" he asked. "Kind of, but not explicitly. Maybe soon," Sid replied.

Sana

I am coming, you were supposed to be here at 7:15… you are way too early. Give me a few minutes.

He smiled and switched on the radio, and the song that played seemed it was written just for him,

Har Shyam Aankhon Par

Tera Aanchal Lehraye

Har Raat Yaadon Ki

Baarat Le Aaye

Maein Saans Leta Hoon

Teri Khushboo Aati Hai

Ek Mehka Mehka Sa

Paigham Laati Hai

Meri Dil Ki Dhadkan Bhi

Tere Geet Gaati Hai

Pal Pal Dil Ke Paas Tum Rehti Ho

Jeevan Meethi Pyaas Yeh Kehti Ho

Pal Pal Dil Ke Paas Tum Rehti Ho…

He saw her coming in with a baby pink top with white pearls spread over and white pants, her hair falling long and wavy in the ends, looking enchanting, captivating, and drop-dead gorgeous. She sat next to him in the car and again her fragrance spread the car, rose and lily.

"Good Morning," she said with a beautiful smile, showing her pearly teeth.

"What a beautiful morning it is…" he replied with his fixed on her, adoring and smiling. She blushed.

"Chale?" she asked. *"Hmm.. ya ya..put on your seat belt"* he started the car and drove towards the company but slowly and in no hurry. He didn't mind the traffic or the signals today, he was in a way thankful that they were giving him time to admire the beauty beside him.

"I did not have my breakfast. You were so early here, so I packed it. Do you mind if I have it in the car?" she asked, wondering. *"Ya sure, waise maine bhi nahi khaya, and sorry I came this early,"* he said. *"Koi na, I have a sandwich with me; you wanna have the half?"* she asked. *"Sure, but I hope that will be enough for you?"*

"Yes, it will be more than enough for me. From tomorrow, I will get extra for you as well. Amma loves to feed; she is like always behind us. Did you have food? Why did you waste this? Why are you not eating properly… blah blah blah…" talking non-stop, she gave her half cheese veg sandwich to him. "She makes the best food; I love to eat what she cooks. I like cooking, but the job I love is eating her food. Appa will demand so many items to her, and she, without complaining, makes it for him." Chewing and devouring the sandwich, she was ceaselessly talking about her parents, and he was enjoying every bit of it.

He could see how much she adored her parents and her family and he also started liking them for the way they were so connected to each other and also connected to their culture.

"The sandwich was so good, and I love Dosa sambhar; it's one of my favorites," he said, finishing the sandwich. "Really, then I should call you sometime. My mom makes the best masala dosa and sambhar in this whole world," she said proudly.

"I would love to come." He said thinking, *'Haath mange toh aana hi ek din tera Janeman tab kayenge'*

She looked at his handsome face and was enjoying the time with him. He was wearing a crisp white shirt and gray pants, looking fully professional and dapper at the same time. Her mind was distracted when she heard one of her favorite songs playing, *'Ban ke Titli dil uda uda uda hain, kahin dur…'* "Ah, I love this song…" she increased the volume and started singing and dancing to it.

"You are so beautiful Sana, I am not able to concentrate on the road, I just want to look at you and admire you." He said brazenly stopping the car near an isolated sideway near the company area. She was shocked to hear his unabashed appreciation and feelings, as well as the fact that he parked the car abruptly on the road. There company must be 15 minutes from there, it was an industrial area so was not very crowded.

"I…I…mmm… can I hold you, Sana, please?" he asked. Vacillating she nodded yes, she became quiet, her heartbeat raised, her cheeks burning, her eyes on him, thinking what was in store. He caught hold of her hand and pecked it lightly, inhaling her scent. He then held her cheek and rubbed it lightly with his knuckles.

"Please don't get scared. I know my limits, but you are so captivating. This is all new to me, and I don't know how to control myself. You know what I am trying to say, right?" he genuinely asked. She nodded again and didn't say anything. "Why are you quiet? Say something," he asked again. She hummed in a low voice, almost whispering, *"Kya bolu."* He chuckled, seeing his goofball, who was so chirpy and lively just a minute ago but suddenly went chickens.

He could understand her situation; she was feeling shy, but he wanted her to be free to him without any inhibitions. He wanted her to open up even when they were physically close. Touching, hugging, and kissing are things that he craved to experience firsthand with her. He thought he would be shameless and say whatever was in his heart if she was so timid and shy. He wanted to be her second skin and be comfortable around him, and it was going to be a tough task.

"Okay, at least see me and tell me what is making you so nervous?" taking his hand away from her cheek but still holding her he asked.

She inhaled and exhaled deeply. Biting her lips, she said, "Woh… actually, this all is new to me." Pausing, she looked at him, sitting straight, and asked, *"Aap mere liye serious ho na? I am not just a time pass for you, right? I have never fallen for anyone until now. I am very orthodox. I have a belief that in my life, I will never fall in love, but if I do, marriage would be the final call. I want to keep myself pious for my husband. Do you love me, like serious wala love, marriage type of love?"*

Chapter Ten:
A Moment To Forever

Sid stared out of the car window, his mind racing. He had always been a career-driven man, focused on climbing the corporate ladder and achieving success. Love had never been a priority for him; it was something he had quietly filed away as secondary. But now, as Sana's words echoed in his ears, something shifted inside him. He felt alive in a way he hadn't before. His brow lifted, his mouth spread into an incredulous smile, and he let out a soft breath.

"Do you even realize what you just said?" he asked, his voice tinged with astonishment and a hint of playfulness.

Sana tilted her head, genuinely puzzled by his reaction. "What? What did I say? Just that... if you really love me, will you marry me?"

Sid's laughter filled the car. "Stupid girl," he said, shaking his head while blushing, "you just proposed to me." He ruffled his thick hair with his fingers and glanced at himself in the rearview mirror, trying to process the overwhelming joy surging through him.

Unable to contain himself, he leaned closer, cupping her soft face in his large hands. His voice softened, and his eyes searched hers with a rare intensity. "Yes, Sana. I love you... truly, madly, deeply. And yes, I will marry you... only you." He pressed a tender kiss to her forehead, his eyes brimming with unshed tears.

Sana felt a warm glow spread through her chest. Her own tears began to spill, but they were tears of happiness. She bit her lower lip to stop a full-blown smile and, unable to resist, threw her arms around him. Sid held her tightly, and the world seemed to fade away. The hug wasn't just an embrace; it was a moment of pure, unspoken connection. They had hugged others before—family, friends, colleagues—but this was different. This was the missing piece of their hearts clicking into place. At that moment, they found peace and a quiet ecstasy that neither of them had ever known.

Still wrapped in each other's arms, Sid broke the silence. "Sana, I fell for you the first day I saw you. I knew then that if I ever wanted a life partner, it would be you. It was an instant connection, love at first sight, just like they say. But I need to know your feelings. Do you love me?"

Sana pulled back slightly, her hands still resting on his shoulders. She hesitated, her mind a swirl of emotions. She wanted to be honest, to give him the truth he deserved. "I don't know, Sid. I mean, I know I like you. I'm attracted to you. Ever since the first day I saw you, you've been in my thoughts. I look forward to seeing you and talking to you. And it's a relief to know I'm not the only one who feels this way. But I'm not sure if this is love. I want to experience that four-letter word with you, dive into the ocean of it, and swim through it. If investing my emotions in you means a lifetime of commitment, then yes, I will do that. I'll be true, loyal, and honest to you. And if that's what love is… then yes, I love you."

Sid's face lit up. He took her hands in his and said, "Sana, the way you just poured your heart out—so honestly, so innocently—shows how wise and mature you are. At your age, to have such clarity and control over your emotions is incredible. I have so much to learn from you, my love."

She smiled and blushed at his words, her heart fluttering. But her gaze suddenly darted to the car's clock. Her eyes widened in panic. "Oh my God! Sid, it's 8:10 already! Drive now, jaldi! Aaj toh siyappa ho jaana hai! I hate being late, especially on my third day at work. Aap ko toh VP hain, but meri toh job chali jayegi! Hey Bhagwan, bacha lena!"

Sid couldn't help laughing at her frantic rambling. He started the car and said calmly, "Kiski itni himmat hogi meri Jaaneman ko job se nikalne ki? Don't worry; you're safe. Tumhare Bhagwan ji ko rest lene do. Why worry when I'm here?"

But Sana was too stressed to relax. "Sid, please drive faster! And starting tomorrow, there will be no distractions and no parking here and there in the morning. Straight to work! I'll set an alarm for 7:55 a.m. so we know it's time to go in."

"Okay, as you say, madam," Sid replied, grinning. He admired her dedication and punctuality, traits he shared and deeply valued. In her, he saw a reflection of himself—a hardworking, sincere individual—and his admiration for her grew with each passing moment. He knew there were still so many facets of her personality waiting to be discovered. Their love was just beginning, and he was determined to give it the time and care it deserved.

When they arrived at the office, Sana hurried inside her heart racing. Sid parked the car and followed, only to find Mr. Gupta questioning Sana about her tardiness.

"What's the issue, Mr. Gupta?" Sid asked in a calm but authoritative tone.

"Oh, Sir," Mr. Gupta stammered, "I was just informing her about the company's punctuality policy."

Sid's gaze didn't waver. "I'm responsible for her delay. You can excuse her. Sana, get back to work."

Sana's eyes widened in shock. She hadn't expected him to take responsibility so openly. Embarrassed but also deeply moved, she felt a new sense of security. Sid wasn't just her boss or her love; he was her partner, someone who would protect her and stand by her. For the first time, her insecurities began to fade, replaced by a quiet confidence in their bond.

Maybe this was what love truly was—having someone who guided you, challenged you, and yet made you feel utterly safe. As she walked back to her desk, a smile played on her lips. Their story was just beginning, and she couldn't wait to see where it would lead.

Chapter Eleven:
Love On The Fast Lane

"Sir, I have moved all your meetings between 8-5 pm. Just tomorrow's meeting at 6 pm with TW & sons has not been moved. They don't have any appointments available before that time, and they are quite busy for the coming 6 months. Also, Sir, this is a very important project for our company; you have been preparing for this for a long." Raj, Sid's PA, spoke out with worry.

"You are right, I will attend that meeting at the scheduled time, no need to change... let it be and thanks for taking care of all other appointments on very short notice, I really appreciate it.Raj."

"My pleasure Sir" Raj left Sid behind wondering how he managed tomorrow's evening car time with Sana. Diverting his mind his phone rang and it was Sumit!! He picked up the call and the first thing he heard was all the curses of the world, *"Ho Gaya bas aur Kuch language ki gali bachi hain toh woh bhi bol de"* Sid smiled.

"Saale... puri duniya jahaan ko pata chal gaya aur sirf mereko nahi pata. When were you planning to tell me?" Sumit asked angrily.

"Kya pata chal gaya? Kya batau?" Sid teased him, making Sumit angry. *"Saale, Bc. Don't play games with me. I should have been the first one to know, and I got the news from whom? That Rahul...!!!! Like, really, bro. Meri toh KLPT ho gayi."* Frustrated, Sumit yelled.

Sid was laughing teasing him holding his stomach, *"Now are you just gonna laugh or tell me who is that Menaka who broke this Vishwamitra's meditation? Hamare pandith ka kya... something... something... brastht karne wali...I am going to wash her feet and take Aarthi of her,"* Sumit was curiously asking Sid and he could just say one thing. *"Sana."*

"Hmm, kya? Phir se bol aur Teri Loudspeaker wali awaaz ko kya hua?" Sumit asked again as Sid was dazed again, thinking about her. *"Her name is Sanaya... Sanaya Iyer. Short main Sana."*

"Oh Teri!!!! Hamare Sharma Ji ko Madrasan pasand aa gayi... sahi hain... Iyer the great... Waise kahan tak pahunchi baath? Did you guys talk or just eyes talking phase going one?"

"We have expressed our feelings for each other!" Sid replied shortly, blushing.

"WHAT!!!!! You are kidding right!!!!! Abey you guys are what Superfast express.... no. Actually, you are a jet airplane..." shocked Sumit said.

"You meet me in the evening, I will give you all the details and also introduce you to her. What say?" Sid asked. "Yes yes, of course, I am dying to meet my Bhabhi, I am so impressed yaar. I will meet you in the evening then. So happy for you man" Sumit happiness was reflected in his voice.

Sid kept his phone down and started to do his work and the day ended very fast as he was very busy in meetings.

It was 5 pm, and Sana wrapped up the lobby and headed towards the restroom before driving back home. She was blushing the whole day; the reminiscence of the morning ride was still lingering in her thoughts. She was exhilarated, beaming with how her life had turned. The new feeling that she had always been running away from, fearing family, heartbreaks, and society, could be so joyful, she never thought. She still had insecurities, but they have taken a back seat for the time being. She wanted to just be in the moment and make the most out of it. Her fear, societal bondages, nothing seemed big in front of what she was feeling for Sid right now. She looked at herself in the mirror and felt beautiful.

She walked towards his car as he was already waiting for her at the curb.

"How was your day? Busy? You are looking so tired!" Sana said, worried.

"Yes, it was busy, but I am fine." Driving the car to the road, he replied, and then their conversation flowed all through their car journey to her home. Mostly Sana talking and him listening. He loved that… as her soothing, innocent, chirpy voice was relaxing him in an unknown way. She had never-ending stories of her childhood, family, summer vacations, and traveling, and he loved every part of it. He felt closer to her. Knowing her more and knowing her family more made him realize how much he missed his own family. She will know his family as she will stay with him after they get married but it is wonderful to connect to her family. He understood her upbringing, her culture, and how she lived up to each moment of her life.

"Tomorrow evening I have a meeting at 6, you will have to take the bus. Will you be fine with that?" Sid asked reluctantly.

"Haan haan no problem, I will take the bus." Sana said with a heavy heart. "I will miss our meeting," Sid said with a heavy heart too. "Arre, but we are together now and also in the morning, so why worry," Sana said making the atmosphere light. They reached her community and it seemed the hour-long drive going by fast.

"I will come in the evening in the park. My friend Sumit wants to meet you. I will text you when I am there," Sid said.

"Hmmm… okay." Sana replied, "I will go now, bye."

Sid held her hand when she was about to exit the car and kissed her knuckles. "I will miss you." Sana blushed and left for her home.

Sid reached home and, after a quick shower, went to his mom and sat next to her on the couch with a piping cup of tea. His mom cherishes this chai time with his son. She was happy that for a few days, he had been coming early, and she was able to spend more time with him. She wondered what might be the reason for his early arrival, so she asked, "Nowadays, you are coming early; what is the reason? I am not complaining; rather, I am very happy, beta."

"Woh. actually, Mom, I want to say something to you." Sid was hesitant about telling her about Sana. Will she like her? Will she accept her? As far as he knows, his mom was very broad-minded and would never deny a love marriage. She supported his sister's love and got her married to the person Kajal chose for herself. She had been more like a friend to both her kids and had always encouraged them both to be independent and free. Still, Sid wanted to hear her thoughts as she was the most important part of his life.

"Bol na bacha, sab teek hain na? Why are you hesitant? Kuch gadbad kiya kya? Company main sab teek hain na?" worried Mom asked.

"All is good, Mom. Sab teek hain kuch gadbad nahi kiya. In fact, I want to share something good." Sid said, pausing, "I have fallen in love, maa! I am in love with this fabulous, beautiful girl."

Surprised and shocked, mouth agape, his mom gave all the reactions within seconds. She smiled with tears in her eyes and said, "I have been waiting to hear this from you for so long, bacha! Who is she? Tell me about her!"

"She started this Monday as a receptionist at my company, and my heart said she is the one. It was instant mom; I couldn't help myself to fall for her. She also feels the same for me. Her name is Sanaya; I will show you her pic…" he poured his heart out to Mom and eagerly opened the phone to show the profile pic she had in her WhatsApp. "I am so happy, Sid, she is so beautiful. Tell me more about her, her family, and where she lives." Mom asked curiously.

"She lives just 10 minutes away. She is from South, Chennai and her father is a bank manager, the mother is a housewife and has an elder brother" he said.

"South Indian?" mom worriedly asked.

"Yes, why?" he asked, bringing his eyebrow.

"They are very particular about their culture, religion, and caste." Mom said.

"There is a long way, Mom. We will talk about that later. Don't worry, she is mine, and I will never let her go because of this stupid system." Sid sternly said.

Chapter Twelve:
Breaking The Shell

Coming back home on the bus felt weird; Sana was missing Sid and the car ride. Her nonsensical talks, which she did with her family and friends, she found it safe to do that with Sid, too. He was so patient with her and a great listener, but she was curious to know about him and his family, too. It felt good to have been introduced to his friend Sumit yesterday evening when he came to walk again in the park. Sumit was an easygoing, jovial person. She connected with him so easily, and his calling her 'Bhabhi' felt so new to her. She blushed just thinking about that.

Looking out the window, she thought about how life had changed within a week. Did she think when she joined the company that she would meet someone who would sweep her floor away and make her heart flutter the way it did whenever she saw him? She spent more time in front of the mirror to look more pretty just for his eyes. There are so many things that she still doesn't know about him, like his favorite color and his favorite song, but she has been an open book to him. He knows almost everything about her because of her nonstop talks.

Her thoughts were completely filled with his presence when her phone rang.

"Hello," she said with a smile, seeing the name displayed in SS🚗

"Missing me?" Sid asked.

"Hmm. yes. aap?"

"Me too darling, I have this meeting at 6 and preparing for it but I can't focus, as this time is ours," Sid said with a frown.

"You should focus on that Sid, I don't want to be your distraction and keep you away from your work. Please don't let this ruin all your hard work that you have done." Sana said sternly and worried.

"You can never be a distraction, baby, never think that. In fact, you are my lucky charm, and talking to you will make things better, never worse." Sid consoled her.

"Hmm.. okay but keep the phone down and work, we will talk tomorrow, and today evening I cannot come out for a walk, we are expecting guests and I will be helping my mom with cooking," Sana said.

"Okay, even though I don't know if I will make it today as this meeting can go long and I might reach home late, I will ride by your community before going home and beep my trademark horn... Just show your face on the balcony. Will you?" he asked.

Sana smiled with his small demand, "Yes... of course. Aur kuch?"

"Yes... a kiss? Milegi?" Sid asked smiling. Sana was shocked and gasped hearing his demand. This was the first time he was asking for a kiss from her. He had been kissing her hand, once on her forehead but she never imagined him asking for a kiss on the phone like this so bluntly. "Hugh?? What??"

"Kiss baby... ek kiss milegi? Like this ummah... not that difficult..right." he again asked shamelessly, even giving her a demo!

"Are you mad? I am on the bus. I am keeping the phone. Bye," Shying Sana said.

"No, dare you to keep the phone down without giving me the kiss... de na.. darling, it's just in the phone.. don't need to be shy. UMMAAHH... see easy... now I gave you two, you also have to give

me two..." shamelessly, Sid was pestering Sana. He wanted her to open up and be free to him. She was free to talk about everything in the world, but when it came to physical, she became silent and shy and changed the topic. Sid was adamant about making her comfortable talking and showing their love physically. It's natural to express love physically as well. He knew his limit and would never cross that limit, but opening her up to him was important to him. So he pushed and didn't feel embarrassed doing that.

"I can't, Sid, please... this is sooo embarrassing. Hey Bhagwan..." with a low voice, she expressed her feelings. *"Ab tere Bhagwan yahan kahan se aa gaye... okay give me a flying kiss... can you do that?"* Sid asked. *"You are too pushy, Sid, you know that..."* Sana said, *"Haan chal teek hain... now quick I have to go to the meeting.."*

After a long pause, Sana said, "Flying kiss, okay..." She looked around and took a long breath, nervous as if she was going to take an exam… she made a flying kiss very soft and quick to phone. He could just hear the soft-clicking voice of her kiss... they were in voice talk, not in the video, and just to get her kiss virtually, even if it was a flying kiss, he felt thrilled. This was her first kiss on the phone; long way to go, but he felt excited. "Love you, Sana, and thanks for your first kiss. Don't feel shy. I will get my second kiss in person from you. Bye and text me when you reach home," and he kept down the phone, blushing and rolling his tongue; he didn't want to make her shy anymore.

He knew she would have been red by now with her face down. He could visualize her clearly in the red top she wore with blue pants. She looked so hot when she came inside the car this morning. He couldn't take his eyes off her, she had this magic to make him forget the world. He felt energized even after a busy day, just hearing her voice and her first phone kiss.

Sana, on the other hand, was feeling too shy; this was her first time doing something so taboo... yes, taboo! She was smiling, but then a fear took over her, fear of society and family. All her life, she had been kept safe and protected by her family, but now she felt as if she was breaking their trust. They had given her freedom and independence. Never kept her bonded or differentiated her, but this world being so cruel to girls, she was always taught to be safe and never indulge in any adulteration. She felt guilty about doing this simple act, though she felt excited at that moment and did it with full love towards Sid, but guilt took over that emotion. She thought of sharing this feeling with her bestie, her solace, her Payal di, to ask her if she did anything wrong in doing this. She would be the best person right now to enlighten her wavering mind.

She reached home and texted Sid that she was home. She freshened up and straight went to Di's house. *"Di, kahan ho?"* Sana yelled, opening Payal's house door.

"Kitchen main aaja, chai peyegi?" Di said. *"Yes, please."* Sana went towards the kitchen and sat on the kitchen slab next to the stove where Di was making chai. *"Bolo kya bolna hain."* Di asked, glancing at Sana; that's how connected they were; though born with different mothers, they were like soul sisters. One would know if the other had anything without even telling the other person. Sana felt blessed to have a sister figure like Payal in her life to whom she could say her heart out without even thinking twice, without any fear. She knows that Di won't judge her. Rather, she will say what's right and guide her to do what her heart feels right.

"Aapko kaise path, ki mujhe kuch bolna hain?" surprised Sana asked, eating the Good Day biscuit. Pouring the chai into a cup, Di said, *"Ab office se aate hi, meri yaad aayi hain toh kuch baath toh hogi, right?"*

"Hayee di, you are antaryami... hmm, super chai.." sipping in hot chai, they sat on the balcony. Payal knew she liked her chai with extra sugar, so they added more sugar before serving her and loved it when Sana relished her chai. *"Di, kaise bolu!!*

Bol du." "When did you start to think twice before saying something to me, haan?" curiously Payal asked. *"Nahi di, this is something sensitive. You know, right, Sid and I confessed our love to each other, but today, while coming back on the bus, he called and asked me to kiss him, Di!"* Sana quickly said in one breath with a guilty frown face.

"Toh, you kissed him right? yeh mooh sada ke kyun bol rahi hain. You must have told me this with an excited and blushing face, why frowning face?" slapping Sana's head Payal said with no surprise which amazed Sana. "You are not shocked? You don't think that I did something wrong?"

"Why do you think you did something wrong? Tu pagal hain Sana? Which century are you born in? When there is nothing wrong with expressing your love in words to the person you love then how can expressing your love physically to that person be wrong?" Payal explained clearing Sana's doubt but still, she was not convinced.

"But Di, I am not that forward-thinking; I feel I am breaking Amma Appa's trust. I don't know di, I am so confused. I felt excited when I did that act, but later guilt overpowered that excitement." Sana said honestly.

"Sana meri gudiya, you are not breaking anyone's trust. You are a human with feelings & emotions, and loving someone and getting attracted to someone is not a 'PAAP' understand this. I understand we are a middle-class family, and our upbringing tells us right and wrong stuff… but get out of this stereotypical thinking. You just listened to your heart; you listened to it and followed it when you fell in love with him, right? So just listen to what it says and shut your stupid mind. Did you ask me or your parents when you confessed your feelings to him? Did you think you are breaking their trust then?" Payal asked. Sana nodded in no with pouting lips.

"Then why did you think today, just coz he asked to kiss you on the phone? He is not wrong, Sana; he is attached to you and likes how you expect things from him like calls him, messages, or drives from him... he also will expect things from you, and men are more physically connected; they have needs, he will ask more kisses, hugs, and many other things later and you should respect that bacha, never judge him and think low of him. You trust him, right? Do you know your limits? Listen to your heart and your conscience. It will guide you to the right path. Eventually, you will tell your parents and marry him, but don't destroy this courtship period because of your guilt and self-loathing!" Payal said, *"Understand? Ya abhi bhi soch rahi hain?"*

"You are right, di, but it will take time for me to come out of the shell, and I hope Sid will be patient till then. It's not easy for me to come out of the patriarchal mindset. I have been fed and consented to it since my birth, and I adhere to it. I think my physical and spiritual nature has to cohere and mature; it's going to be a process, and I want to experience this journey with Sid. I want to find myself with him." Sana replied back with a stance and confidence, clearing her battle of mind over heart. The clarity, the point of view given by Di was giving her some thought to think. She felt lighter, guilt gone, and clarity surrounded her chirpy, bubbly persona again.

Chapter Thirteen:
First Kiss, Forever Memory

It was a weekend, and that meant an hour more of sleep for Sana, which she loved to take, though with a lot of noise from the house, but she did not mind as she was used to it. Her father is a firm believer in the 'Early to bed, Early to rise' concept. He would wake up daily by 5 am and make a nice filter coffee for both himself and his wife. Sana's mom would never get up from bed unless she got her bed coffee made by her dad. He would then make all the noises in the world to wake up both the kids. Put morning Tamil suprabatham (devotional) songs, push the steel cloth stand from the balcony, open the curtains, and switch off the fan, and cooler. Pour water into plants, and give bread to stray dogs from the balcony. This was his daily routine. By 6 am, all the members of the house would wake up without him specifically calling their names. But on weekends, he would not switch off the fan and cooler till 7 am and let both kids sleep, but after that, he would again start making disturbances to wake them up.

He would do his morning prayer routine with Guru Anna. He was a firm believer in following the Brahmin customs of prayer, like Sandhya Vandhanam and Veda chanting, which they would religiously follow. Sana loved to hear the Veda chanting from his father's voice, which was melodious, it was a kind of meditation for her, spiritual and divine. The whole house would be illuminated with positive energy.

Her mom, on the other hand, would make a feast on weekends, and all the family members would eat breakfast, lunch, and dinner together. They always had a lot of guests in their house, their relatives and friends who would just come to have food made by her mom. She was very particular about cleanliness and would make sure everyone did their part of cleaning chores, which Sana loathed. Guru Anna is very obedient and disciplined; he did his work diligently and was never reminded. Sana, on the other hand, was pampered by her dad and would always escape doing her part, which Guru Anna does eventually so that she does not get scolded by her mom.

Sana would spend her time listening to music, dancing on the numbers, and reading books, but now she had one more distraction and that was her mobile phone where she waited for Sid to call or message her. She would carry her phone all the time now, being careful of the family, so that they do not pick up Sid's call or see his message and question her about him.

Sid, on the other hand, usually was laid back on weekends. He would wake up late, go to the gym, and would work out, taking extra time. Go to a club to swim, catch up with friends, and watch a cricket match. His mom would make his favorite food, just a simple healthy lunch and dinner, the way he liked. Life was good for him, and with the new addition to his life, it was more blissful. He would message her good morning and good nights and ride around her community whenever he went somewhere just to take a glimpse of her, horning the trademark horn, Beep. Beep. Beep beep beep… and she would show up smiling and looking for him from the balcony.

They were having the time of their life; it had been a month since they met for the first time in the company. Sana wanted to celebrate the day, and as it was a weekend, she asked Sid if they could meet. Sid was more than happy to meet her outside of her company and car rides. He immediately responded with a yes as this would be their first time, and that too, coming that request from Sana was huge. He always gave her the space she needed and respected her request about the physical proximity. She was not comfortable with kissing and was still apprehensive about it. They have not had their first kiss yet! And Sid was impatient to experience that with Sana, but he waited for her to get comfortable and trust him with that.

They decided to meet in a Mall, watch a movie, and have dinner later. But she could not come alone and came with Payal di in her scooter taking due permission from her parents as they would never deny her if Payal was going with her. Sid too asked Sumit to accompany him as he wanted Sana all for himself and asked Sumit to entertain Payal when he was with Sana.

"Hi Sid, hi Sumit," Payal and Sana said together, hugging them.

"Hi Sana, hi Payal, nice to see you both, kaise ho dono," asked Sumit.

"First class, Sid tickets le liye? Let's go I don't want to miss the ads that come before the movie." Sana said, making Sid and Sumit laugh out loud. Payal was not surprised she knew Sana and she knew how fond Sana was about not missing even a single thing that showed on the big screen and she just rolled her eyes.

"Han le liye, Chalo... we will get popcorn and drinks for you guys, tere liye Fanta and you Payal what will you have?" Sid asked, as he knew that Sana didn't like any black color soda drink as she said, but Fanta was her favorite mango juice.

"Coke for me, please. Thanks, Sid," said Payal. They waited for them at the entrance of the gate, and they came happy and excited. Sana was very excited to be with Sid, and being with Di helped her to overcome her fear of someone seeing her with Sid.

Sid took the tickets from the topmost back row; there were not many people, which was the best part. It was an Akshay Kumar movie full of entertainment, Bollywood masala. Sid sat in the corner, Sana next, followed by Payal and Sumit.

Sumit was a talkative, funny guy who was fully entertaining Payal, who was enjoying his company. They both clicked instantly, and Sana was pleasantly surprised to see her friend enjoying it. Sid was happy to be with Sana, and he enjoyed her company, too. They both held their hand and looked at each other from time to time during the movie in the dark. She laughed during the comic scene, cried during the emotional, and blushed in the romantic scene. There came a kiss scene, too, where Sid looked at Sana with expectations. Sana could feel his eye on her lips, and she also looked at him. His eye radiated all his passion for her. She held his muscular arm and kept her head on his shoulder, rubbing his arm and making him calm.

There were some things that were untold, untouched, but they knew their soul and could understand each other's emotions. "I want to kiss you, Sana, please." He asked, kissing her forehead. It was dark, and Sana looked at Payal; she was engrossed in a movie, eating popcorn. They were reclined back to the seat, and Sana couldn't stop herself either; the ambiance and his handsome face in the dark made her nod to him yes. Her cheeks were hot, her stomach fluttering in anticipation, and she looked up at him and his lips.

Sid didn't wait anymore he held her face and took her lips and kissed her, a peck first, and then took her lower lip and kissed her opening her mouth. It was his first kiss too, and he didn't know if he was doing it right but it felt right. He kissed opening her mouth taking her upper and lower lip, tongue rolling and exploring her mouth. His right hand held her face, a slow but passionate kiss.

Music in the background was fading for them at that moment. They were enjoying their first kiss, a memory they will cherish lifelong.

Chapter Fourteen:
Passion's Silent War

It's been a week since their first kiss, and now Sid couldn't help but keep away from her. He wanted to kiss her whenever she was with him. In the car, in the office, he would stop his car in the middle of nowhere and kiss her fervently, call her during her lunchtime, break time in his office room, and kiss his heart out. He was getting crazy for her lips. He was addicted to that.

Sana, on the other hand, was meek; she was in a demurred state. She liked it when Sid showed his passion by kissing her, but he behaved like a dam broken, never leaving a moment to kiss her. The only time they talked was when they were on the phone; otherwise, all the time, he would just kiss her when they met. The drive in the car was more silent and reticent. Lunch times were spent more on kissing than eating lunch. He was a passionate man; she understood that clearly. Her lips were swollen all the time these days, though she applied lipstick, but they never stayed on her lips long! She always blushed when she saw herself in the mirror these days.

Also, questioning the eyes of her mom was bothering her. She asked her once the reason for her swollen lips and she gave a lame excuse of lipstick allergy, which she loathed.

"Sid, I am going by bus from now on; I am not coming with you anymore bas ho gaya mera. Jab dekho you kiss!!! "Sana exasperated with a very low voice. It was Saturday, and Sid called her almost at midnight; she was in bed in her room, and they had been on the phone for an hour.

"Arre, baba what should I do, I cannot take my eyes off your lips... and please jayda bakwas mat kar samjhi.." Sid said, "Aur sunn tomorrow meet me na, we will go to Delhi and roam around, maybe watch a movie, chal na moti." he requested. They have opened up a lot; formal talks have taken a back seat. Their relationship has grown steadily and they feel much closer to each other.

"MOTI!! kon moti.. main na tumhara sar phod dungi Sid.. main nahi jaa rahi kahin apke saath.." angry Sana replied. Sid laughed, imagining her angry, pouted, round face. "You are my moti, my sweetheart, my jaaneman.. and please, you call me 'tu' only… When you call 'aap,' I feel like an old man."

"Toh aap.. tum.. manthe ho that you are a Budauuoo.. hehehehehe..." Sana teased him.

"Acha, bathauu yeh Budha kya kya kar saktha hain? Bol.. aauuu" Sid said..

"Pagal ho tum.. majak kar rahi thi!" Sana feared them as she knew he was crazy and could do anything if challenged. "Make an excuse for tomorrow at home and come. I will wait in the car at 12, and we will be back by 6, I promise…" Sid ordered and pressured her to meet him.

"Dimaag karab ho gaya hain tumhara Sid, kya bolungi amma appa ko ki kahan jaa rahi huin and above all Guru anna is at home and you know he is a Sherlock Holmes. I can't… sorry!" Sana tried to make him understand. She also wanted to spend time with him but making excuses, and lying to her family was not her forte but she has been doing that a lot these days. Not big ones but still it hit her conscious.

"What is your problem? Haan, you don't want to spend time with me? Am I the only one dying to be with you, and don't you even care to say a lame excuse to your family? Jab dekho, I can't do this, I can't do that. I am just fed up!! Even when I come close to you to kiss, you just make me feel as if I am forcing on you. Don't you feel anything for me? Haan.. Damn!!" he shouted and yelled at her making her hurt, shocked for the first time!

She felt hurt; her eyes watered hearing his harsh words; why was it difficult for him to understand this? It was her belief and something she had been taught since birth: to be honest and truthful. Even at school and college, she would never cheat, bunk, or lie to her parents just to freak out with friends. She would always ask for their permission if she wanted to go with friends and watch a movie or go out. "Aa..aap gussa kyun ho rahe ho? Please understand it is very difficult for me to lie and come out of the house..... helloo.. helloo.." Before she could say anything, Sid cut the call abruptly.

Sid was frustrated; he could not take any more of the principles she followed. He loved her and wanted to spend time with her. Was he anywhere wrong about that? He questioned himself. He was patient enough with her and understood her, but now, in this phase where he wanted all of her to himself, and when he couldn't get that, it was frustrating. He cut the call angrily, drank water, and went to sleep, but sleep was nowhere. He made up his mind not to talk to her until she realized what he wanted.

Sana cried and was shocked as to why Sid kept the phone down. Was meeting her that important that it didn't deter him from hurting her and then cutting the call on her? Why was he so angry about it, she wondered. They met daily, and they spent almost all day with each other; it was just weekends that they were away, but even in that, they would call and see each other on the balcony, in the park. Was that not enough for her to lie more to her parents to meet him? She was already doing so much out of her way. She called him again, but he didn't pick up her call. She was hurt, and she thought she was not wrong.

This was their first fight and it was hurting them both, sleep nowhere, one watching the ceiling and proving himself right, and one crying and wetting the pillow understanding where she was wrong. Both of them ached, straining each other for inseparableness but what an irony it was. Malady that accompanies love is inevitable, they drifted off to sleep in the crack of dawn!

Chapter Fifteen:
Through Her Eyes, Through His Heart

Sunday went by with the amiable bovine faces of Sana and Sid. Sid made himself busy in the gym, club, cricket matches, and in-office work. His phone was in silence, and he had not bothered to look at that since last night, not even charging it. He was sulking, disappointed, and distracted himself from this sour feeling which he detested. She was in his mind all the time. He missed and worried about her even though he did not want to talk to her. He was acting like a small kid, adamant and validating his demand for her to realize the thing important to him.

Monday, when he woke up, he checked his phone, and it was switched off due to no charge. He charged his phone and went to get ready for the day. He was standing at 7:15 am near Sana's community entrance to pick her up, which was a usual working day for him for 1.5 months now. Anticipating her glimpse, he missed her, her face, her voice, her smile, her lips, her aroma, her antics, her dancing eyes and hands, her gimmicks… everything about her. He thought of ending this fight and asking her for an apology, saying he would never behave the way he did. This was testing his sanity, and he did not have a good feeling to dwell on.

He decided never to yell or shout at her; she was young, and he admired how she respected her parents' trust. He had never seen such a disciplined and honest girl in recent times, and he felt proud of her and his choice. He thought that he would be more understanding and would never push her and make her do what she hated.

Fidgeting his fingers in steering, shaking his leg, eyes fixed on her flat gate. She didn't come. It was 7:20. She is very punctual and is never late. He picked up his mobile and switched on the phone. It had 32 missed calls from her and 112 messages from her.

He was shocked and felt guilty for avoiding her calls and messages. He checked the messages, which mostly said sorry and details about her point of view, then one message which caught his attention, she had waited for him yesterday on the road for their meet up. She lied to her parents and agreed to meet him and fulfill his demands... his heart felt heavy, heavy with guilt, heavy with ignoring her and doubting her intentions. The message about her not coming to work today!

He felt low about himself for torturing her and giving her so much hurt. She didn't deserve this. He felt ashamed of himself; he was mature between them but did not show the maturity that she showed, which made him feel disappointed. He called her, but she didn't pick up this time. He felt that he deserved this, which is how she must have felt when he did not pick up his call. He slammed the steering with how vulnerable he felt! Eyes getting wet, he felt ashamed.

Then suddenly his phone rang, it was Sana, his heart fluttered seeing her name on display. He picked up the call immediately with relief that she might have missed his call and that he was wrong to think that she deliberately didn't pick up his call.

"Hello, Sana..." he said... "Hi Sid, sorry I missed your call... Sorry aap gussa mat hona," she said, fear in her voice evident by adding so many sorry.

"I am sorry, Sana, I am sorry for behaving like an asshole... my phone was out of charge, and I did not check it till now," Sid replied. "Oh, it's okay!" Sana said, her answer clipped short.

"Why are you not coming today to work? Are you sick?" he asked.

"No, I am not sick" again a short reply from her. She was distancing herself from him, he could feel that. She is going back to her shell again, which he managed to break through their car rides and talks.

"What is it, Sana? Hmm... I am still waiting outside, come now... get dressed. I will wait for you here, take your time, but I want to see you; I know you have taken off for today, but I will also take my day off. We can go out somewhere and talk this out. Please come, Sana..." he almost begged her.

"I am sorry, Sid, but I cannot come; I am at the airport," she said... making Sid shocked.

"Airport, why airport? Are you going somewhere? Why didn't you tell me? No, you cannot leave me, Sana... please don't give me such a big punishment. I know I was foolish to shout at you, and I regret it... I do. Please Sana... sorry yaar aisa mat kar," he cried, questioning, retaliating his deeds.

"Nahi Sid, aap pareshan mat ho. Aap, sorry, mat bolo... I am not going anywhere, came with Guru Anna to drop my parents and my mama. They are going to Kerala, as yesterday night we got the call from my eldest mama that my 'Ammuma,' I mean my Nani, is hospitalized as she had a heart attack. Amma cried the whole night; she was very sad. So, Appa booked the tickets immediately, and they are going for a week. I will come back home soon." She clarified, giving a sigh of relief to Sid.

"Ohh... Thank God! Main darr gaya. I am sorry to hear about your Nani's health. Let me know when you come back home; I will pick you up. I want to meet you, Sana," he asked politely this time, not pushing her and ready to accept if she could not make it. He has to practice that a lot and not be pushy and bossy with her. He has been bossy the whole of his life, and that's why he is in a good position in the company. However, the relationship does not work that way; he understands that it is just because of his first rift with her.

"I will call you Sid, Guru Anna is coming back, and I cannot talk in front of him. Sorry and please don't get upset. I will call you once I get back home and we will make some plans, definitely. I hope you understand! And I request you to go to the office now as it will take 2 hours for us to reach home." Sana said quickly as she could see his brother coming back to the car.

"Yes, yes Sana, I do understand. Bye..." She kept the phone down before he could complete and get a reply from her. He understood her situation and has learned his lessons well. He knows that he has to be more considerate towards her and emphatic about her situation and beliefs.

He drove back to the company till he got a call from her, missing her, still with a heavy and guilty heart. The scene in which she waited for him in Sun out on the road just to fulfill his demand, lying to her parents and breaking her ethics and beliefs, made him cringe. He felt empty without her in the next seat. He got habitual of her being with him all the time in the car. This car didn't feel good enough without her being on the side. Life without her felt empty, just like the seat beside him...

Chapter Sixteen:
When Love Knocks

The way back home was silent, with a heaviness in Sana's heart. It was the most painful and cruel Sunday she had ever experienced in her life. She could not express how she had been feeling for those 24 hours. It was grueling, exhausting, and extremely tiring. Her eyes were heavy without sleep, and her stomach was growling from the lack of food. Well, it's true when they say, "Na bhook lage na pyaas," but for her, this happened while she was experiencing the pain of love.

Being in love felt good, like a paradise, but she was unaware that it also came with so many other feelings—sour and bitter ones—that she had not anticipated. She was naturally a very happy, positive, and unambiguous girl all her life, and this was the first time she faced her vulnerable side. It was taking a toll on her.

She had called him so many times and messaged him several times on Sunday, but he neither replied nor bothered to look at her messages and calls. She wondered what if he decided to come and stand there at 12 to pick her up for the meeting. She decided to go and meet him if that was the only way to calm him. She didn't want to upset him further, so she resolved to go against her beliefs and lie to her parents.

She gave the excuse that her college friend was having a get-together and had invited her too and that she really wanted to be a part of it. Her parents agreed without any questions, only asking how she would commute. She lied about that too—as they say, one lie leads to another—and said her friends would pick her up. Somehow, she was getting the hang of it. Earlier, she thought she would fear giving excuses, but love makes you do things you never imagined!

She dressed up, making an effort to look good. She hadn't had proper sleep or eaten well, but she wanted to look good for him, to cheer him up.

She messaged him that she was ready to meet and that she would wait for him at the usual spot. She waited... but he never came. She waited for an hour, called him, and messaged him again, but he never picked up her calls or read her messages. Disappointed, she went back home and had to tell another lie—that her friends couldn't come to pick her up—and gave some lame excuse for it.

She thought that this was it—Sid hated her and had broken up with her. How will she face him at work? Will he ever talk to her again? she wondered. She cried, thinking about the time spent with him and their short-lived love story. She felt this was her destiny and was overcome with hopelessness. To add fuel to the fire, a call from her uncle that night brought more sadness. She cried with her mom, mourning not just her Nani but also her ill-fated love life.

The next morning, she messaged him again, assuming that she was blocked and that he wouldn't bother reading her messages or seeing her at work. She had lost all hope and was disappointed to believe that he had ever loved her. She regretted trusting him with her feelings—all her emotions for him felt wasted. It was her first love, and now it had given her her first heartbreak, her first pain.

Later that day, they left for the airport to drop off her mom, dad, and uncle. She was standing outside in the parking lot when her phone rang from inside the car. Hearing it, she sat back inside, waiting for Guru Anna, who had gone to the restroom before they began their ride back home. Her heart skipped a beat when she saw the name in the missed call list. Hope flickered back, and with a small smile and her eyes lighting up, she called back. To her pleasant surprise, he answered.

Hearing his voice and his apologetic tone melted her heart. She never expected him to apologize, but the relief was overwhelming. He still cared, still anticipated seeing her—and that felt so good to her.

When they reached home, the first thing she did was eat. She had been starving and was almost on the verge of blacking out. Afterward, she took a small nap, only to be woken up by Guru Anna.

"Sana, get up," he said, shaking her vigorously.

"Kya Hain, Anna? Some do mujhe..." she murmured sleepily.

"I need to go to work. It's urgent. Can you manage on your own? Payal is also not here, or I would have asked her to stay with you," he asked.

"Ya, I will. Aap jao... Did Appa call? Have they reached safely?" she asked, still half-asleep.

"Yes, they have reached safely and are still on their way to the hospital. Okay, I'm leaving. Call your friends if you want, but don't go out. Lock the doors. Bye," he said hurriedly and left, driving out of the community.

Sana was still in a daze, catching up on her sleep. She closed the door and realized she was all alone in the house, which had never happened before. She called Sid, and he picked up the call in one ring.

"Hello... thank God you called. I was so worried about you. Itna time kyun laga call karne main?" he bombarded her with questions.

"I am sorry, woh... when we came back, I felt sleepy and went to take a nap. I didn't sleep last night, that's why... so I forgot to text you," she replied nervously, her voice low, fearing his anger or reaction.

"Don't say sorry, please, Sana. Kyun itna formal ho rahi ho? Please, baby... tu mujhe maaf kar de. Itna affect mat ho." He almost begged her, wanting her to come back to her usual self and leave the fearful shell she seemed to be in.

"Hmmm..." That's all she replied.

"Baat kar, Sana. Have your parents reached safely?" he asked.

"Yes, they have. And Guru Anna also just left for the office. I'm all alone at home. Payal Di bhi nahi hai yahan..." she complained, pouting.

There was silence from the other side.

"Hello?" Sana confirmed his presence.

"Ya... you said you are alone?" he asked as if he didn't believe what she said.

"Yes... kyun, kya hua? It's fine, aap worry mat karo. Waise bhi, I'm tired. I'm going back to sleep. It's just 2 p.m.," she said, thinking he was worried about her.

"Can I come? Main aau?" he asked bluntly, thinking this was a good chance to meet her at her home. She was alone, and he could get some time with her to clear the misunderstandings. Besides, he missed her and wanted to hug her—he missed her scent. This seemed like the perfect opportunity if she agreed.

"Par... aap... you are in the company, right? What if someone sees you coming? Nahi, nahi... I'm scared. Please, aap gussa mat hona, par I don't think it's a good idea. You coming when I'm alone will make it look fishy to anyone who sees you coming inside," she said anxiously, biting her nails.

"Don't worry, Sana. I'll be careful. I just got back home. I'm coming in 10 minutes. Open the door when I knock. I miss you, sweetheart. I want to see you... and I'm coming. No further discussion," Sid said firmly and hung up the phone without waiting for her response.

He quickly changed into jeans and a T-shirt and walked out toward her home, excited to meet her.

Sana was skeptical. She sat down on the bed nervously, looking around the house. It was messy. This was the first time he was coming home, and she looked messy, too. She got up—there was no time to think about her reservations. She quickly gathered the clothes scattered on the bed, tidied up the house a bit, and rushed to the restroom to wash her face. She applied kohl to her eyes and tied her hair into a ponytail.

She thought about changing her clothes as well since she was wearing a gray skirt and a simple white T-shirt—her comfortable house clothes. She went to the cupboard to grab a churidar, but before she could change, she heard a knock at the door. Her heart stopped for a second, and she felt dizzy, anticipating his presence.

She quickly put the churidar back, closed the cupboard, and walked toward the door. There were two doors—the wooden one inside, which she opened, and a steel mesh door outside. She saw Sid standing there—handsome, splendid, and smart.

Love can make you feel an intense elation that takes you high. It can make you vulnerable to pain that drags you down. Your heart beats as fast as your partner's, and it can also make you a daredevil—something both of them were becoming in that moment.

Chapter Seventeen:
Held By The Clock

Sid hastily came inside and closed the door before giving Sana a tight hug—a hug they both desperately needed, one they yearned for, showing how much they had missed each other. It was a hug that felt like it lasted forever until he heard her sobbing. She whimpered, clutching him tightly, venting out all the pain and fear she had of losing him.

"Bas ho gaya... mat ro Sana... please yaar... I'm already drowning in guilt. I will never shout at you again. I won't promise, but I'll try, okay? Mujhe gussa jaldi aa jata hai... I'm short-tempered," Sid tried to pacify her.

"Kitna rulaya tumne…" Sana said, smacking his chest. Her words brought a smile to Sid's face as he heard her say 'Tum' again—a significant moment, he thought, letting out a small laugh.

"Ab darwaze mein hi khada karogi? Andar nahi bulgogi?" he asked, now relaxed, still hugging her tight with his chin resting on her head.

She jerked, parted from him, and asked him to come inside. "Oh, sorry... aao na..."

"Nice home," Sid said, sitting on the sofa in the living room.

"Thanks! Paani piyoge?" Sana asked, smiling, her brightness returning to her face.

"Bhook lagi hai... kuch khila do. Aur coffee ho toh woh bhi pila do, yaar. I have a headache," he asked without hesitation, like how he would have asked his mother with full rights.

Sana felt exhilarated hearing his demand. She smiled, her teeth gleaming. "Sure, abhi layi..." She ran toward the kitchen, with

Sid following her, standing at the entrance of the kitchen. He stood with folded arms, legs crossed, his right shoulder leaning on the wall, sporting a bright smile.

Her mom had made roti and potato sabzi in the morning, which they packed for the flight journey, saving some for Sana and Guru. Sana heated the sabzi and rolled fresh rotis for Sid, sneaking small glances at him. He stood in the doorway, striking a pose, looking absolutely handsome.

She also cut some cucumber for him as salad, made boondi raita, and heated milk for coffee. Suddenly, Sid came up behind her and hugged her, holding her waist.

"I missed you, baby," he said, pecking her cheek.

Sana blushed at the proximity, though she loved it. She had always admired her dad holding her mom from behind in the kitchen, and now that it happened with her and Sid, she felt happy and blessed to experience this moment with the love of her life.

"Me too..." she said, then went into her silent demur again, thinking that her happiness could fade, and she controlled her emotions.

"Come, food is ready. Sit at the dining table; I'll bring the coffee," Sana said. Holding the plate and a glass of water, she walked toward the table and placed the plates down. Sid held her arms and pulled her toward him.

"Kya hua hai, Sana? Kyun udaas ho?" he asked.

"Kuch nahi... I'll sit, just give me a minute. I'll grab the coffee and come," she replied, running back to the kitchen. She returned with piping hot filter coffee.

"Eat na, it will get cold," she said, urging him to eat.

"Hmm... wow, aloo curry is so good. I am famished... subah se kuch nahi khaya. You also eat; come," Sid said, feeding her a morsel of roti and sabzi. She happily ate it from his hand while sipping her coffee.

"Wow, yaar, kya amazing coffee banayi hai... this is too good. Never had South Indian coffee before..." he said, enjoying his food and coffee with no worries, no inhibitions, as if he were at his own home, comfortable.

But Sana was in a different zone. She was having a cyclone of emotions running inside her—anger toward him making her feel vulnerable and pathetic, fear of being alone with him at home, fear of society, people, neighbors, and family. Her face reflected all of it. She couldn't hide it from Sid.

She didn't want to share her feelings with him for fear of his anger and judgment, but Sid could see everything. Her face was like a mirror of her heart and mind; she couldn't hide anything from him.

He washed his hands, rinsed his mouth, and then went to the kitchen where Sana was. Without warning, he picked her up bridal style. She couldn't gather her thoughts, not expecting what he was doing. He just lifted her like she weighed nothing and asked softly,

"Where is your room?"

"Kya kar rahe ho? Neeche utaro..." an ambivalent Sana asked him.

"Where is your room, Sana?" he asked, this time sternly.

"That one, on the left... but please put me down..." she requested, feeling shy in his arms. No one had picked her up like this before, and she felt coy.

"NO," he said, continuing toward her room. He took a glance around before sitting on her bed and placing her in his lap.

"Ab bol, kya hua hai? Kyun mooh sada rakha hai? Sit here; don't move," he said, tightening his hold on her waist and legs as she tried to stand up. She stilled and submitted to him, her face down in her lap. One hand held his neck; the other rested on his arm that was holding her leg.

"I am hurt, I am in agony, pata hain how much I suffered this last 24... no... 36 hours when you just shunned me off. I couldn't sleep, couldn't eat, I was not functioning, and I hated it. I don't like myself in that state. I am a carefree, cheerful girl, Sid, and this side of yours, shutting me off, made me shrink," she poured her heart out like she always does without any wariness or hesitation. "Never, I said never, ever do that to me. Problem hain baath karo solve karo.. but dare you to detach and isolate yourself. I cannot handle you distancing from me. I thought we would never talk or meet!! I had this sour fear of losing you.." she cried, tears pouring down again.

Sid got emotional, too. He hugged her tight, and Sana hugged him for her life, too. "Never, I will never do that. You are my life, Sana, a very important part of me; I also was in pain but also an asshole to behave the way I did. I should have understood you. I will try to be more considerate with you, Sana... thoda time de, I will change for sure. I have been independent almost all my life and have thought the same way you do. My sister Kajal never had to go through any of these limitations, or I should say she never had this ideology. I am sorry, baby, and thanks for speaking clearly with me." he made her look at him and wiped her tears. She pouted and nodded her head, "Ro mat yaar, kaisa haal ho gaya tera ro ro ke.. dark circles aa agaye hain.."

"Kya dark circles.. hato.. dekhne do.." crying was gone, and now she got worried about dark circles around her eyes. Such is her personality; she is carefree, like a baby who can be easily distracted. She got out of his hold and went to check herself in the mirror. Sid chuckled, smiling, seeing his innocent, naïve ladylove. He lay on the bed with his legs down and arms holding his head behind and admired her. He got up and hugged her again from behind and looked at the mirror, "we look good," he smiled. She smiled too and nodded in yes, seeing their reflection in the mirror.

He turned her, pulled towards him, and devoured her lips for a kiss. He waited too long for this; he had craved to kiss her since the time he saw her, but before he could do that, he wanted to clear the misunderstandings and give the trust back to her. It was a kiss of eternity; they took breaths in between, but again for a deep, long kiss. Even in those simple clothes, she looked no less than a diva to him. Simple, no makeup, yet gorgeous. It was mostly him dominating the kiss, and she just let him do what he wanted. His hand roamed around her body behind; he wanted more. His left hand slightly went inside her top and touched her back, skin to skin, and pulled her close. Right hand touching her neck and slightly shifting the top from her shoulders kissed her neck and earlobe and her skin in the shoulders.

Sana was breathing heavily with the ecstasy she was given by him. She was not on the floor as Sid had picked her up from one hand, which was inside her top at the back, fondling the hooks of her bra and giving her the euphoria of kisses on her neck and shoulders. He fondled his hand down and groped her left bosom above the top. She gasped and returned from her trance to realize what they were doing. He stopped, too, when he felt her stiff and looked up, keeping his forehead on hers. "I love you, Sana; you know that right?" he asked softly, breathing hard, eyes closed, still both hands where they were. "Tell me, Sana, you know that?" he asked again when she didn't respond. "Yes, I know that, and I love you too…" she replied, trembling. "You trust me?" he asked. She nodded, "I want words, Sana. Do you trust me?" "Yes!!" she replied back again, looking at him eye to eye. "I know my limits, and I will never make you uncomfortable or regret my actions." With that, he kissed her again, bringing her down and bringing both his hands cupping her face and hugging her tight.

"You should go now, Sid. It's almost 2 hours since you've been here. My mami ji will come after her job at 6, and she'll be with us for this week since mama has gone with amma and appa," she said, worried but still hugging him, not wanting him to leave.

"Hmm... I'll go, just a little longer..." he replied, reluctant to leave her and go.

Right now, the differences and distance didn't seem to be their enemy, but the time they had to separate and wait to hold each other again was.

Chapter Eighteen:
The Promise Of Soon

"Sid, you should go now... shaam ho gayi hai aur bahar koi dekh na le tumhe..." Sana again requested Sid as she was getting anxious and worried.

"Mann nahi kar raha tujhe chod ke jaane ka... Kal aayegi na office? I will pick you up... same time," Sid asked, looking down at her. She was petite in front of him, small and feather-like. He couldn't resist himself from holding her up. He swiftly bent down and picked her up in the air.

"Aaaahhh… Ammaaaa... kya kar rahe ho... utaro mujhe yeh kya Bahubali Bahubali khel rahe ho... ab moti nahi lag rahi tumhe!!!" Surprised by Sid's action, she held him tight around his shoulders.

He laughed at her antics and facial expressions. "Meri moti baby hain tu..." he replied, smiling.

"Amma… utaro mujhe!" she almost begged him. She was feeling weird but at the same time, she felt wonderful, looking down at the most handsome man pampering her and giving all his love to her.

They were in their own world when her phone rang. Sid brought her down, and she picked up the call, seeing the display name: Appa, her dad. Her heartbeat wavered as if she had been caught red-handed doing some mischief by her dad. She gestured to Sid to be silent and answered the call. "Helloo Appa..." she then spoke in Tamil; Sid couldn't understand anything she was talking about, except for some Hindi and English words in between.

When she hung up, Sid asked, a worried expression on his face, "All good? What did he say?"

"My Nani Ji is not doing well. She is still serious, and Appa is saying that we might have to travel to meet her as she is taking her last breaths," she said, with water filling her eyes.

"Oh... will you go then?" The atmosphere turned serious, and Sid rubbed his face in worry. How would he survive without her around? He would miss her, but he couldn't stop her either. This was about her family, and he would not stand in her way. It was important to her, and he needed to understand that. A turmoil of thoughts churned inside him.

"Yes, I think so... that's what Appa was indicating. Let Guru anna and mami ji come, we will decide. I will let you know if we make any plans to travel to Kerala. I also have to inform the company for leave," she said, speaking non-stop, her confusion and worry evident.

"Call HR or Mr. Gupta and let him know. You are still in the temporary period, you might not have accrued enough leave, but I will handle that, don't worry, but please come back soon... I will miss you, yaar," Sid said, hugging her again.

"Hmmm... I will miss you too... but I will call and text you," said Sana.

"I will leave now," Sid said after a pause. "Wait, let me check the surroundings..." Sana nervously said, worried that anyone would see him getting out of her flat. She went out, peeked from her balcony to see the crowd outside, and then went towards the door, opened it, and checked if the stairs were clear of her neighbors upstairs and downstairs. "Okay, all clear, jaldi jao..."

He left her home and walked towards his home. It was an adventurous meet, he thought. Misunderstandings cleared, and they came more physically close. Her house gave him such positive vibes—neatly kept, simple, and clean. This was the best meet they had so far. But her going to Kerala was bothering him, and he couldn't do anything about it either.

He entered his home and went towards the fridge to drink some cold water.

"Chai piyega, beta?" his mom asked.

"Sure, maa," he replied and sat down on the couch, exhausted.

"Aaj kaise jaldi aa gaya? Sab theek hai?" his mom asked, bringing in chai and some snacks.

"Woh aaj Sana office nahi aayi. Her Nani had a heart attack, so she went to check on her. Her parents left early this morning. Woh bhi shaayad jaye Kerala!" he said with an upset tone. He was very attached to his mom and never felt any need to hide anything from her. She also encouraged her kids to be open and free with all aspects of their lives. She would never judge them and would always give advice and guide them with her experience.

"Oh! Hope she is fine," she asked, concerned.

"Ya, she is a bit upset," he replied, sipping the chai and switching on the air conditioner.

"Tu usse mujhse kab mila raha hain? When she comes back, bring her here. I want to meet her," Mom almost demanded.

"Ya, I will... Is Kajal planning to come here? I thought I could make her meet you both at the same time. Nahi toh Kajal mera dimaag kha jayegi. She is already pestering me to give Sana's phone number to her to talk, but I want to introduce you guys first, face to face, before you all can make daily calls to gossip about me!" Sid said sarcastically, smiling.

"Yeh acha hain, when did we gossip about you, badmash? But I like that idea. I will ask Kajal to make plans to visit us soon. I can't wait to see Sana. If not, you just make me meet her, na. Kajal will wait," Mom said excitedly.

"Ya, sure, I will do that," he replied.

They both had a little more conversation, and after a while, Sid excused himself to complete some pending office work.

Sana lit the evening Diya in her puja and cooked a simple dinner. Payal and her family had gone out for a week for their relatives' marriage. She was missing her Di very much. The emotional turmoil she had been in over the weekend and then Sid coming home made her want to share everything with her Di. But her Di was busy and having fun, and Sana did not want to interrupt her family time and make her stressed thinking of her. She did send her routine texts to her, though.

Her Mami came home, and so did Guru anna, and everyone discussed the plan to travel. They called Appa again to know about Nani's condition, and he recommended booking the flight as soon as possible, as her health was deteriorating. Guru anna started looking for flight tickets and booked the early morning one for all three. Sana immediately texted Sid, telling him the details about her flight.

SS🚗

How long are you planning to stay? When is your return?

Sana

Right now, I have no idea, but I called Mr. Gupta after you left, and he said I can take 3 days off maximum. I don't know what to do!! I told Anna about it, and he said he would keep the tickets open for me. 😟

SS🚗

Don't worry, Sana, I will take care of the office protocols. You do not need to take stress. Pack the bags for 3 days and try to be here soon. It is going to be a tough 3 days for me as well... I will miss you...

Sana

Hmmm... I will miss you too. Bye for now, and I will text you later.

Like the saying goes, "Distance makes the heart grow fonder." They knew distance would make them suffer and long for each other, but they also knew that their love was right, and it was real.

Chapter Nineteen:
A Love That Crosses Miles

Sana and her family left home for the airport before the crack of dawn. She was shocked to see his blue car at the entrance of the community early at 4:30 a.m. She never thought that he would wake up that early just to see her, but was even more shocked to see him following their car beyond the Ghaziabad-Delhi borders. She texted him, curious to know his intentions!

Sana

Why are you following? Are you planning to come to the airport or wait... don't tell me that you are coming to Kerala. 😲

SS🚗

I am coming to the airport... just put your windows down; I want to see you!

Sana

Are you mad!! Go home, Sid...

SS🚗

No, do what I said now...

Sana put down her windows immediately when she saw the reply from him. Her phone was on silent, so no one in the car guessed what she was doing, but Guru anna asked why she put her window down when the AC was running. She gave the excuse that she needed fresh morning air. Then he drove parallel to their car with his windows down on her side, and both peeked glimpses of each other.

Sid looked just out of bed, heavy-puffed eyes with the same t-shirt he wore yesterday when they met in her house. He was looking at her with distress and passion, the feeling of being apart from her giving him a pang in his heart, and his face reflected it all. Looking at him, Sana could not stop her tears from flowing; her heart twitched, and she felt a gnawing pain in her stomach.

Sid followed them to the airport, behind their cab, taking glimpses of her until she went inside the terminal. He reached home and got dressed for the day's work. It was the second day without her in the car next to him!

He had a usual day with less enthusiasm than he would have otherwise. He got a text from Sana about her reaching safely and then another text after a while, which disturbed him. She told him that she had lost her Nani and that she might have to stay for 13 days, which just shook him to his core. There are usually 13-day rituals if someone in the family passes away in Tamil Brahmin tradition, and she tried to explain that to him. She was upset with Nani's loss, and he did not push her much, understanding her situation.

She also was sad with the pain around her, and seeing her mom crying and in sorrow made her condition even worse. She had never faced any deaths in her life, and this was the first time she experienced it firsthand, and it was brutal! By the end of the second day, she wanted to escape the place and the remorseless atmosphere around her. She was in constant touch with Sid through text but was unable to call him due to the family crowd around her, and he, too, understood that.

On the third day morning, she went to her parents and requested them, "Appa, Amma, after today's ritual, can I go back home, please?"

"Why, beta? We all will go back together after the 13th day, and how will you go alone and live at home by yourself? No, no, we can't take that risk, bacha," Appa said, concerned and worried.

"I have not accrued enough leave, Appa, and I don't want to lose this job. I just joined that company! I will manage, Appa; I am not a kid anymore, and also, Payal didi and her family are coming back today; she will be there with me," Sana insisted, adamant with her request.

"But Sana, tu akeli kaise jayegi aur akele kaise rahegi, woh bhi 10 din?" her mom asked anxiously.

"Reh lungi, amma, trust me... yahan nahi reh sakti, mera dum gut raha hai yahan... aur my job is important to me, please understand, ma..." persistent, she replied back.

Her dad called Guru and asked him for his opinion, and he suggested that he could travel too with Sana, as he was also having problems at work, and him going with her would provide them both the needed comfort. They agreed to that, giving Sana much-needed relief. She sighed a long breath, bringing a small smile after days! After the day's ritual, they packed their bags to travel back home on the night flight.

She texted Sid about her changed travel plan and asked him to pick her up for work tomorrow.

Sid was ecstatically happy, overjoyed to see Sana's message. He had been missing her, and this message gave him the hope he needed. He was elated. He constantly texted her to know her whereabouts — from when she landed to where she reached. He was there at the community entrance when she arrived at her flat in the cab. She had no idea that Sid was standing outside just to catch a glimpse of her.

She was tired and sleepy, unaware that Sid had stayed awake late at night just to see her. She took her bags from the trunk and walked towards her flat when she suddenly turned as if someone was calling her soul. And there he was, standing tall, smiling at her from a distance, looking at her with all the love in his eyes.

She couldn't believe her eyes at first. How could someone be so crazy for her? Just to have a small glimpse, could someone put in so much effort to wake up early or stay up so late? She felt blessed to have a man like Sid, who adored her and understood her. The perseverance he displayed during the difficult time she was facing was undaunting. This was something she had to learn from him. Her respect for him grew even more.

Sana:

Love you, Sid 🖤☕

SS🚗:

Wow, someone is in a good mood. I am happy you are back, Moti. Love you too. Good night, rest well... can't wait to meet you tomorrow and hold you in my arms.

Sana smiled, seeing the message. The 'Moti' tag didn't bother her anymore; in fact, she loved that nickname, which was just for him to use.

Sana:

Me too ☺ Good night and sweet dreams ☺🖤

Chapter Twenty:
Steps Into His World

The next morning was busy for Sana and Guru. Without their parents around them, the kids tended to take on the roles of their parents and became responsible for doing their chores in their absence, and both Sana and Guru were doing exactly that. Guru was doing what his dad would have done—watering the plants, feeding the street dogs, dusting the house. Sana was busy in the kitchen, making breakfast and packing lunch boxes for both, doing the dishes, which otherwise her mom would have done. She made a simple breakfast: mixed veg Upma and chai and called Guru anna to have that at the dining table.

She had already taken a shower and was ready to go to work after breakfast when her brother joined her.

"Anna, aap Diya jaala dena and give the house keys to Payal di when you leave for work. When will you be back in the evening?" Sana asked while stuffing food in her mouth.

"I will try to come early. You come at 6, right?" he asked.

"Yup," Sana replied, looking down at her phone.

"Don't you think you're hooked to your phone a lot lately?" he inquired.

"Haan, tho, I have so many friends and followers... I am world-famous, you know... not like you, just always serious and critical... have some life, Anna! Make a girlfriend; waise bhi you look old and bald, better do it now, or kunwara hi maarna padega!" Sana said, teasing him.

"Acha toh ab tu batayegi life and fun ke baare mein!! Jayada nahi bol rahi tu... buddhi hogi tu…" They continued their sibling banter, except that their parents were unable to stop them.

Sana left home at her usual time to find Sid missing in his usual spot! That was the first time! She was wondering why he hadn't texted her since morning, nor did he reply to her good morning messages. That was very unusual of him, and lately, he had been very prompt in responding to her. She called him this time while waiting in the spot, and he did pick up after a few rings.

"Hello..." he said, picking up the call with a very heavy and stiff voice.

"Kya hua? Are you not well, Sid?" Sana asked, worried.

"Yaa... I don't know; I think I have a fever. What time is it? I think I turned off the alarm while still half asleep," he replied feebly in a thick voice.

"It's 7:25 am now... I think you should take some medicine or, better yet, go see a doctor," she said, worried.

"What the hell!! How did I sleep so much? Maa didn't even wake me up... Where are you? I will come now, wait... Sorry, Jaan, are you waiting for me? Shit, shit, shit!!!" he said, perturbed.

"Sid... Sid... listen to me first... I am taking a cab, you should rest, take medicine, and take your day off... Understand?" Sana said in a stern voice.

"No yaar... it's been so many days I haven't seen you, please, Sana," he requested.

"Tumhe meri kasam, Sid, you have to take rest; you sound so weak. This is the result of staying up late... If you feel better by evening, we can make some plans to see each other, okay?" she pleaded with him.

"Ab yeh kasam-wasam main nahi manta... What is this stupidity, Sana?" he said, frustrated.

"Ab aisa hi hain, you have to listen to me and see, we're talking, right Sid? Please, go now and take fever-reducing medicine. If that doesn't work, go see a doctor," she asked him softly this time. But she was disturbed. She missed him and had thought of spending the morning drive with him, which now seemed impossible. How the universe conspires—what we plan to do and what actually happens!

She reached the company, talking with him the whole time. He did take the medicine and ate bread before that, as she instructed. He lay in bed and was almost asleep when she put the phone down.

The day seemed long, never-ending for Sana. He was gloomy all day and just concentrated on work, completing all the pending tasks. She messaged Sid during her lunch break, but he didn't see or reply to her message—maybe he was sleeping. She was worried and concerned for his well-being but could only pray for his quick recovery.

It was evening and time to end her shift. She checked her phone for any reply from Sid, but he didn't even see the message. This disturbed her on another level. She booked the cab and headed home, feeling edgy and afraid, thinking about him. Tears welled up in her eyes; her mental state was already shaken by Nani's demise, the distance from Sid, and now his fever, which was frightening her to death.

She thought of calling him and disturbing him, even if he was sleeping. He didn't pick up, and that was the last straw for her disturbed mind. She asked the driver to turn towards Sid's house, as the suspense was killing her soul. She didn't care what his mother might think or what people might say. Right now, Sid was her priority, and she would go to any lengths to know about his well-being. She was familiar with his house and knew that his mother was aware of them, even though they had never met or talked to each other.

She reached his house, opening the front gate with a twitching stomach and a rapid heartbeat. This was the first time she was going to enter his house. The house was huge from the outside, with a small garden on the front left side, filled with different colored roses, making it look beautiful. His car was parked on the right, in a passage that led to a side door. She could also see a bike there, which she didn't know he had. There were two outdoor sitting chairs kept on the entrance porch. She removed her sandals, and with trembling hands, she pushed the bell near the front door.

An elderly woman with long white hair, slim, dressed in a peach-colored churidar, opened the door and gave a shocked look upon seeing her. "Sana? You are Sana, right?" she asked, startled.

"Huh... Yes... I am Sana," the tense Sana replied.

"Oh my goodness, kitni pyaari hain bacha tu! So beautiful in real life... Come here, give me a hug!" Sid's mom pulled her into a tight hug. Sana felt overwhelmed. She hadn't expected that. She got emotional and hugged her back, missing her mom, and Sid's mom gave her the sense of comfort she craved at that moment.

"Arre, why are you crying, bacha? Come, come inside..." Sid's mo bm asked, guiding her into the living room. Sana wiped her tears and stepped inside. "Woh, actually, how is Sid? Is he okay? He was having a fever, and he didn't answer my calls or messages, so I got worried. That's why I came here to check if he's doing well," Sana asked in one breath, worried, holding Sid's mom's hand. She gave off positive vibes, and Sana felt comfortable around her, contrary to the assumptions she had about her. She placed her purse and lunchbox on the sofa and felt mentally drained.

"Haan, haan, samaj gayi. Saans le le, bacha. Wait, I will get you some water. Drink it; you look so exhausted," Sid's mom said, caressing Sana's head. Still holding her hand, she walked towards the kitchen to get cold water from the fridge. "Sid has been sleeping almost the whole day today. He still has a high temperature. I gave him kichdi and medicine in the afternoon. He's a baby when he gets sick—needs pampering and all the attention. If he rests well, he usually gets better soon. Come, I will take you to his room," she added, giving Sana much-needed relief. Sid's mom seemed like a strong woman, and Sana realized that she had to learn to be invincible like her.

His room was on the far end of the house, and it was dark when his mom opened the door. She called him softly and switched on the light. "Sid... beta... get up... see who is here!"

Sid twitched his eyes, looking sick and tired, which made Sana emotional again.

"Sana..." he could only say that hoarsely with a sore throat when he tried to sit up.

"Please don't get up; keep lying down. How are you feeling?" Sana asked with a shaky voice.

Sid smiled, seeing her in front of him, in his home, with his mom. He thought he was dreaming, but when he heard her voice, he realized it was real, and she was standing next to him in his room! His sickness seemed to fade away, and suddenly, he felt alive again.

"I think I'm feeling much better now, seeing you here," he said with a smile. "Sit," he gestured to her, inviting her to sit on the left side of his bed.

"I am so happy to finally see you, Sana! Sid has been telling me about you non-stop. At least there's some benefit to him being sick," his mom said, admiring Sana and caressing her hair again. Her face showed how delighted she was to meet Sana and how happy she was to see that Sana cared so much for Sid. She was in awe of Sana and happy that Sid had chosen a girl who loved and cared for him just like she did.

Chapter Twenty-One:
A Hug That Heals

It felt surreal to Sana—how she got so lucky with her life, the man who loved her madly and his mom who adored her. She felt blessed and thought maybe she might have done some good to be blessed with such a blissful partner.

"I will freshen up a bit, Sana. Wait here," Sid excused himself to the restroom attached to his room.

His room looked clean and spotless, with minimalistic furniture—just a bed with side tables on both sides, a wooden dresser with a big mirror that matched the huge wall-attached cupboards covering the entire right side wall. Very simple and modest, just the way she liked. One wall had a split AC, which was why she felt cold in the room, though it was powered off.

She was quietly observing every corner of the room, sitting on the corner of his bed feeling contented, when his mom came in with a tea tray filled with hot chai, ladoo, and some snacks. Sana got up and took the tray from her hands.

"Arre... I will take it, Maa Ji, but why did you trouble yourself?" she said, placing the tray on the side table. She picked up a teacup and served it to his mom. "Lijiye..."

"Ruk, sabse pehle mere haath se ladoo kha. Pehli baar aayi hain ghar mein, mooh meetha kar," his mom said, filling Sana's mouth with a boondi ladoo while taking the chai from her hand.

Sana hadn't expected that and swallowed the mouthful ladoo, making her face look like a balloon.

"Hmm... thank you, this is so good—yummy ladoo! Aapko pata hain, I love ladoos! Amma—my mom—makes so many types of laddoos. Aur Appa, my dad, to puchho hi mat—he just demands them, and she readily goes and makes them for him. He has never-ending demands, Maa Ji, and I love how she willingly, without any grudge, makes them for him. Aur aapko pata hain..." she continued her chatter nonstop while his mom smiled warmly, watching the chatterbox who had filled the otherwise silent home with liveliness.

Sana was now comfortably sitting on the bed with her legs folded up, tea in one hand, and her yellow churidar with a pink dupatta giving her a special glow.

Sid came out to witness a beautiful picture of his mom and Sana comfortably chatting and sitting on the bed. He wanted to capture this moment—both his lifelines together, bonding so well. It felt like paradise.

He felt much better after a full day of rest and a little wash-up. Though he wanted to take a shower, he couldn't resist being with Sana and spending as much time with her as possible while she was at his home.

"Aaja beta, how do you feel now? Kuch khayega? Drink this ginger tea first with some biscuits… I will make some soup for you for dinner," his mom said, gesturing for him to pick up the tea kept on the table.

"Teek lag raha hain, but still feeling weak. Tu kaise aa gayi yahan? What a pleasant surprise," he said, dipping biscuits in tea and eating them while asking Sana.

"Haan toh, meri fatt gayi thi when you didn't see my messages or reply to them… I was so worried for you, Sid. Then I just impetuously decided to come here!" Sana said with a sulk.

"Acha hua tu aa gayi, bacha. Dekh, yeh bhi uth gaya. Since morning, he has been sleeping… lunch bhi sote sote khaya," his mom said.

Sana gave a smile to his mom and stood up to keep the teacup back on the tray. "Acha, toh main jau? Bahut late ho gaya hain. Tum rest lo, Sid," Sana said hastily.

"Arre, abhi toh aayi hain. Ruk na thodi der… Abhi kaun hain tere ghar jo teri class lega?" Sid asked restlessly.

"Haan, bache, thodi der aur ruk. Abhi toh aayi hain… and also, sorry to hear about your loss… Sid told me about your Nani."

"It's okay, Maa Ji. Woh Appa Amma wohi hain Kerala mein. Only me and my brother came here, and he said he will come early today as he didn't want me to stay alone at home for a long time," Sana said.

"Yes, that is also true. It's not safe, either. Acha ruk, I will get something for you. Tum dono baat karo," his mom said, leaving them alone to catch up.

Sid had been waiting for this moment—when his mom would leave, and he could embrace Sana in his arms. He quickly stood up, jumped toward Sana, and grabbed her tightly for a hug.

Startled, Sana screamed, "Aah! Ammma! Kya hain, darra diya tumne!" But she quickly relaxed, hugging him back tightly, her arms lacing around his waist while he hugged her from her shoulders.

It was a hug that comforted both of them—a release of the longingness they had for each other, calming them down. The power of the hug eased Sana's stress and soothed Sid's agitated mind.

"I missed you, Sana," Sid said, feeling peaceful after a long time, squeezing her tighter and kissing her hair, with no plan to release her from his embrace.

"Mereko rona aa raha hain, phirse! I missed you too…" Sana said, getting emotional and beginning to cry again, still hugging him with her face buried in his chest. She gave a small peck there, finding comfort in his closeness.

"Pagal Moti... koi bol ke rota hain? Tu one piece hain is duniya mein," he laughed, cupping her face, wiping her tears with his thumb, and kissing her forehead.

Sana was still holding him tightly, her arms intertwined on his back, her eyes closed as she cherished his forehead kiss. She rested her head on his chest again and said, "You should take rest for two days. You look so tired. This might be viral, you know. No office for two days. I'll come here and meet you in the evening every day, okay?" She looked up and instructed him.

He smiled with a crinkle in his eyes. "Okay, aur kuch, madam?"

She shook her head, smiling. "I will be perfectly fine by tomorrow, don't worry. I'll take care and rest completely," he said, looking down at her lips and leaning in to kiss her.

But she distanced her head, still holding him.

"Kya Hain, baby? Ek kiss de de... kitne din ho gaye," he complained.

"No! Tum bimar ho. Kahin mujhe ho gaya toh? No kissing when one is in fever. Bacteria transfer hote hain, and I can't afford to take any leaves now," she said, parting from him.

"Yeh kya logic hain?" he sighed and sat down on the bed. Though he was complaining, he knew she was right and didn't want her to get sick.

"Bas aisa hi hain," she said firmly. "Listen, I think I should go now. What's the time? Oh! I left my mobile in my purse on the sofa..." She rushed toward the living room, with Sid following behind.

"Shit, it's past 7. I have a missed call from Guru Anna and Payal Di. Wait, let me call her—ek minute, Sid," she said worriedly, sitting down.

He nodded and sat on the couch near her.

"Hello, Di! … Haan… Oh!!! Woh, Sid is not well, so I came to see him at his house… He's recovering… I'm starting now… Arre, aap kyun aa rahe ho? I will come by walk na… Acha, teek hain… Woh Shiv Mandir wale road pe main wait karungi… Haan, haan, Di, in 5 minutes… Okay, bye!"

Sana looked up at Sid and said, "Maa Ji kahan hain? I have to go now. Di is coming to pick me up from the outer road. Guru Anna is coming anytime now, and he called Di when I didn't pick up the call. She told him I'm with her since he was worried."

She kept her mobile in her purse and started hurrying.

Just then, Sid's mom entered the living room with a bag.

"Maa Ji, I have to leave now. Bahut late ho gaya hain," Sana said.

"Yes, Bache, take this," his mom said, handing her the bag.

"Yeh kya hain, Maa Ji?" Sana asked.

"Dinner for you and your brother. Ab ghar jaake kya banayegi? You are already tired. Aur yeh churidar material, pehli baar aayi hain, aise khali haath nahi bhejungi. Stitch karke pehenna, aur phir mujhe dikhana, teek hain," his mom said, caressing Sana's face and kissing her forehead.

Sana hugged her, overwhelmed by the love and care she was receiving. "Thank you, Maa Ji, so thoughtful of you!"

She parted from her and said, "I asked him not to come to work till he gets completely well. Dhyaan rakhna, Sid. Main kal phir aaungi. Chalo, I will leave now."

She hurriedly took her purse, the lunch bag, and the bag Sid's mom had given her, then marched toward the front door, putting on her sandals.

"I'm coming too, till the road… wait," Sid said.

"Haan beta, chhod ke aa ja. Raat ho gayi hain," his mom said.

"Arre, but don't strain yourself by walking! You're already feeling weak, na, baba," Sana said, yelling over her shoulder.

"Chup chap chal! Koi weak nahi hoon," Sid replied.

"Bye, Maa!" Sana waved to his mom.

"Bye, bache. It was lovely meeting you. Khush reh," his mom waved back with a contented smile, watching her son and his would-be daughter-in-law.

She felt at peace, knowing her son had chosen a perfect soulmate for himself. With the experience and wisdom life had given her, she could sense in just one meeting that they were made for each other. She silently blessed them both for a lifetime of togetherness.

Chapter Twenty-Two:
Sana's Eventful Day

Walking past Sid's home, they turned towards the main road, where Payal said she would pick Sana up.

"Maa bahut achi hain. When I came from the office, I was so worried and tense for you, but when she saw me and hugged me, I felt as if all my troubles flew away. She has so much positivity in her. I want to be like her—strong and calm," Sana, as usual, said her heart out.

"You know, I feel so blessed to have you and Maaji. Pichle janam main maine jaroor kuch punya kiya hoga," she expressed herself with gratitude, a smile filling her face.

How one moment or one person can change your day—rather, your life. In the morning, she had been sad, worried, and tense for Sid and his health. The whole day had gone by thinking about that, and yet, just one person's persona could change her fickle mind and bring it back to stability. She wondered how.

"If that is what you think, then I must have done some punya too to get you in this life. Maa had to become strong when she lost my father. Bringing up two kids when you were a housewife, fully dependent on your husband, and then suddenly in his absence—it makes one strong. She brings calmness into my life. She is my anchor, showing me the right way and advising me whenever I feel lost," Sid, too, expressed his feelings.

"Indeed, parents are our anchors. They bring stability and safety into our lives, teaching us enormous values," Sana replied.

Just then, Di drove in, honking on her black Honda Activa.

"Hello, Sid! How are you? I heard you were not well… Feeling better now?" she asked.

"Yes, Payal, much better. And after Sana's visit to my home, I can run a marathon now…" he chuckled, saying that.

"Wah! Kya baat hain… Sahi hain… Chalo, take care! Sit, Sana, we have to be there before your Hitler bhaiya returns," Payal hurried and turned her scooter.

Sana looked at Sid with buoyant eyes. Sid blinked and gave her the assurance she needed—no words spoken, no physical touch, as they knew they were on the curb of the busy road—just understanding what each other felt at that moment. She sat on the scooter, waving him goodbye.

Sid came back home feeling much better, and the medicine was doing its work. A contented smile appeared on his face when he saw the respect Sana gave his mom and how his mom adored Sana. He thanked his stars for witnessing such a great bond between them in just their first meeting.

His mom was on the phone, and he knew exactly who it would be!

"Main rakhti hu, Kajal. Aa gaya Sid. Baath karegi usse?" Mom asked her daughter.

Sid took the phone and greeted his sister, telling her what their mom had said about Sana.

"Haan baba, baat kara dunga. Now stop complaining. I will call you tomorrow and ask Sana to talk to you… Abhi kaisa hai? And how is Dinesh? Say hi to him… Okay… Make plans to come here… Chal, goodnight… Bye… Take care."

"Maa, why do you have to tell everything to Kajal the moment it happens? Thoda bhi wait nahi kar sakti ho aap? She just climbs on me whining!" He complained, wondering how both his mom and sister wanted to share every little detail as soon as it happened. Couldn't they keep something to themselves? They weren't like this before Kajal's marriage. He had noticed this habit developing after Abhi's birth. Now, the two had become inseparable over the phone—gossiping, sharing, and talking about whatever came to their minds. He wondered if Sana would be the same with her mom. If so, then it would be three women versus him... He chortled at the thought.

"You won't understand how important it is for a woman to have a heartfelt conversation. We think differently, act differently, solve problems differently, and are more emotionally driven than logically driven," his mom tried to explain.

"Acha, okay... Now have your heartfelt conversation with your son also... Ya phir, is that exclusive for your daughter?" he complained, slouching down on the couch.

"Chal hatt... pagal, kuch bhi bolta hai... Who is whining now?" His mom playfully hit his arm and took his head onto her lap, massaging his hair and giving him a much-needed sense of relaxation.

"I love Sana, beta. She is so appealing and graceful and has a positive aura around her. She is such a delight to have. I can't wait to bring her home," his mom told him, sharing her impression of Sana. "You know, she is just made for you. Tere jaise serious aadmi ke liye woh chirpy gudiya hi perfect hai. You will both balance each other. I am so relieved that you chose the best life partner for yourself. Der aaye, par durust aaye," she said, laughing as she expressed her feelings.

"In just one meeting, you guessed all that about her?" Sid asked inquisitively.

"Acha? Toh tune usse kitne din mein jaana? Love at first sight sirf tere saath hi ho sakta hai?" his mom teased. He laughed—she was right! Even for him, he had been drawn to Sana like a magnet without knowing her background, her nature, or anything else.

On the other side, Sana and Di managed to reach home before Guru Anna. Sana freshened up and looked for Di, who was in the kitchen at Sana's home.

"Kya kar rahi ho, Di?" Sana asked.

"Paani pee le… I will make some chai," Di said.

"Nahi Di, I just had some at Sid's place. Aap pee lo… His mom also gave dinner for us. I'll bring it, wait…" she said proudly and ran towards the table where she had kept her stuff.

She placed her lunchbox in the sink to be washed and opened the boxes packed by Sid's mom—her Maaji now! She smiled at the thought. She already loved her and got a motherly vibe from her. Inside the boxes, there was baingan bharta, khichdi, and roti.

"Oh my God! All my favorite items! I just love her! Aapko pata hai, Di? She is so fascinating…" Sana continued chattering, telling Di all about the morning's events—how she had impulsively gone to Sid's home, her meeting with his mom, and her impressions of it all.

"Saas-bahu already bonding, haan… Sahi hai!" Payal said.

"Kya Di, aap bhi!" Sana blushed, hearing those words.

"Hayee, hamari Sana sharmati bhi hai! Not bad, huh?" Payal teased.

Just then, Guru Anna came in, frowning.

"Kahan thi tu, Sana? Why didn't you pick up the call? Why so irresponsible?"

"Sorry, Anna… Woh… phone was in my purse, and I didn't hear it ring. That's why," Sana stuttered, fearing her brother's anger.

She knew neither her parents nor her brother tolerated it when they weren't informed of her whereabouts.

"Otherwise, you're glued to your phone at home, but when you really should carry it, or when we call, you never take it! This is not acceptable, Sana. You know, Appa gave me your responsibility, and I want you to pick up my calls every time. I get worried, understand?" he hollered at her.

"Guru, you're unnecessarily creating a scene. She was safe with me, and we were engrossed in our talks about your Nani and the Kerala trip. She's already so stressed—she doesn't need you yelling at her pointlessly," Payal Di came to Sana's rescue, for which she was grateful, as she was on the verge of crying.

"Whatever. But tell her not to repeat this," Guru said and marched off to his room.

Sana went and hugged her Di. "Thank you, Di, for rescuing me," she said, grateful. "Agar aap nahi hoti toh yeh jallad Hitler ne toh meri poori class le leni thi."

"Tu bhi, Sana! You know your family—be careful. What if I wasn't here? You're planning to go to his place tomorrow, too, right? Then, keep your phone in your hand. When he calls, let him know you're at your friend's place. I'll come again to pick you up. Mujhe bhi bata dena, theek hai? Another thing—say what you're saying convincingly and be strong, Sana. You're not doing anything wrong! Pyaar karti hai tu, and it's not a crime. Stand up for yourself rather than sulking all the time," Payal instructed, almost counseling Sana.

"Hmm, I will… Ab aap kyun class le rahi ho? Chalo, khaana khate hain… Bhook lagi hai," Sana said, pouting with a frown, too tired and exhausted from the day's tension and stress. It had been an eventful day for her—full of incidents, good and bad, but certainly not boring…

Chapter Twenty-Three:
The Fire Between Us

A new day, a new morning. Sana finished her morning chores and prayed for Sid's health, lighting the Diya in the prayer room. She told Guru Anna that she would take the company bus, but he insisted on dropping her off at work, even after she denied it, knowing the trouble he had to go through by starting early.

"Anna, I could have gone by bus only. Why trouble yourself so much, taking a detour to go to your work and that too so early?" she pouted, complaining.

"No trouble for me. This way, I can see your company as well," said Guru, driving the car towards the Ghaziabad-Noida borders.

"Yeah, right... Let me call Appa and Amma," she said, dialing her father's phone and connecting it to the car's Bluetooth.

"Hello, Appa ji... How are you?" she asked when he picked up the call.

"I am good. Kya kar rahe ho dono?" her father replied.

"Anna is dropping me at the company today, so we are in the car. Talk to Anna; we're on speaker," she replied, and they had their regular chat of the day.

On the other side, Sid was feeling much better. He woke up late, took a shower, and headed up for breakfast.

"Maa, why didn't you wake me up? It's already 10 AM! How am I sleeping so much?" Sid grumbled.

"Tu so jaa, beta. You are sick, and I know that only by resting will you get better quickly. You work so hard, and you hardly spend any time at home with me. Even during weekends, you have club plans and friends and no time for your mom. At least iss bahane, tu mere saath thoda time spend kar. Main toh bore ho jati hoon ghar mein warna," Maa said, bringing in poha and chai for Sid.

"Sorry, Maa. Aisa nahi hai… I will try to spend more time with you, I promise."

Sid was famished, and he gobbled down the food, spending a good amount of time with his mom, talking about random topics. He also asked for a hair massage and got pampered like a sick child hooked to his mom. However much kids grow, they remain babies in front of their moms, and Sid, being attached to his mother, was no less than a child.

He slept more, and by the time Sana's workday was coming to an end, he felt fit and stronger. He texted Sana that he would pick her up from work in the evening, but she strongly denied it, asking him to stay at home and assuring him she would take a cab back. But Sid, being adamant, reached the company just before 5 PM and texted Sana that he was waiting outside in the parking area. He didn't want to miss this time with her, a time when she had no restrictions about reaching home on time, no fear of her parents and their rules.

Sana smiled when she saw the text. She, too, wanted to spend time with him. The time she had now was rare, and she was happy that he was here, though she worried about how his health was recovering. She stepped outside, mesmerizing in a white calf-length dress with a short, light denim jacket over it, her long hair flowing in the wind. Sid just stared at her like he was seeing her for the first time.

She opened the passenger side door and sat inside, keeping her bags in the back seat. She glanced at Sid and was shocked to see that he was wearing a white T-shirt and denim pants.

"Arre wah! We are twinning!" she exclaimed and pinched him hard on his arm. "Same pinch!"

"Aaahhh... kya hai, itni zor se kaun chutti maarta hai, Sana?" Sid jerked and rubbed his left arm.

"Waise, you are looking very handsome, dude... I love white! It's my favorite! Actually, I love all colors—pink, yellow, blue, orange, black—" Before she could complete her sentence, Sid threw his arms around her neck and pulled her toward him for a searing kiss. No permission asked, no time given, with all rights...

He had waited long enough for this moment, and with no patience left, he rushed in for a sizzling kiss—hard and intense. He savored her lips to his satisfaction, taking in her flowery fragrance, catching a glimpse of her aesthetic face. He hadn't planned this, but seeing the prodigy sitting in front of him, he couldn't resist.

He had merely come to spend some time with her, to see her face, listen to her talk, and know more about her. But the physical magnetism he felt toward her was matchless. His heart was beating faster and faster. He slowed down his swift intensity, making her cling to him, both of them feeling dizzy. His demanding mouth parted her lips and savored her trembling ones, evoking sensations never known to him. And when she kissed him back, the passion was paroxysmal.

The car stood still in the parking lot, its dark-tinted glasses shielding them from the world. Sana was drawn into his passionate kiss; his sudden action, his arms around her—it all surprised her. He kissed her repeatedly, ceaselessly, as if she would vanish if he stopped. His lips moved in a slow, languorous motion. She lifted her arms, patted his chest, and parted her lips, slowing her movements. She wanted to bring him back from his unending intensity.

Sid reluctantly parted and looked at her blushing pink face, her dress riding up to her thighs, her jacket slipping down her shoulders, revealing sleeveless straps and soft skin. This was the closest they had ever been. Still holding her in his arms, he hugged her tightly, zeal and fire coursing through his body.

"Sana, I... I love you... I missed you... You are the most alluring person I have ever come across, and I am unable to control myself around you. You have the upper hand here. Please, let me hug you for a while... let my heartbeat slow down a bit. Hold me, Jaan," Sid said in a grave voice.

Sana held him tight—tighter than he had asked for—as she was no different. Her heart pounded with emotions. She felt safe in his arms, comforted, a tranquility giving them both strength.

They drove around the city, going beyond borders to places they had never been together, with old Kishore Kumar songs playing in the background. Sid was an ardent fan of Kishore Kumar, and most of his collection consisted of his songs—something Sana had realized in just a few days of their car rides. She preferred new, peppy dance numbers over old classics, but she loved how he shared his love for music and spoke about his admiration.

He played a song, saying it was his dedication to her. She blushed when she heard it—it was one of the many songs he had dedicated to her, which he made her listen to repeatedly.

"Roop ye tera jisne banaya vo

Kahin mil jaaye to haath chum lu

Kahin mil jaaye to haath chum lu

Rang ye tera jisne sajaya vo

Kahin mil jaaye to haath chum lu

Kahin mil jaaye to haath chum lu

Roop ye tera...."

They reached her home on time today. She had informed her brother and also Payal Di about her whereabouts, letting them know that Sid was dropping her home.

Somehow, even with the fire inside them, they remained in control, managing their emotions, comforting each other with their limitations known. Getting to know each other deeper—emotionally, mentally—felt more significant than physical needs at this moment.

Chapter Twenty-Four:
A Weekend to Remember

"You have a bike? I saw that at your home. Do you ride it?" Sana asked Sid.

They were driving to the company as usual in the morning.

"Yes, why?" Sid replied.

"I would like to go around on a bike with you someday... will you take me?" she asked.

He was amused by her request. This was the first time she had asked him for something, and how minuscule that request was.

"Of course, sweetheart! We can come to work on it tomorrow if you want," he said, smiling, his happiness pouring out onto his face.

"Nahi, not to work... maybe Saturday. Appa and Amma will come next Thursday, so we have this weekend, and I want to spend both Saturday and Sunday with you. You always ask me to spend time with you on weekends—this time, I am asking you..." Sana said excitedly, regretting the times she had denied meeting him and their first fight that followed.

Sid was flabbergasted. He was shocked when she said that.

"Yes... yes... oh my God, Sana! I can't wait for the weekend to arrive now. I will plan everything for us, sweetheart," he said, overwhelmed with happiness.

But a sudden question popped into his mind.

"Waise, have you ever ridden on a bike before?"

"Nahi na, tabhi toh! Appa had a scooter, and then he bought a car, which Anna drives. It's my dream to ride on a bike—with my hair flowing, chunni lahrake, standing up and feeling the air, aur phir—"

Before she could finish, Sid interrupted, "Oh, hello! This isn't some movie, and you're not a heroine. No hair flowing, no standing up. You need to wear a helmet, and no chunni or anything like that. Wear comfortable clothes like jeans or something—nothing hanging down. I don't want any mishaps, please," he said sternly, looking at her with a serious expression.

"Yeh kya, Sid! I wanted to feel like a heroine for once—get that movie-like feeling. You're such a sadu, just like Anna! He also keeps giving strict orders like this... huh!" She twisted her mouth, crossed her arms over her chest, and looked out of the window.

"No. Do whatever drama you want, but I can't compromise on safety, and that's final," Sid said as he focused on the road, about to enter the company premises.

"Now don't sulk, na, baba... just plan where you want to go."

He grinned. "Come now, give me my kiss dose."

Sid parked the car and pulled Sana towards him for a kiss again. They had been doing that a lot lately, unable to keep their hands off each other.

"Let's go, warna phir se late ho jaungi," Sana said, applying lipstick after a steamy kiss.

"Hmm… chal," Sid agreed.

They walked out of the parking lot together and entered the company. Rumors had already started spreading about them, as Sana spent most of her time in Sid's office during lunch and breaks. Their carpooling had also become the talk of the town. However, neither of them was bothered. Sid, being in a higher position, was someone no one dared to question, and Sana, too, remained untouched by gossip, as everyone was well aware of how professional and strict Sid could be. His dominant demeanor was enough to make people fear him.

By evening, they were back in the car.

"Let's go to your home, Sid. I want to see Maa ji. She texted me today, asking if I could drop by to meet her," Sana said.

"You guys are texting? When did that happen? And why don't I know about this?" Sid was stunned by the revelation.

"Yes, Maa ji asked for my number when I came to your house, and she texted me for the first time today. So, let's go to your house. Loitering around the city, we can do that tomorrow. Okay?" Sana explained.

They reached Sid's place in 45 minutes, and she jumped out of the car to open the gate and go in. Sid chuckled, seeing her excitement at seeing his mom.

"Namaste, Maa ji," Sana said when his mom opened the door for her, and she hugged her.

"Kaisa hai mera bacha?" his mom asked, kissing her forehead.

"Mast," Sana replied with a big smile, walking inside and placing her belongings on the couch again.

"Main bhi hoon... koi mujhe bhi pooch lo!" Sid came in, complaining and shaking his head.

"Pata hai, Maa ji? I think he's getting jealous of our bonding. Car mein bhi itni enquiry kar raha tha... Jalkukda," Sana teased him.

His mom laughed, enjoying their banter.

"Jalkukda toh hai yeh... no doubt! Kajal aur mere phone pe baat karne se bhi jealous hota hai yeh."

"Make a team of three against me... I think I'll soon get the tag of 'Satayi Hui Bahu' because of you all," Sid groaned at his mom's teasing and walked toward the fridge to grab a cold water bottle. He drank some and handed it to Sana. She took the bottle and drank water without sipping, tilting it, and pouring it directly down her throat.

His mom noticed and asked, "Arre bacha, mooh laga ke pee le. Or Sid, get her a glass from the kitchen."

"She drinks like that only, Maa. It's some custom in her religion… Jhootha nahi karti woh. I don't understand the logic—when I have already sipped from it, why can't she do the same?" Sid said, wondering aloud.

"It has become a habit now. Since childhood, we have been taught to do certain things a certain way. But it's not a restriction—I actually like it. Being a Tamil Brahmin, we are very orthodox. In Chennai, where my Appa's family lives, they are extremely strict. Whenever we visit during vacations, we have a tough time adjusting to my Paati's—I mean my Dadi's—rules. Here, my parents are much more lenient, and we have adapted to a North Indian lifestyle. Thank God for that, warna meri toh band baj jaati!" Sana explained with a chuckle.

"You are doing it right, Sana. Do whatever you want, bache. Here, in this house, you are free and independent. You are my daughter, and I will treat you like one. I will never stop you from following your customs or force you to follow ours. We love you, and we will love you as a whole package—which includes your customs, rituals, and family," his mom said, holding Sana's hand with complete sincerity.

Sana had a satisfied smile, silently thanking her fate for blessing her with such an understanding and loving mother-in-law.

"Thank you, Maa, for respecting and understanding me," Sana said, hugging his mom, her eyes brimming with tears.

His mom hugged her back, smiling. "Ab thank you bolegi Maa ko? Khush reh, bacha," she said, caressing Sana's head.

"I also want a hug! What is happening here? Everyone is ignoring me, yaar!" Sid complained and hugged his mom from behind, wrapping his arms around both her and Sana.

They all laughed and spent the evening enjoying chai and snacks, with nonstop chatter from Sana, who charmed everyone with her liveliness.

A little while later, his mom's phone rang—it was Kajal, her daughter. Sid picked up the call and asked her to switch to a video call.

When she did, she was shocked to see Sana sitting with their mom, waving and saying, "Hello, Didi!" in her melodious voice.

"Sana? Oh my goodness! Finally, I get to see you. Sid ko toh keh keh kar thak gayi thi!" Kajal shrieked in excitement.

"Haan toh ab mila raha hoon na… mil le! Zyada bakwas mat kar and calm down, kitna chillaa rahi hai, gadhi," Sid scolded her, cutting off her complaints.

His mom, Sana, and Sid talked to Kajal to her heart's content. Sana and Kajal exchanged numbers and planned to meet in August when Kajal was visiting Ghaziabad for Sid's birthday, which was just two weeks away on August 6th.

Sana instantly liked Kajal. She was talkative like her, and Kajal was overjoyed that Sid had found such a beautiful girl.

"Waise, you look more like a Punjaban than a Madrasan. And you speak such fluent Hindi—doesn't even feel like a South Indian accent," Kajal remarked, surprised.

"I've been told this many times by several people. My Hindi slang also resembles Punjabi a lot because I have many Punjabi friends from school and college. Plus, my bestie—my soul sister, Payal Didi—is also Punjabi. I guess I've picked up a lot from them," Sana explained.

Suddenly, she realized she hadn't informed Payal Didi or Guru Anna about her whereabouts. She facepalmed.

"Hayee Ram! Main Di ko aur Anna ko message karna hi bhool gayi... Main toh gayi aaj! Sid, please mujhe chhod do na... jaldi! Kitna time ho gaya, maine realize hi nahi kiya... Shit yaar!" Sana panicked and requested Sid, grabbing her belongings and hurriedly saying goodbye to his mom and sister.

Sid drove fast and dropped Sana in front of her community, asking her to message him if she faced any problems. She walked quickly toward her flat, praying she wouldn't run into her brother.

Relieved not to see his car parked, she exhaled deeply and ran up the stairs to her home. She rang Payal's doorbell to get the keys.

Payal Di was worried about her and, as usual, gave her some advice.

Later that night, Sana texted Sid, thanking him for another beautiful day. Lying in her bed, she looked out of the window, admiring the full moon and the twinkling stars.

The moon was a beautiful and delightful sight to behold. Without the dark, we would never see the stars. There they stood—the innumerable stars—shining in order like a living hymn written in light. There was always something new to be seen in the unchanging night sky.

Chapter Twenty-Five:
Tides of Love

It was Saturday morning, and Sana was getting ready for the bike trip with Sid. She wore comfortable, baggy, Capri pants, going with a purple turtleneck, full-sleeve top. She was sensitive to sunburns and prepared to cover herself well with sunscreen and clothes to protect her skin. She was excited and jumping around the house. She prepared food and did all the chores at home for the day.

Giving an excuse to Guru Anna to go out was a big task for Sana. She was getting the hang of it, though, and was able to anticipate his response. So, she prepared well with the help of her ally, Payal Di. She didn't feel as guilty about her brother as much as she regretted it with her parents when she had to lie to meet Sid. She didn't look forward to that in the future, and she wanted to discuss this with Sid and find a solution. He didn't have any compulsion to do that with his family, as he was clear, and everyone knew about their relationship there. She also desired the same for herself—clarity, honesty, truthfulness, and freedom towards her family. She valued that a lot, and she felt that she was ready to tell her parents about her alliance with Sid if he was ready as well!

They planned to meet at 11 a.m. at Sid's house, so Payal di planned to drop Sana there, and that gave Guru some relaxation as well. He was getting doubtful of Sana's movements these days but trusted her as he knew how social she could be. Now, with a job and new friends, it can be pretty challenging for her to keep up with all the friend circles she has. Though her visits were limited to their houses and friends' houses, she rarely went out to meet friends. She was his responsibility in their parents' absence, so he was extra vigilant. But he also had some office work to finish, and Sana would have been a big distraction. Her not being around would give him the peace he needed for the weekend.

"Put your legs on both sides, Sana. Two legs on one side would be uncomfortable for you, and we are going for a long ride," Sid instructed, noticing her hesitation to sit.

"Hmmm... okay," she replied.

"Abe yaar, pakad le, mujhe itna kyun sharma rahi hain?" Sid grumbled.

"Maa hain na Sid... woh kya sochegi?" Sana whispered, waving at his mom, who was standing at the gate.

"Woh kuch nahi sochegi. And wait, why is this helmet slanted? Let me correct that." He pulled her toward himself and fixed the helmet. He got her a new ladies' helmet, pink with white designs, keeping in mind her favorite colors. She looked adorable in it. She had her sunglasses underneath it, and she looked delightful. He just couldn't stop looking at her. The helmet looked fine, but just to admire her a bit more, he pulled her toward himself and acted as if he was fixing it.

She had a small gray ladies' backpack around her shoulders, with white sneakers on her feet. She looked like a bairn.

"Chal, baith," he slightly pushed her hand to his shoulder and asked her to sit.

Sana was excited about the bike ride. She sat comfortably on the bike, holding Sid's shoulders, and waved to his mom.

"Bye!" she called.

Mom had a big smile, waving at them and asking them to be careful. "Take care, bacho. Drive safe and enjoy."

"Chale?" Sid asked Sana, slightly shaking the bike.

"Aaahh amma, kya kar rahe ho? Chalne se pehle hi darra rahe ho?" Panicking, Sana held his waist tight.

"Now you know how to hold!" Sid chuckled and started their first bike ride.

Sana was having so much fun; she was cherishing the experience. It was a special one, as it was with Sid, and how handsome he was looking with his toned muscles protruding out in the rolled-up sleeves of his blue polo T-shirt. She had wrapped her arms around his waist, hugging him close, and she could feel his toned chest. She was blushing and biting her lips, whipped with the thrill.

They reached Connaught Place (CP) in Delhi. He parked the bike, and they walked around CP and ate special chaat and juice. Sid loved all the street-side food, and Sana was crazy about it as well. They relished it together. Then, they went to feed the pigeons. She also did some petty fake jewelry shopping in Palika Bazaar and the local market.

He asked if she wanted to watch a movie, to which she denied it and said, "Nahi Sid, I want to talk to you. Let's go towards the water fountain. There are a lot of benches to sit on," she suggested.

"Nice idea... chal," Sid was happy about her suggestion as he also didn't like the idea of going to a movie. But he had said it because he knew Sana's fondness for Bollywood movies. He wrapped his left hand around her shoulder, and she held his waist from behind with her right hand. They walked towards the fountain like lovebirds, as if no one was watching, free and unburdened.

They both were silent, sitting on an empty bench away from the crowd, watching the water and kids playing around it from a distance. A large drop of the sun lingered on the horizon, sprinkling an orange façade across the sky.

"You know, Sana, dusk is just an illusion because the sun is either above the horizon or below it. And that means that day and night are linked in a way that few things are: there cannot be one without the other, yet they cannot exist at the same time. How would it feel, I wonder, to be always together yet forever apart?" Sid said, watching the Sun while Sana laid her head in his arms, holding it, tired and sleepy.

"The journey of the sun and moon is predictable. But ours is our ultimate." Sana looked up to see Sid's charming face, and he bent down to peck her lips. She pecked him as well in return.

"I want to tell Appa and Amma about us after their return from Kerala," Sana said in a hushed tone, looking up at him.

Sid jerked and faced her, cupping her face with both hands. "Sachi, I was waiting for you to say this! I've been waiting to take you home and make you mine forever, but I didn't want to force you with any of my wishes. You are young, and you might have aspirations, so I thought I would wait for you. I know you are my ultimate, and I will wait for you lifelong. Thank you so much, Sana... let's do it. Let me know when to come and talk to them or whatever you say, dear..." Overjoyed, Sid expressed his happiness, hugging her tight.

Sana was relieved hearing Sid's feelings. She thought he might ask her to wait and would tell her to enjoy this time of their courtship, but she was pleasantly shocked hearing his eagerness.

"Should I come next Saturday? What do you say?" he asked.

"I will talk to them on Saturday first. Let me check how they react first, and then you can come Sunday, maybe!" she said.

"Yeah, that would be right. Let me also know. I will prepare myself accordingly. Itna toh board meeting mein bhi nahi nervous hua yaar..." he huffed out some breath, combing his hair with his fingers.

"Nervous toh mujhe hona chahiye, in our family no one has done a love marriage, and mine would be the first... that too out of our caste... I don't know what is in store, but I am somehow confident that they will initially disagree but will agree later," she said, looking at him questioningly as if seeking an answer from him.

"What if they deny? What will we do then?" he asked.

"I will try to make them agree, compel them, pressurize them, make them understand that you are my happiness. They are parents; they will understand," she said confidently.

"What if, even after all that, they don't agree?" he pestered her again.

"I will not go against them, Sid, if that is what you are asking. They are my parents; I will give up my happiness and my love for them if I am unsuccessful in making them understand. They are more important to me, Sid, and because of them, I am here with you... They are my God. How can I scuffle with them?" she said honestly again, making her point clear and surprising Sid but also making him proud of his girl, who values and respects relationships so much. He was also the same; his mom was everything to him. Given a choice, he would have chosen his mom, like Sana said. He would never judge Sana's love for him based on the fact she said so innocently and honestly.

"We will see that. We have to think positively and believe that they will agree, and if not, we will make them realize our love for them. Together, we will face any challenge as deep as the ocean and as high as the sky. Although we may come from vastly different stories and very different walks of life, we are one people who possess common values and common ideals. I think we will make them recognize that together." He tried to clear all the confusion that was misting their minds, giving himself solace.

"Yes, we will, together!" Sana smiled, giving him assurance, and laid her head on his shoulder, intertwining their fingers, watching the sunset, which was promising the new dawn.

Chapter Twenty-Six:
A Night of Love and Promises

Sana was at Sid's house with his mom and his sister, Kajal, who was finally able to meet Sana. Today was also Sid's birthday. They celebrated his special day with a small gathering of his close friends—Sumit, Rahul, and Vishal, his childhood buddy. They cut the cake, and Mom, with the help of Kajal and Sana, made dinner arrangements for everyone.

It was a Friday evening, and Sana had already informed her family about her plan to attend a friend's birthday party. Payal was also invited, which made it easier for her to spend extra time, as she planned to return with Payal.

"Tu toh bilkul bahu-type kaam kar rahi hai, Sana! Lag hi nahi raha tu hamari Sana hai, full responsible-type feel de rahi hai," Payal teased as Sana served hot puris to Rahul and Payal.

"Haina? Mujhe bhi laga! Kya baat hai, Sana! Looking duty-bound... good, good," Rahul said, agreeing with Payal.

"Haan toh, hone wali bahu toh hoon na main iss ghar ki! It's good that I'm giving you both that feeling, which means I'm on the right track," Sana replied, giggling and laughing with ease.

She already felt like a part of the family—that's how Sid and his family treated her. She felt comfortable around them; they were progressive and liberal, and she felt positive and free in their presence. She could be herself with them, just like she was at home with her parents and brother. But when she was in Chennai, she felt burdened by the need to wear a "manner mask" in front of her Dadi and other elders. It was such a paradox. Still, she felt lucky to have Sid and his family and always thanked her God whenever she got the chance.

"Sana, let's go. We'll also join them; the puris are ready. Make yourself a plate," Mom said, switching off the stove and drinking some water.

"Haan, Maa, chalo! I think Kajal Di has also fed Abhi. I'll ask her to join us, too," Sana said as she walked toward Kajal, who was feeding Abhi in the living room. Sid and everyone else were sitting there.

"Kajal Di, khila diya Abhi ko? Chalo, we will also eat," Sana said.

"Haan, ho gaya! Bas last bite," Kajal replied as she pushed the last portion of food into Abhi's mouth. He then ran toward Sid, jumping on him.

"Mamaaa... I want ice cream," he demanded.

"Fridge mein hai, come, I'll give you," Sid said, picking him up and walking toward the fridge.

"You guys eat, na! What's taking you so long?" Sid asked, looking at his mom and Sana.

"We're going now, just waiting for Kajal," Mom replied.

The trio then made their plates and sat in the living room, surrounded by everyone, talking and having fun.

"Sana, I heard you're going to tell your parents about Sid tomorrow?" Kajal asked.

"Yes, Di. I'm a bit nervous. I had planned to tell them immediately after their return from Kerala, but Amma fell sick, and after that, Appa also got the flu. So, I had to postpone it for two weeks. But finally, the day has come," Sana said.

She had planned and prepared a lot—thinking about what to say and how to start the conversation. But when her parents returned, her mom was depressed and had a high fever, maybe due to the change in water and weather. Seeing their condition, she couldn't bring herself to say anything. She didn't want to add to their stress.

Things at home had been getting back to normal over the past few days, so she thought this weekend would be the right time to open up to them. She had also discussed it with Sid, who supported whatever decision she made.

"We will leave now, Maa. It's getting late, and Sid also has plans to go out with his friends," Sana said after finishing dinner and helping Mom clean the kitchen.

"Haan bacha, theek hai. Today, after so many years, Sid agreed to celebrate his birthday like this—thanks to you, Sana," Mom said.

"Arre, kya Maa ji, why thanks and all? It's a special occasion, and Kajal Di has also come, so we had to make it special, na," Sana said.

Just then, Sid came in.

"Kya ho raha hai? Why are you both in the kitchen the whole evening? Aap dono ki agar baat khatam ho gayi ho toh, can you please join us outside?" Sid said, almost frustrated. His eyes had been searching for Sana all evening, but she was either busy helping his mom with food, talking to Kajal, or chatting with his friends. His only interaction with her had been brief eye contact here and there.

"Haan, chal. We were just coming. Sana is leaving now; she was just saying that," Mom told Sid.

Mom walked past them, and Sana followed, nodding with a smile. Just then, Sid suddenly grabbed her wrist and gestured for her to come with him. She looked surprised but followed him as he pulled her by the wrist, leading her upstairs toward the terrace.

"Kya hai, Sid? Sab kya sochenge? Leave my hand... chhodo mujhe," she whispered, trying to resist. But he wasn't listening. He opened the terrace door, pulled her inside, and shut it behind them, leaning against it.

"The whole evening, you've been avoiding me! Itna kya kaam kar rahi hai tu?" he complained, pulling her close and wrapping his arms around her waist.

"I was with you the whole day, na, Sid? In the car, in the office... ab yahan Mom needed my help, and there are so many people. Samjho na... I can't be glued to you all the time, na, dear," Sana tried to explain, resting her head on his chest. She was tired, and his chest felt like the coziest place.

He was tall, and she barely reached his chest. He loved their height difference, though Sana always complained about it. She hated wearing heels—just a few inches were fine, but she often wondered how girls managed to wear those pencil heels. She was a Bata-shoe girl—comfortable yet chic.

"Now you're leaving, too? So soon? Why?" he asked.

"You have plans with your friends, right? You said that, remember? And it's getting late. I have to go," she reminded him.

"Right, right... but where is my gift?" he asked with a smirk.

"Gift? Yeh kya hai jo tumne pehna hua hai?" She poked his chest, pointing at the shirt he was wearing—the one she had gifted him.

A baby pink khadi cotton shirt, which she had given him in the morning while they were in the car on the way to work. He had paired it with khaki-colored pants after they got back, looking absolutely suave and charming.

"But I want a kiss," Sid demanded.

"Subah hi 10 baar le chuke ho!" she grumbled

"That's what! I'm always the one taking it. When are you going to give me my kiss?" he smirked, being adamant.

"Very funny. Ha... ha... It's always give and take. Zyada na chant mat bano tum," she fussed.

"Now, are you giving me my gift, or should I get it myself?" he asked, stepping closer.

"Hayee Rabba mere! Kya karu main?" she face-palmed, then cupped his face and gave him a strong kiss on the lips.

She had to lift herself to reach him, but he held her up effortlessly, lifting her slightly off the floor and pulling her tighter into his embrace, wrapping his strong arms around her hips.

She was now comfortable around him and was also becoming a pro at kissing. She, too, craved it whenever they were together. Sometimes, she was even the first one to do it, and Sid loved that—especially when she took control, just like now. She was kissing him with all her heart, making him feel special on his birthday.

She finally parted, resting her forehead against his.

"I love you, Sid. Happy Birthday..." she whispered, smiling as she kissed his forehead, then his cheek, nose, chin, and once again, his lips, showering all the love she had for him.

"I love you, Sana," he replied.

He loved her pampering sessions. Lifting her up a little more, he held her from the bottom and thighs and swung her around, laughing. She giggled, feeling like she was touching the sky with happiness, her arms wide open in the air as she looked above. They both felt elated in each other's arms—worried and nervous for tomorrow but not losing the present.

The places of happiness are infinite, the sources never-ending. And you inhabit those places not because they have been pursued but because you have opened your heart and allowed them in.

"Waise, I have kept one surprise gift in your bedroom. Baad mein batana kaisa laga," Sana said as she came down from Sid's hold.

"Why so many gifts, dear? But I'm excited to see it! Let's go down; I want to check it out," he said, locking his fingers with hers and walking down the stairs.

"Nahi, not now. Go with your friends, enjoy the time, and see it before you go to sleep," she said.

"Hmm, okay," he replied as they reached the crowd waiting for them.

"Aa gaye lovebirds... kahan guttergoo karne chale gaye the?" Kajal teased, making both Sana and Sid blush.

"Pagal hai, kuch bhi bolti hai gadhi..." Sid lightly slapped her head.

"Toh kya galat bola maine? Maa, dekho na, jab dekho marta rehta hai!" Kajal complained to Sana.

"You both fight just like Sana and her brother, Guru... Chal Sana, let's go; we are already late," Payal said, and they left after saying their goodbyes.

Sid also went out with his boys' gang to the club for some catching up over drinks. Though he didn't drink, he wanted to treat them when they insisted, and he happily obliged.

When he came back home, he went straight to his room, freshened up, and changed into his comfortable shorts and tee. As he walked towards the bed, his eyes fell on a photo frame placed on his bedside table, decorated with a red bow. He picked it up, removed the decoration, and was astonished to see the framed picture—a selfie of him and Sana taken at Connaught Place, with a flock of pigeons flying up in the background.

He was mesmerized by the picture—so serene, their faces beaming with wide smiles, their cheeks glowing. It was such a simple yet beautiful gift, one he would cherish for a lifetime.

Both of them wished each other good night over text, looking forward to another day filled with hope, potential, and promise...

Chapter Twenty-Seven:
The Test of Tradition

"Appa... Amma... ummm... I want to tell you something..." Sana said in a dubious voice to her parents.

It was already Saturday evening, and she had been waiting since morning for the right time to have the conversation with them, but she couldn't besiege the courage the whole time. She was reassuring herself, talking to herself, preparing the talk, and even took help from Sid by texting him and calling him once in between to get an energy boost. She was stressed out and nervous to an extent that couldn't be described.

She had planned to talk at lunchtime, and when it was lunch, all four of them were sitting at the dining table, having food made by her mom. Amma had made a feast after a long time—Sambhar, Rasam, potato fry, beans curry, and even Payasam (Kheer). Everyone was happy, relishing their favorites and chatting. She didn't have the heart to spoil the good time they were having after almost a month. She thought she would wait and maybe talk during tea time when they would all sit together again after their noon nap.

But then Payal di's mom came in, followed by aunty from upstairs, then the one from downstairs, making chaos at home while talking to her parents. She missed that opportunity as well…

Now, it was 7 PM, and silence finally prevailed at home after everyone had left. She had lit the Diya at 6 PM and prayed to her God for a little longer—praying for strength and hoping her parents would understand her situation.

They were in their bedroom—Appa in his wooden recliner, scrolling through his phone, maybe checking WhatsApp messages or browsing Facebook. He wasn't a tech geek; whatever little he had learned from his kids and friends, he used that for social media browsing. Amma was busy with something in the armoire—that was her pastime—cleaning, sorting, even folding already folded clothes again, or cleaning places that were already clean. Sana always wondered why her mom always found unnecessary tasks to do. That's why she often teased her about having OCD, or she wondered if all moms were like that.

"Come, Kulandai (baby), enna achhe? (What happened?)" her dad peeked over his reading glasses. He was wearing a half-sleeved white inner tee and a white lungi. He was a stout man but tall, with a protruding belly and salt-and-pepper hair. His sharp features made him look quite handsome.

"Why are you so dull today? You're not yourself. I hope the flu virus hasn't been transmitted to you..." Her mom suddenly got up to touch her forehead, checking her temperature.

Her mom was a caring and loving lady, very simple yet gorgeous in the chiffon sarees she wore. She had been married at the young age of 18, and both kids were born immediately after, making her look quite young. She always adorned a big maroon bindi on her forehead—something traditional in their Hindu culture, where women wear bindis since birth. That was also the reason Sana always wore one herself, except when she wore western clothing, that too due to peer pressure at school and college.

"Temperature toh nahi hai, thank God! Today, just have Kaanji (rice broth) for dinner." Her mom sat next to Sana on the bed, looking worried.

"I am fine, Amma, but I want to tell you both something," Sana said again, meekly, tense, her hands getting cold while her face heated up, turning red.

"Please listen and stay calm... and don't judge me," she started, the tension in her voice making them look at her with full concentration.

"What is it, Sanaya? Do you want something, or did you make a mistake? Tell me!" Appa questioned her this time.

He would always call her by her nicknames—Sana or Sanu—but when he said "Sanaya," she knew he was in his stern self, and she couldn't tease around.

She took a long breath and looked at her parents, who had to interrogate her eyes.

"Appa, I like a boy. I love him and would like to have a future with him," she said quickly in one breath, her forehead sweating in anticipation of their reaction.

"WHAT?? What did you say? Do you like a boy? Do you know what you are saying? Don't joke around, Sana. This is not funny at all!" her mom scolded her, slapping her arms.

"It is not a joke, Amma. I really love him. He is the VP of VS Corporations, and he loves me too. He wants to marry me and wants to ask for your blessings." Sana spoke, gaining a bit of confidence now that she had disclosed the main thing. She knew she could now give other explanations to their questions.

"Isliye bheja tha tujhe job mein? Tune toh hamara bharosa hi tod diya, Sana!" her mom shook her furiously. "Kuch toh bolo aap, Guru Appa..." she asked her husband, who was just staring at Sana in shock, his glasses in his hand and his phone falling onto his lap.

Sana jumped toward her dad, sitting down on the floor, catching his legs, and pleading, "Appa, please listen to me. He is a very good man—well-to-do, respectful. Just meet him once, Appa. He will not disappoint you; I can guarantee that. Ek baar milke faisla lena, Appa."

Her dad remained statue-like

"What is his name?" he finally asked.

"Sidesh... Sid..." she said, shivering.

"FULL NAME," he asked seriously in a high tone.

"Sidesh Sharma," Sana said, tears welling up in her eyes as she saw her father's authoritative, tough side. She had always been her father's pet. He would always cajole and coax her, never raising his voice. Seeing this side of him was breaking her heart.

"At least he is a Hindu... and not from a different caste," he stated.

"He is also a Brahmin, Appa, a North Indian Pandit," she added quickly, not thinking of any logic right now, just wanting to paint Sid in the best light before her father.

"Sana, we always trusted you and never thought you would do this to us. What will we say to our family? Pyaar karne se pehle kuch toh soch leti... How will we ever face them now?" her mom cried and yelled again, face-palming her forehead.

Sana abhorred the scene her mom was making. She had somehow known that her mother would be the most upset, but now that it was real, she despised her reaction. Her mom had only studied until 10th grade, was married young, and had lived in her husband's shadow for most of her 44 years. Sana knew that it was mostly fear of her father's reaction that was making her behave this way. She was confident that if she spoke to her alone, she could make her understand.

But her father was a hard nut to crack—difficult to convince because of his rigid thoughts on caste, religion, ethos, and prestige. He had never compromised his Hindu Brahmin lifestyle in his 57 years of life.

"Amma, please think about me right now! Not about the relatives. Koi sochke pyaar nahi kiya, ho gaya bas... I haven't committed a crime, Amma! I just love someone and want to spend my life with him," Sana cried, sitting down on the floor.

Just then, Guru came inside, hearing the chaos.

"Kya hua? Why are you all shouting?"

Her mom wailed again, explaining to him the so-called treacherous, hideous act Sana had committed.

"Can you keep quiet, Seetha?" her dad yelled at her mom this time, standing up with his hands clasped behind his back.

"Sana, it might not be a crime for you, but for us, this is something horrendous. In our family, no one dares to marry outside of caste, language, or religion. He is a North Indian. Though a Brahmin... still, he is not a Tamil Brahmin."

He paused, taking a deep breath before continuing.

"But you are my daughter, and I want to believe you. I want to give you a chance. I want to know if he is the right person for you or not. Call him, and I will see after that," her Appa announced.

"Par..." her mom tried to protest but was stopped by her dad.

"No more talks about this now. Guru, go. And Seetha, go prepare dinner. I don't want to discuss this anymore. Sana, call him and tell him to meet me tomorrow at noon."

When it comes to social consequences, different people react in different ways. It is difficult to even have a proper criterion of logic. Changing the norms and the very focus of a cultural system is a far more complex task than changing an individual's attitudes and interests. It wouldn't be easy for Sana and Sid. But where there is a will, there is a way!

Chapter Twenty-Eight:
The Silent Struggle

Exhausted... worn... weak... that was how Sana was feeling at that moment. Not physically, but mentally drained. She usually never closed her bedroom door, but she did today after a grueling moment with her parents for some privacy. She somehow fathomed them and knew this would happen, but in her thoughts, the reality was cruel! Never in her 21 years had she seen her house so riotous. Her mom was still yelling, her brother was arguing with Appa, and her father seemed to be doubtful, quiet, and silent, which was uncanny.

She called Sid, and he didn't pick up. Tears flowed down her cheeks. Nothing seemed right at that moment. She wailed, doubting herself. Were her parents right? Did she do something that atrocious? So many of her friends loved someone; even Payal Di said that loving someone is legitimate. Can religion stop someone from falling in love? Is there a law written somewhere that a Tamil Brahmin-born girl cannot love someone from a different caste?

"Where are you, Sid?" she screamed inside. Just then, her phone rang, and it was him—SS🚗.

Just his name popping up on the screen gave her anguished heart some comfort. She hadn't done anything wrong by loving him, she told her heart, and picked up the call, much calmer compared to a while ago.

"Hello... Sana... sorry, main bathroom mein tha... kya hua, bola tune?"

"Sana... hello... are you there?" he asked again, disturbed and worried for Sana, who was always mirthful on the phone but now unnervingly silent.

"Sid... I told them and... and..." she paused.

"And what?" he pondered.

"They are very upset... Amma is accusing me of tainting their image and how she will face society! Appa is also very serious... Sid... he is so quiet... just like the silence before the storm..." she said, pouring out every detail to him—what she felt, her state, her feelings... everything. Who else would she express this to? It was him, and only him, her soulmate.

"Appa wants to meet you tomorrow at noon, Sid... mujhe bahut darr lag raha hai. He said he wants to meet you and then decide! What will he decide, Sid? I don't understand anything..." she said, biting her nails, sitting up straight in her bed, feeling much more relaxed after sharing her concerns with Sid. Somehow, she felt that he would solve everything for her.

"Tu tension mat le, relax and be calm... you must be feeling hungry now. Go and find some junk to eat, and I'll come tomorrow to meet him. Don't worry. Bata diya na, main part over, rest we'll see..." he said, pacifying her.

"Haww... how do you know that I'm hungry and craving junk?" she surprised him with her question, as whenever she gets stressed, she eats junk—sweets, chocolate, chips, namkeen—all the junk items you can name. She always wondered if she was the only unique person who got ravenous when anxious.

"In these three months I have known you enough to know what you need right now, meri jaan," he said with a smile, thinking how easy it was to change his sweetheart's mood. How much of a baby she could be!

"You are not tensed for tomorrow? What might he ask? What are you going to say? Hayee, meri toh saans hi atak rahi hai..." Sana said, making all the expressions while talking to him, frowning and pouting.

"Honestly, I am tensed... but I know what the result will be... you will be mine, and I will be yours. Jab destination malum ho, toh journey asaan ho jati hai. Muskilen aayengi, hardship aayengi, par hum unse ladenge aur jeetenge," he said convincingly.

"True. You know, I was doubting myself; so many negative things passed through my mind. But you are my true anchor. I am immature, and your wisdom always brings mindfulness to my ignorant brain. I feel much more relaxed now," she said with gratitude.

"We balance each other, Sana. You calm me. You give peace to my agitated soul... Tu tension mat le, zyada. No negative thoughts... We will conquer this phase with flying colors," he said, giving her the boost she craved at that moment.

"Hmmm... Positive sochoge, toh positive hoga... Haina?" she said, with a smile covering her face.

They chatted a bit more, giving each other energy—a much-needed vigor to prepare for the big day tomorrow. After she hung up the call, she slowly opened the bedroom door to find a much quieter house. She wondered what happened and where everyone was. She walked toward the kitchen, expecting her mom to be there, but she wasn't! She drank some water and grabbed the Aloo Bhujia savory, which her mom diligently keeps in a container—something she didn't quite understand. Why keep biscuits, chips, and namkeen in containers when they can just be kept on the original cover?

She could hear muffled voices coming from her parents' room. The door to that room was closed, which was rare, too, as no one in her house ever closed the door of their respective rooms. She got curious and walked closer to the door to listen, wondering if they were talking about her. She heard her father's voice and went dumbstruck by what she heard.

"We need to prepare Sana's Jhadagam (horoscope) as soon as possible. I will let the relatives know that we are seeking an alliance for her marriage. Seetha, you also tell your brothers and relatives," he announced to her mom and brother.

Just then, Guru's harsh voice added his opinion, "Appa, we have to stop her from going to work. This is where everything started. I told you guys not to send her and, instead, make her apply for a Master's degree. But no... Who listens to me? She was adamant about going to a job and earning money. Now see what she has earned... utter disgrace!"

"Aap dono shaant ho jao. She must be having an infatuation with this boy. Love doesn't happen in three months. Zindagi beeth jaati hai, to understand what love is. See him tomorrow and then decide. Bachi hai woh hamari, Guru ke Appa... Don't be so stone-hearted. We cannot marry her to any boy. Please calm yourself and think," her mom pointed out who Sana thought was the most averse, but now was giving some sense to the men of the house.

"Tomorrow's meeting is just a formality. Woh kitna bhi accha kyun na ho, I am not going to accept him. Whosoever he may be, but a boy with a different background cannot be my Mapilai (Son-in-law). I have some respect in front of my relatives, and I cannot sacrifice that due to this immature girl! I faulted somewhere in my upbringing... all your fault, Seetha, aur bhejo kaam mein, gumne phirne..." her father callously said in a high pitch, accusing his wife and daughter.

"Ab maine kya kiya? Aap nahi maante uski baat. I am always strict with her, but you are the one who pampers her. Don't blame me. She has always been a good girl; I never had any complaints about her from school, college, or anywhere. In fact, hamesha sabne hamare bachon ki tareef ki hai. This may be the first time she has disappointed us... So give her a chance."

"Call Ganeshan (Sana's Mama) tomorrow. We will need him too when that person comes. And stop supporting your daughter," Appa warned Amma.

"I am not supporting her, but please don't take any decisions hastily. That is my only request. She is so young and innocent, our only Chella (loving) daughter... Bache galti karte hain toh hum maa-baap unko sudhaarte hain, punish nahi karte hain..." Mom sat down crying, disheveled.

"Amma, aap kyun ro rahi ho? Please mat ro... We will find a solution. I will talk to Sana and try to make her understand. Okay?" Guru, seeing his mom cry, melted and toned down his anger.

"Yahi toh problem hai, she is my Chella kutti (loving child). Even I don't like to be guileful, but she has left me with no choice. We will see what we can do to rectify this now. I am calling my astrologer in Chennai to make her Jhadagam (horoscope) and spread it across. I thought I would get her married at age 24-25, thode saal aur hamare saath rehti, but now no option left. I have to hurry up and find a prospective groom," Appa said in a grief-stricken voice. He loved his daughter but was bound by social norms.

Sana felt wretched and devastated by the conversation she overheard. Tears flowed down her face without any emotion as she walked back toward her room. She felt responsible for her parents' miserable condition. Her mental state was fluctuating back and forth. Positive thoughts came in when she talked to Sid and felt right about what she felt for him, but listening to her parents' thoughts made her feel dejected. She loved them, actually more than Sid! How long did she know Sid? Just 3 months... but her parents had been with her her whole life, and she wanted them to be a part of her future. She would be berserk without them.

She laid down in bed, tired, and prayed to the almighty to show her the right path. If He had instilled the emotion of love in her heart, it would have been for a reason. She left it to Him to decide her fate. If her fate was written with Sid, then she would be the happiest person. But if not, she would not fight with her living God, her parents, who gave this life to her.

Chapter Twenty-Nine:
A Ray of Hope

Sid was taciturn, silent since evening. He had been in his room for a long stretch of time. He usually would play around with Abhi or banter with Kajal when they were at home. His mom was concerned about what might be the reason for his silence. Was it related to work? If that were the case, he would be working on his laptop or calling someone at work to solve it. He was a hard worker, and the reason he was in a good position was his work dynamics. He had been an achiever, an eager beaver... but this was unusual. He never looked jaded the way he was now, so indifferent and engrossed in his thoughts.

Mom called him, but he didn't respond. She came forward and flapped his shoulder. "Sid... kahan khoya hua hai?"

"Hugh... haan... kuch nahi maa, bas aise hi!" Sid said, getting up from the bed and sitting down, massaging his eyes and forehead.

"Pareshaan hai beta, let me give you a head massage," Mom said, walking toward his dresser to get coconut oil for his hair. "Chal... get up and sit down," she asked him, and he obliged.

"What happened, kuch problem hai... mujhe nahi batayega? You didn't even join us for dinner, and Abhi was asking for you. Kajal was also worried for you. We didn't want to bother you as we thought you were in some work stress, but I can see you are disturbed with something else! Kuch hua hai... is Sana fine?" Mom asked him, reflecting her concern.

"Maa, you can sense everything, right? How do you do that?" Sid said, enjoying the massage his mom was giving him.

"Maa hoon... they know everything. A mother's instinct towards her child is very strong; they just know!" she said with a smile.

"Hmmm..." he just hummed.

"Ab bolega bhi?" she asked again, pausing the massage.

"Sana... maa... she... she has told about us her family, and they are creating a big hue and cry about it. Her father has called me tomorrow to meet him, and then he will decide if I am right for his daughter or not... Hugh!" he said with a smirk, nodding his head in disappointment.

"Good that they know now, and we already knew, right? They will behave that way... How is Sana doing? Poor girl must be going through a nightmare," Mom said, guessing right about Sana. She was indeed going through an ordeal, Sid thought.

"Haan maa, she is, and I gave her some hope and showed her the positive side, but I am worried myself. I don't know what will happen tomorrow. I hope I keep calm and don't lose my temper in front of Sana's parents. I cannot tolerate their thinking towards this societal discrimination. Hadd hai, sahi mein! Even in today's generation, there are people like this. I don't understand this patriarchy!" Sid growled with anger, frustrated by the preposterous mindset of people who still clung to backward rituals.

"You have no right to judge them, Sid. We need to acknowledge their way of thinking if we want THEM to acknowledge our way of thinking. No one is right, and no one is wrong here. Who are we to judge their beliefs? To claim that you can't judge me is then an ethical condemnation, and so it applies to itself. Aur doosri baat, beliefs are passed on to generations after generations... there is no 'today's generation' or 'old generation' for that," his mom made him understand with a tough tone.

"Now I know where I got so much wisdom from!" he was amazed with what his mother just said.

"How do you know so much, matlab, how can you think so clearly? I was so frustrated thinking about their beliefs, but you are right—who am I to judge them?" he said, assenting to his mom's words of thought.

"Struggles and pain teach you a lot in life, and like it goes, experience is the best teacher... ab dhoop mein safed nahi kiye yeh baal!" she said with a smile.

"Par maa, I am nervous. What if..." he couldn't finish that line and fell into deep thought about the uncertainties that might occur during the visit.

"You know, first impressions are very important, and you have to make sure that you are yourself with them. Remember, this is not some company deal to crack; this is your life. So be calm and say what's in your heart and what you feel for Sana. Dil ki baat agar sachayi se bolega toh doosre ke dil tak zaroor pahunchegi," she said with conviction.

"Hmmm..." he closed his eyes and enjoyed the hair massage, which was taking out all the stress.

"Waise, I have a plan..." Mom said after a while, with a twinkle in her eye!

"Plan?!" he turned to look at her, holding her legs.

Mom got up, holding the bed, put the oil back in the dresser, and said while walking out of the room, "Yes, plan... let me go and wash my hands, and you come to the living room, eat your food, and I'll call Kajal to discuss."

He wondered what his mother's plan could be. She had been a great influence in their life and had always been inclusive. He knew that whatever she was thinking would be for his well-being, and he waited for the day tomorrow to unfold.

Sana had a tough night with no sleep, docking her eyes, twisting and turning till the break of dawn. She woke up and went to her balcony to watch the sunrise. She would usually miss that on normal days. She was a sleeper and loved to sleep late, at least on weekends, until her father forced her to wake up with his noisy, irritating indirect tricks. She was craving some nice filter coffee to watch the sunrise. She went to the bathroom and freshened up, as she always brushed her teeth before anything went inside her mouth—she wouldn't even open her mouth without brushing. She loathed morning breath or any disgusting odor.

She went toward the kitchen and very silently made herself a coffee, as everyone else was still sleeping, and she didn't want to disturb anyone. With her small steel tumbler, she admired the morning beauty—the fresh air, the orange sky, the sun peeping out, and the birds chirping. It was meditative. She was feeling energized from within. The universe was giving her the strength to face the eventful day ahead.

She silently prayed for herself and Sid. She was an ardent believer in the powers of prayer. It gave her faith and felt like the easiest thing to do for more power, healing, strength, and comfort for her soul.

She felt awkward to face her parents, knowing their intentions for her future. She did not want to confront them, so she opted to be silent. She cleaned her room, tidied it up, and ironed a new parrot green churidar for the day, along with matching accessories. She wanted to be positive, just like Sid said, and believed in what her dad always says: everything happens for good, and if you think good, good will happen. She decided to be confident, decisive, and optimistic.

She greeted everyone with a good morning, as always, though the responses she received were different. Amma had a sympathetic look on her face, puffy eyes, and a sad, upset expression. Appa, who would usually be active and do his chores, seemed absent today, reading the newspaper for the longest time while sipping his third cup of coffee. Guru Anna didn't even bother to answer.

She helped her mom in the kitchen, where she was preparing breakfast—rava upma and chutney, simple comfort food.

"Have you told him to come?" Amma asked.

"Yeah, he will be here at 12," Sana replied.

"Clean, dust, and change the sofa covers after breakfast. What will he eat? It's lunchtime. Should I serve him lunch or snacks?" Amma asked casually, as she would any other visitor or relative.

"Anything will do, Amma. By the way, he loves your Sambhar, Rasam, Kootu (vegetables with coconut and lentils), sandwiches, and Poori with Aloo masala," Sana said with a sweet smile.

"O... Naijamaa va? (Really?) When did he eat my food?" Amma asked, curious, with a small smile.

"We eat lunch together at the office, and he would snatch my lunch and eat it daily, and I end up eating his food. He's a big fan of your cooking. Remember one day I asked for extra Rasam? That was for him! He also says that you look like my sister—very beautiful, natural, and homely," Sana revealed, making her mother blush with a shy smile.

"Uske papa kahan work karte hain?" Amma asked, becoming more curious, which gave Sana a positive sign. She nervously and eagerly answered, "His dad isn't around—he passed away from a heart attack 16 years ago. His mom raised Sid and his sister with a lot of difficulty. He has worked really hard to reach his high position. Kajal Didi, his sister, is married and settled in Kanpur. You should see her son, Abhi—oh my God, he's so cute! Chubby, totally pink!"

"You've seen them?" Amma asked, curiosity growing, to which Sana nodded in agreement.

"They know about you? Has he already told them?" Amma's questions came one after another, but Sana was delighted to answer all of them. She wanted to share everything she knew about him—his family, his nature, his likes, and everything else—so her mother could understand a little more about him, to see how worthy he was of being their son-in-law.

"Haan Amma, he's been very vocal about me to his family, and they are all so good. His mom is just like you, so loving and caring. She adores me like a baby... When you were in Kerala, she used to pack dinner for me and Anna. She took such good care of us. Her hug brings so much comfort, just like the way I feel when I'm with you," Sana said with a proud smile, raising her eyebrow.

Amma didn't ask any more questions after that. She fell silent and just announced, "I'll make Puri, Aloo masala, and Kesari (sooji ka halwa with saffron). Mama and Mami are coming too. You go eat breakfast and do the work."

Sana felt light, happy, and hopeful. Being optimistic was good; it was a way of seeing the best in life, no matter the situation. Whether one was dealing with something good or bad, being optimistic made you always strive to see the most positive outcomes.

Chapter Thirty:
When Culture Collide

"SANA... SANA!!!!" Guru shouted from his room.

"Aayi!!! Ek minute, Anna." She came in with a duster cloth in her hand, tired and weary. "Kya hai? Why are you shouting so much?" she snapped back, wiping the sweat from her forehead with her long kurta sleeve.

"Sit here; I want to talk to you," he said with a stern face.

"Bolo," she said with a disinterested face as she sat down in the office chair, keeping the duster cloth on the table and grabbing the water bottle to quench her thirst.

"You are not ashamed of what you are doing? Itna attitude mat dikha mere saath, samjhi?" he said, frustrated.

"Why should I be ashamed? Kissi ka murder kar diya maine, chori ki hai? Have I done some crime? Have I been convicted for a jail sentence that makes your head spin?" she shot back. "Sharam se... Please, Anna, keep your thoughts to yourself." She was pissed with her brother. She knew he was very orthodox, but the way he behaved yesterday in front of their parents and then confronted her behind her back was unacceptable.

"Haan, bas ussi ki kami reh gayi hai... zyada na baatameezi mat kar mere saath," he yelled at her again.

"Aur aap kar sakte ho? Behind my back, planning and bitching about my life. Even I didn't expect that from you..." she rebelled back, shocking him as he didn't know she had heard what they said.

"What about you? Are you not having an affair behind our back? That too with a North Indian boy! Chaee!! Our parents have not brought us up to see this day. They've always been clear to us that we need to have our life partner from our caste, religion, and culture. Even if they are Hindu, they are different, Sana! Didn't you know that? Why did you do this? They are so upset!!!" he said, giving his point of view, opposing her to make her see some sense.

"He is a human, Anna. Maine insaan dekh ke pyaar kiya, caste dekh ke nahi! I know how our parents brought us up, and they taught us to love and not discriminate or hate anyone. I value my upbringing and will always follow what Appa has instilled in me." She stated her point of view firmly.

"What about our family reputation, our prestige? It will all be ruined just because of your stupid love! Have you thought about Paati (Daadi), Periaappa (Tau, father's brother), and Periamma (Tai, Periappa's wife), our cousins? What will they think of us… you??" he asked.

"No, I did not think of anything when I fell for him. Love doesn't hit you with rules, protocols, reputations, and prestige. It just happened too quickly, and now I cannot step back. Sid is my life, and I cannot fathom my life without him. I will be a living dead Anna!" she said, getting emotional and tired of the turmoil she had been through.

"We have lived here in this place in the North part of India since I can remember… I have friends who are from here, including my school, my college, my teachers, and my neighbors. We follow so many rituals, festivals, religious practices of theirs that are not part of our 'SO-CALLED TAMIL BRAHMIN' customs," Sana said, agitated, quoting with her fingers. "Do we have the Holi festival in Tamil Nadu? Do we have Raksha Bandhan? But still, I tie Rakhi on your wrist, Anna, and you still promise to protect me. I speak Hindi more than Tamil… I am more of them than my genes… It's fine when we opt to live here with them and blend in with their lifestyle and culture, but when it's about choosing our husband or wife, it should be from our side. Why… Why this prejudice? Why this bias?" she questioned him, fire in her eyes, rage in her body language.

Guru was quiet. He did not have anything to answer her back as he knew that she was right. Even he liked it here in Ghaziabad, in Delhi, where he was brought up, schooled, and worked. He accepted what she said. He would prefer a life partner from this part of the state but also of his caste—someone who would understand the lifestyle they live, which was way more lenient and forgiving than what he had seen in Chennai when they visited for vacations.

"I have always told myself, Anna, never to fall in love with anyone here, as our parents have been very particular about that factor, but I couldn't help myself from falling for him. Bas ho gaya, Anna! Kya aap kisi ki bhi shaadi mere saath kara doge, like what Appa was saying yesterday? I heard you guys… koi bhi aira-gera aa ke shaadi kar le matlab, main kya chahthi hoon uska koi value nahi hai! I feel safe with Sid and protected; his family is so good. I will be happy with him, Anna. Do you want me to be cheerful, peaceful, and content, or do you want me to suffer in this orthodox culture and caste purgatory??? Answer me, Anna! Bolo kuch…" she questioned him, much calmer, with sadness on her face. Disappointed with her brother for being so trapped in societal norms, she felt he was not empathetic toward her feelings, her life, and her chosen one.

"Sana, I understand what you are saying. I also live here with you, and we will never give you away to anyone, my Kanna (baby); please don't have that fear. But it is easy to adjust to people who are your friends, teachers, or neighbors from different cultures. But when it comes to your life partner, you will be more comfortable with someone who is associated with our culture, as you have been brought up in this environment. Try to understand that this is not a game. You will not get any lifelines here. This is about marriage, and it is a lifelong commitment. Appa and I are only thinking about your welfare. We are not your enemies," Guru replied back, figuring out ways to make her understand.

"I know that, Anna, but I know I will adjust to him and his lifestyle. We girls are trained that way since birth to be like water and adjust and take the form of whichever vessel we are poured into. We are told not to be assertive or rigid but to find a way around it. I am confident that if I am put in my choice of vessel, I will find my way and be lively... I will be responsible for any adversities, and I will find ways out of them. But if I am poured into your choice, I will be stagnant there. Can you guarantee that there will be no misfortune in that life? Will you or Appa or Amma take responsibility for that?" Sana said, replying to Guru, who was astonished to hear such insightful words from her mouth but still troubled inside, wondering how their parents would agree to this and how it would work with his relatives and family.

Sana's father was standing outside Guru's room, overhearing all the conversation between the siblings without them knowing he was there listening to their discussion. He bowed his head down, hands clasped behind his back, and walked toward his bedroom. His wife was preparing herself to take a shower, pulling a saree from the armoire.

"Seetha, what will we say to Amma? She will be so mad! I really hope that boy fails to impress us, and we get a good Varan (alliance) soon. I've spoken to Anna about Sana's Jadagam (horoscope). He was surprised, but he will visit the astrologer soon and get it ready for us by tomorrow," he said, distressed.

"Are we doing this right? I think we should give her a chance, please don't take a hasty decision, Bala Appa," Sana's mom said to him, calling him that name, as she usually did when they were alone.

He sighed. "You go take your bath and come back soon. I need to shower too and pray before Ganeshan (Mama) and Lalitha (Mami) arrive," he said, lying down on the bed, shaking his leg and thinking deeply with his eyes closed.

It was almost noon, the time for Sid's visit. She knew how punctual he was, just like her. She dressed up prettily in her parrot green churidar, newly stitched. Sid's mom lovingly gave the gift during her first visit to his home. She wanted to make this special for them and show him how much he meant to her. This gesture may give him confidence, and whatever may be their fate today, she was with him to support him and give him the assurance.

Sana

Kahan ho?

SS 🚗

Just starting... all the best to us ☺

Sana

☕❤ Love you

She was nervous and didn't dare to venture out of the room. Her parents, brother, mama, and mami were all sitting in the living room discussing, but she preferred to stay in her room and silently prayed to her Almighty for favoring her side.

Just then, her mama came into her room. She adored him very much. He was her favorite mama out of her four mamas. He was the youngest of the siblings and was very easygoing and funny.

"Kaisa hai mera bacha?" he asked, sitting next to her on the bed, wrapping his arms around her shoulders and giving her a hug. She wanted this at that moment—a warm hug from someone for her nervous state.

"Bahut darr lag raha hai, mamu. You are with me, right?? Please don't ditch me; support Appa. I am warning you, mamu." She told him. He was more like a friend to her than an elder figure, and he always pampered her like his own child.

"Koi shak... tera mamu tere saath hi hai. Don't worry when I am here. Waise tera hero kaisa hai? Why haven't you shared anything with me?" he asked, trying to lighten the mood.

"Thank you, Mamu jaan. I wanted to tell Appa first and then you... that's why... sorry." She said, pouting her lips and pinching her ear. "Like how you are the best, he is the best in the world. Jab aap dekhoge na, you will know." She said, happily smiling and glowing.

Just then, she heard the car horn beep... their code signal... Beep... Beep... Beep, Beep, Beep...

She got up and peeked through her balcony, seeing his blue car entering the community. Her heart was palpitating, expectations running high, with anxiety and stress, but also a feeling of pride and happiness that Sid was about to meet her parents.

She just thought at that moment that there is only one way to happiness: to cease worrying about things that are beyond the power of our will. She had Sid, the love of her life, with her, loving her selflessly. Tension could not exist in the presence of that... right?

Chapter Thirty-One:
Against All Odds

Sid took his time to get out of the car. He relaxed his rapidly beating heart, took a deep breath, and stepped out of his side of the car door. The first thing he saw was his beauty standing on the balcony, wearing the dress gifted by his mom. Her lips curled up into a smile as she blushed and waved at him. Her hair flowed down to her waist, glowing in the sunlight, highlighting the dark red ombre color, making it mesmerizing. Their eyes locked, giving each other the much-needed strength. She blew him a flying kiss, making him smile even more. She then complimented him, signaling with her hand 👌, as usual, making the air light and relieving their stress.

Sana was equally admiring her handsome hunk, dressed in a crisp white shirt neatly tucked into silver-gray pants secured with a matching belt. He looked aristocratic, well-groomed, and majestic. Excited, she rushed inside to tell her mother about his arrival and asked her to inform her parents. She glanced at herself in the mirror again and gave herself a reassuring wish, **"All the best, Sana! 👍"**, and rushed towards the front door to open it for him.

At that moment, Payal came out and noticed Sid's car outside.

"All the best, Sana... Sab theek hai na? Wow, kitni pyaari lag rahi tu!" she said.

"Haan di, aap mere saath rahoge na?" Sana asked, holding her hand.

"Haan haan, yeh bhi koi puchne ki baat hai? I am always there on your side," Payal said, reassuring Sana.

Just then, they heard some voices coming from the ground floor. Curious, they peeked down the stairs and were left astonished.

Sana couldn't believe what she saw... Sid was climbing up the stairs with his mom, Kajal Di, and Abhi in her arms, followed by Rahul Bhaiya.

"Maa... aap?" Sana said, her face a mix of shock, surprise, and happiness. She was elated to see her and Kajal Di.

"Haan, main..." Mom said, smiling, as she hugged Sana tightly and kissed her forehead. "Kitni pyaari lag rahi hai tu, bacha! Bahut sundar, nazar na lage meri gudiya ko," she added, wiping some kohl from her own eyes and placing it behind Sana's ear.

Sana smiled, tears welling up in her eyes.

"You live so close by, Sana. Never thought it would be this close," Kajal said, breaking the moment.

"Hi, Di! What a pleasant surprise," Sana said, taking Abhi from her arms. "Hello, Abhi..."

Sana's parents witnessed the bond between the elderly lady, the child, and their daughter. They didn't yet know who they were but sensed who they might be. They were equally surprised to see the family. They had expected to meet only the boy, but when his entire family came along with him, they were overwhelmed. The ease with which their daughter interacted with them was evident to them.

"Please come inside. Sana, bring them in. Bahar hi khada rakhogi?" Sana's mama said.

"Aayiee na... Please come, Maa," Sana added, inviting them warmly.

They all walked into the living room, removing their shoes and sandals outside.

"Namastey," Sid said. I am Sidesh Sharma. My mom is Priya Sharma, and my sister is Kajal." He politely introduced his family.

"Namastey, have a seat, please," Sana's dad said with a smile. He joined his hands in greeting and gestured for them to sit on the couch.

Sid, his mom and his sister sat on the three-seater sofa. Guru and his dad took a single-seater each. Sana's mom stood next to her dad. Around the dining chairs placed in the living room, Rahul, Payal, Mama, and Mami seated themselves while Sana stood near the door entrance.

"Sorry for not informing you about our presence, Bhaisaab," Sid's mom started, breaking the awkwardness. "But we wanted to join Sid and introduce ourselves to you. I thought, along with the boy, you should also meet his family to clarify how serious we are about making your beautiful daughter ours."

"Yes, we are happy to see you all," Sana's dad said hesitantly. This was not what he had expected. He had thought this was just a formality to meet the boy his daughter claimed to be in love with—only to reject him for some reason and then make Sana quit her job, marry a groom of his choice, and send her far away. To him, love and attraction were just momentary things, never meant for the long run. But now, with the boy's family showing up alongside him, it was a shocker. He was unprepared for this, and his face showed it to everyone.

"Maa… this is Appa, Guru Anna, Amma, my Mama, and Mami..." Sana introduced everyone. They all joined their hands, bowing slightly as they whispered, "Namastey."

"Sana, Payal, go get some water for everyone," Amma instructed them both. They nodded and went toward the kitchen.

"Aap log chai, coffee, ya sharbat—kya prefer karenge?" she asked Sid and his family.

"Sana has praised your filter coffee so much, Bhabhi. We would prefer that, thank you," Sid's mom requested.

"Haan haan, abhi laayi..." Sana's mom happily went toward the kitchen with a smile. She had always been a simple lady, and receiving praise from someone always pepped her up.

Just then, Sana came inside with a tray of six steel glasses filled with water and served everyone.

"Sana, come sit here," Kajal patted the side of the sofa armrest. Sana readily handed the tray to Payal Di and sat beside her, fondling Abhi's hair as he sat in Kajal's lap.

Sid, all the while, was nervous. His legs were shaking vigorously, but his mom, sitting beside him, gave him the much-needed strength. He had dealt with numerous meetings, projects, and business deals, but nothing compared to the anxiousness he felt at that moment. This was his life he had come to discuss—his future—and it was crucial, a do-or-die situation.

"Uhmm... Sid... Sidesh..." Guru called out, breaking Sid's trance.

"You can call me Sid," Sid said with a smile.

Sid had an aura—a majestic persona, a charm—that was not hidden from anyone in the room. He looked extremely handsome among the lot.

"Tell me something about yourself," Guru asked as if he were an interviewer assessing a candidate for a job. He simply wanted to start a conversation and know more about him. He was already impressed with Sid's looks and gave him full marks for that. Standing more than six feet tall, muscular and fit, Sid effortlessly captivated everyone's attention in the room.

Sid spoke about his background—his education, work, and current position—so masterfully and effortlessly that everyone was in awe of him.

"If you don't mind me asking, what is your age? I mean, how did you achieve so much at such a young age?" Guru asked, genuinely impressed and curious. He wondered how someone so young had reached such great heights. Maybe Sid could mentor him in the future for his career growth. Judging by his looks, he seemed close to Guru's age—perhaps 25, maybe just three or four years older.

"Uhmm... I just turned 35 this week," Sid said, staggering a bit, fearing that his age might create more hurdles in this already shaky alliance with Sana's family. He had always been conscious of the age difference between him and Sana, carrying a deep-seated insecurity about it. But Sana, as always, had reassured him, making him feel accepted and confident.

Will her family feel the same? He wondered.

Chapter Thirty-Two:
Hearts Against Caste

"Actually, I think the success of a relationship depends on the extent to which partners share similar values, beliefs, and goals about their relationship—how they support each other in achieving personal aspirations, foster commitment and trust, and resolve problems in constructive ways. These factors have little to do with age. While an age gap may bring some challenges, as long as couples work on their relationship, age should be no barrier. Haina, Appa?

Appa and Amma are a perfect example of that. They are the most compatible and satisfied couple I have ever seen. The trust and commitment they share cannot be found in any of my relatives that I know of. What do you say, Anna? Do you agree with me?" Sana jumped in, supporting Sid, knowing how much of a complex he had regarding this factor. She genuinely wanted to express her thoughts and stop anyone from judging him based on their age difference.

She smartly questioned her father and brother before they could put Sid in the spotlight and used this point as a reason to reject him. She felt so happy and proud when Sid told them about his accomplishments, but the question about his age soured her mood. She couldn't hold back her thoughts on this evolutionary phenomenon!

"Ya ya... I agree with Sana. Seetha and I have a 10-year difference, and we are very happy. That is not an issue at all," Appa said, feeling awkward at how Sana was already supporting Sid in front of everyone without hesitation or restraint.

"Yes... but a 14-year difference seems like a big gap!" Guru said with concern, looking toward Appa.

"It's 13, Anna... I will turn 22 in January—just four more months to go! If that is the case, what are your thoughts about our grandparents' age gap?" Sana said with élan and certainty, putting Guru in shock at seeing his resilient sister.

Sid and his family were astonished—flabbergasted—by how boldly Sana was standing up for him in front of her family. The way she brazenly defended him and cleared his stance left them completely stupefied. A newfound respect for her took root in their hearts.

Just then, Sana's mom walked in with coffee, and her Mami followed closely behind, carrying a tray filled with plates of pakoda and kesari (sooji halwa with saffron) for everyone.

"Bhabhi, aap bhi hamare saath baithiye. You should also know everything about Sid and us," Sid's mom requested Sana's mother, noticing how she was getting busy with hospitality.

"Haan, bas coffee hi bana rahi thi... aap lijiye na... I have made lunch as well... aap—" Before she could finish her sentence, she was interrupted by Sid's mom.

"Arre... please don't trouble yourself. Come, sit here with me. Sid, get up and sit somewhere else—I will not allow Bhabhi ji out of my sight now!" She grabbed Sana's mom's arm and made her sit beside her.

Sana's mom blushed at the unexpected warmth from a stranger—though, in that moment, she didn't feel like one. She found a friend in her. She liked her a lot—her lively, positive persona.

Sid immediately stood up to give her his place. He was offered the dining chair that Sana's mama had been sitting in while Mama went out to get an office chair from Guru's room.

"Humein aapki beti bahut pyaari lagti hai. She has become our daughter in just a few days—humare dil mein bas gayi hai! We came here to ask for her hand for my son. They like each other, and as parents, we only want their happiness, isn't it?" Sid's mom got straight to the point, expressing her heartfelt wish to Sana's parents and formally proposing the alliance.

"Sana told us about her feelings as well, Bhabhi ji, but we are very orthodox people. In our family, we do not encourage love marriages. It has always been our tradition to find a life partner for our children—within our religion and caste—for generations. This inter-caste marriage system… we object to that. My brother and my mother back in Chennai won't accept it, and they might even disown us. I am sorry, but this is off-limits for us," Sana's father stated, his voice firm as he clearly laid out his concerns and thoughts.

After a pause, he continued, "It's not that we dislike your son—he is perfect in every way: looks, family background, financial status—no issues at all. He can get any girl… Please don't take this the wrong way, but I don't even know what Gotra you belong to or what beliefs you follow. I can't go against my society… Please understand." He joined his hands and bowed his head slightly, declining Sid's mom's proposal point-blank with a miffed voice.

Silence filled the room. Some nodded in disbelief, some were disappointed, some lost hope, and some silently agreed with his words.

Then, Sid's mom spoke up—stern yet composed, her tone mellowed but authoritative.

"We belong to Bharadwaja Gotra. We are Hindus from a Pandit family. My late husband and Sid both wear the sacred thread, Janeu, around their bodies. We follow the same traditions and beliefs that you do—the only difference is geographical diversity.

I do not believe in discrimination, but I wanted to clear this with you—we are not from any other caste. And even if we were, I would have never let my beliefs stand in the way of my children's happiness.

But, to give you some relief, I am telling you this!"

Sid stepped forward, his patience wearing thin. He had remained calm and composed all this time, but he could no longer hold back from supporting what his mother had just said.

"Bas Maa... we don't have to explain ourselves or prove that we are 'good enough' based on his beliefs."

Turning towards Sana's father, he continued, his voice resolute.

"Who created religion, Uncle? Us! Humans! Do any of our holy scriptures—the Bhagavad Gita, the Vedas—ask us to discriminate based on religious concepts or ethical principles? No! In fact, they emphasize that one must rely on love while rejecting anger, ignorance, and ego. They teach selflessness. I follow my religion for my spiritual and emotional growth—to enhance my cognitive process—not to build fear, restrictions, hatred, bitterness, or resentment!"

His voice was rising, turning hoarse. Sana, sensing his emotions, quickly walked over and handed him a glass of water. He took a sip, trying to steady himself.

Sana turned to her father, her eyes pleading.

"Appa, for us, love is our religion. We will be happy with each other. Please let go of this shortsighted thinking."

She walked over and sat on the floor beside her father, gently holding his leg. Her voice softened.

"Appa, do you remember when we went on vacation to Chennai? Paati (Dadi) said that boys should eat first and then girls, but I was so hungry. You fought with her and made us girls eat with our brothers. She was upset because you broke a rule that had been followed for centuries. But you stood tall and made her understand that all children are the same, that there should be no difference between boys and girls.

That day, for the first time, you, Amma, even Periappa (Uncle), and Periamma (Aunt) sat together and ate your dinner—unlike the old days when husbands ate first, and their wives ate later.

And don't we still follow that even now? You brought that change.

Why? Because you believed it was right. Because you had the courage to stand against blind traditions.

Our situation is the same here, Appa. Please think..."

Sana's father fell silent. He was deep in thought.

Her words struck a chord—Sid's argument, her plea, their unwavering stance.

He had always treated his daughter and son as equals. He had fought against his own mother for their rights, making her understand why those outdated customs were unfair. He had always believed that what is truly right should triumph—even if it challenges long-standing traditions.

Was he now contradicting his own principles?

Sana saw the shift in his expression and pressed on, her voice trembling.

"If Paati (Dadi) or any relative objects to my marriage with Sid, we will make them understand. We will show them that caste discrimination is unethical. Yes, people argue because of their core beliefs, but beliefs can change when faced with truth.

If they criticize us, we will stand strong. If they refuse to accept us, we will wait. Because when they see us happy, when they realize love is stronger than prejudice—they will understand, they will accept, and they will forgive and forget.

We can be an example, Appa..."

Tears welled up in her eyes.

Payal rushed to her side, lifting her gently from the floor and leading her to the chair beside Sid. She placed a comforting hand on her shoulder and handed her a glass of water.

The atmosphere in the room was tense.

Suddenly, Rahul stood up. His voice was firm, his frustration evident.

"Uncle, I have known Sid since our school days. He is the best man I know—honest, committed, caring.

I have known Sana since childhood, and I see her as my sister. If I had to choose a groom for her, I would blindly choose Sid. They are made for each other.

Please, Uncle… come out of this casteism mindset."

He exhaled sharply, shaking his head.

Then, turning to Sid, he said, "I'm going, man. I can't handle this senseless belief system anymore. I'll see you later." With that, he walked out, leaving his final words lingering in the air.

Challenging someone's core beliefs is never easy.

It forces people to be honest with themselves. To confront their fears. To step out of the comfort of tradition and into the unknown.

Sana's father remained eerily quiet.

But Sana's mother had already changed.

She walked up to Sana and Sid, placing her hands on their heads in blessing. Tears shimmered in her eyes.

"I know you will take care of my daughter," she whispered. "I give you both my blessings. I don't know what Sana's Appa will say, but I am with you, Kanna (Bacha)."

Sana let out a small, relieved sob. She wrapped her arms around her mother's waist, resting her head against her, smiling through her tears—grateful, hopeful, and strong.

Chapter Thirty-Three:
Bound By Fate

"Seetha, you go and prepare lunch; Lalitha, you help her." Sana's father gave the instructions curtly. His voice was laced with a tension that didn't go unnoticed. Sana's openness, her unwavering acceptance, and the blessings she had given Sid were slowly eating away at him. He wasn't ready for this. Not yet. He needed to speak to his family first to sort his thoughts before any decisions were made. His mood was sour, and at this moment, the closest person to vent his frustrations on was none other than his wife.

Seetha, who had been quiet, understood immediately. She had shared 26 years of her life with him, more than half her lifetime. She knew every nuance of his moods, every word that held weight, every sigh he gave. She stood up silently, her heart heavy, and walked toward the kitchen.

"No, no, Bhaisaab, let her stay. We don't need lunch. We're full from the coffee and snacks." Sid's mother interjected gently, stopping Sana's mom from leaving the room. "Please, sit here. Let me know if you have any questions or if there's anything you'd like to clarify or know about us."

Sana's mom hesitated, sensing the heavy atmosphere in the room, but sat back down. "Well… Sana mentioned Sid's father, and I'm sorry to hear about his loss. You are such a strong lady, especially in the way you raised your children. It's truly admirable." She spoke with genuine admiration, her voice softening.

Sana's mom resembled her daughter in many ways: fair skin, a round face, and big, expressive eyes. Her long black hair was braided neatly, and the maroon bindi on her forehead added a beautiful touch to her already graceful appearance. She wore a simple gold chain around her neck, radiating a quiet elegance.

Sid's mother's voice wavered slightly as she spoke. "He had a heart attack. One fine morning, he just... left us. He worked as a Bank Manager at the SBI branch in Navyug Market. After his passing, I struggled a lot. But Sid was always there for us. When he graduated, he got a job, and Kajal also helped by taking tuition classes. We started to breathe a little easier after that." She paused, her eyes clouded with a bit of sadness and continued. "Sid did more than I could have ever asked for. He grew up so quickly. He had to, for us."

"Hmm... Sana's father also works as a Bank Manager... at the SBI near the Railway Station." Sana's mom said thoughtfully, her words creating a brief connection between the families.

"Oh! Really?" Kajal's interest piqued as she asked. "Uncle, do you know my papa? His name was Surendar Sharma."

Abhi, who had been quietly playing with Guru on his lap, kept distracted by a game on his phone. Kajal had been quiet up until now; not wanting to add to the tension but sensing an opportunity to lighten the mood, she asked her question.

Sana's father, who had been in a cloud of his own thoughts, looked up at Kajal's words. There was a flicker of recognition in his eyes, though it wasn't certain. "Surendar Sharma..." he murmured, his voice thoughtful. "I've heard that name before... but I'm not sure if I remember him well. I've been working in this bank for twenty years, and I have a terrible memory of names. Perhaps we've met, but I just don't recall, beta."

A small, rare smile appeared on his face as he spoke, his first since the family had arrived. For a moment, the tension in the air seemed to ease just a little.

"Oh, okay... We live very near Uncle Ji, just 10 minutes from here. I came here to celebrate Bhaiya's birthday, and Abhi's school had a holiday, so I thought I'd give him a surprise. But Sana is so lucky—her Maiyka and Sasural will be so close by, and she can visit you here daily... Haina? I miss my mom so much sometimes, her food, her pampering... but I video call her daily." She said nonchalantly.

Sana's father breathed hard, blowing out air. "Acha hai... It's always good to have your kids and parents near you. I'm not that lucky either. My Amma is far away from me in the South, but what should I do? We have to live here now, and she doesn't want to come here. Compromise karna padhta hai."

"Do you have your son's horoscope?" Sana Amma asked Sid's mom. "We're getting Sana's horoscope done by tomorrow, so I thought we could match it."

"One minute, Seetha, before you answer that, Bhabhi ji, I would like to say—please don't expect anything from us right now! I need to talk to my family and relatives before I give you a decision. It might take a few days." Appa said rigidly.

"Take your time, Bhaisaab... I have Sid's horoscope with me for you to match, Bhabhi. Here it is." Sid's mom dug into her purse and pulled out a red-colored envelope, handing it to Sana's mom, who took it and went to the Puja room. She placed it in front of the deities and prayed for her daughter.

Amma and Mami went to the kitchen to make fresh puris for everyone, joined by Kajal. Sid's mom and Appa were conversing about Sid's dad, their house, and other general topics, which she thought he should know. She felt this was the best time to talk about it and give some more brownie points for the match. He also relaxed with them, leaving his rigid persona behind.

Meanwhile, Sid and Mama had started getting along well with small talk, sitting at the dining table. He was impressed with Sid's immense knowledge and maturity. Guru also joined them when Abhi got distracted and followed his mom to the kitchen.

"Di, aaj pata nahi kahan se mere andar Mata jaag gayi... I never thought I would be so bold in front of Appa." Sana whispered to Payal, feeling much more relaxed with the dispersed, distracted crowd chattering individually to each other.

"Tu chal na ek minute, I want to talk to you..." Payal said, grabbing Sana's hand and walking towards her room.

"Kya hua, Di? You are scaring me... What do you want to talk to me in secret?" Sana sniffled.

Payal hugged Sana when they reached her room in private, which startled her. "SAAANNAAA... I am so proud of you... Tujhe nahi pata, aaj tune mera jeevan safal kar diya... All the lectures and philosophy that I preached to you didn't go in vain! How bravely you took your stand and faced Appa... My God... I was stunned. Tune mera sar garv se uncha kar diya, baache..."

Sana smiled, jumping and blushing. "Hayee, sachi... kasam lage Di... I was so annoyed when Guru, Anna, and Appa talked against Sid... My BP just shot up... I cannot tolerate anyone saying something wrong about him... Pata nahi, apne aap hi ho gaya, bas." Pouting, she said, hugging her Di again.

"Good, bas aise hi lagi reh apne rights ke liye. Don't ever fall out of this zone. I know they are your parents, who gave birth to you, and you respect them a lot, etc., etc... But when elders get lost in their stupid ideologies and start doing stupid things, we as kids should guide them to show them the right path, like how they show us when we do something wrong. Never, I repeat, never compromise for anything, Sana. Everyone has the right to be happy, and your happiness is with Sid. Fight for it... Okay?" Payal, like always, guided Sana and showed her the right path, and she was always grateful to her for being there as her guiding angel in her ups and downs.

"I will, Di... Thank you for being my strong pillar of support. Love you... What would I have done without you?" Sana kissed her cheeks and came out with her to join the kitchen gang.

Everyone ate a simple yet delicious lunch silently, praising the chef... Sana's Amma.

Sid was feeling awkward, though he loved Amma's food, as eating in a place where he was not yet accepted felt weird to him. He just had one puri and a little rice with chole, which Sana's mom forcibly put on his plate.

"Don't be shy, ache se khao, tumhara hi ghar hai..." Appa said that in a flow, like he was used to saying it with other guests and relatives. But everyone was shocked to hear those words from his mouth. Everyone looked at him in disbelief. He wondered why everyone was giving him such a shocking look. "Kya hua? Why are you all looking at me like that?"

"Sometimes Saraswati Mata sits in our tongue, and what we say happens... May this also come true, Athimber (Jijaji)," Mama said loudly, and all the people nodded in agreement. Sid and Sana looked at each other and blushed. Amma joined her palms and looked up at the roof, praying. Maa and Kajal smiled in contentment. Guru gave no reaction and just concentrated on his food, while Appa was just wondering, confused, why everyone was suddenly giving so many reactions.

"Aap aur puri lenge?" Sana's Amma asked him, not giving him any explanations, distracting his confusion and leaving it for destiny to decide for the match made by God for their daughter.

It's rightly said when we say, "Man proposes, but God disposes." Man has limited intelligence and knowledge of the outcome of his efforts and freedom. Naturally, when something goes against his wishes, he cannot blame himself or anybody but must say that destiny is more powerful than the free will of man.

Chapter Thirty-Four:
A Battle For Love

Nervousness is something that everyone experiences at one time or another. It feels like a combination of anxiety, dread, and excitement all at once. Anything that causes apprehension or fear can lead to feelings of nervousness. They can be brought on by good experiences and negative ones, like Sana and Sid had the same complex feelings after facing the big day of their life. Nothing could compare to the feeling they experienced today. It felt like a judgment day where society would either accept or reject the love they have for each other. Sometimes, they wonder who others are to decide for them what they feel for each other. But this is the world they are living in, and they have to follow certain norms to be included in the part of the world they are in.

Visiting Sana's parents was stressful for Sid, but he finally accomplished it, and now he felt much more relaxed. His mom coming with him was a relief, and the 'Plan' that she made to accompany him was a blockbuster. The support he and even Sana got from her was immense. Now, when he visualized what it would have been like to handle all of that alone, it gave him an adrenaline rush. They reached home after having lunch at Sana's place, and everyone was mentally tired. His mom was very quiet; Abhi had fallen asleep in the car, and Kajal took him to her room and excused herself for a nap. Sid came to his mom's room after changing into something more comfortable. She was in bed, lying down with the air conditioning on.

"Kya hua, maa? You don't seem to be fine since we came back. Sab teek hai? Itni chup chap kyun ho?" he asked with concern, sitting by her leg and massaging it.

"I hope sab teek ho jaye, beta. Bas thodi tension ho rahi hai... Sana's family seems to be very honest, simple, and innocent people, just like her... but... her father seems to be very adamant with his ideologies. Now I have this fear about your horoscope match. I hope aur koi problem na ho... already it hurdles ho rahe hain," Mom said, worried, massaging her forehead.

"Aap zyada tension mat lo. Don't take so much stress. You always told me to be positive, 'Acha socho toh acha hoga,'... and now you're talking like this? Not done, maa." He crawled to her headside and started massaging her head. "You take a nap, and I'll make you a Jhanatedhar chai later..." he said, smiling, and switched off the light, closing her room's door slightly.

He took his mobile out of his pocket and texted Sana.

Kajal suggested him, "Sid, I would say give her time, Kal toh miloge na when you go to work... let her take time; you never know what she is going through, so wait till tomorrow. I am sure she will text you by night and tell you her whereabouts. Be patient na, Baba!"

"Haan teek hain... teek hain... teek hain... got it... I am going to my room, some pending office work is there, let me complete it. Call me if you need anything," he said, walking out of the room.

Sana

Kahan hai tu? I am worried! Please call when you see this message...

He texted again... and sat down in his bed with his laptop, keeping his phone to charge near him with the full volume up of his ringtone.

It was past 10 pm, and his phone rang with Sana's ID popping up. He rushed to take the call.

"Hello... Sana?" he said.

"Hello Sid, sorry I couldn't text you, gussa mat hona please..." she said in a feeble voice.

Her voice gave him the calmness for his rapid heartbeat and frayed mind. "Pagal hai tu? Why would I be angry? I was so worried for you!!! You are okay, right? Kuch problem hua kya?" he asked her, perturbed, his hands rubbing his face and hair. All negative thoughts roamed in his mind.

"Woh actually, after you left, Appa had a heated argument with Amma and Mama... I did not pitch in as I was already drained and tired... I left my phone to charge and forgot to check... I saw your message just an hour before but just waited for everyone to sleep so that I could call you and tell you what happened!" she whispered, keeping the phone close.

"Okay okay okay... I get it... tu tension mat le... just I wondered what happened to you! Thought of calling Payal but then skipped it. We will talk in detail tomorrow morning in the car... I will wait for you... ho sake toh jaldi aa jaana by 7 maybe..." he said.

"Pata nahi kal aa paungi ki nahi!" she muttered.

"What do you mean?" he questioned, as he didn't understand what she was saying.

"I mean... are you sick? Dhyaan rakhna chahiye na Sana... kya hua?" he said, worried.

"I am good, but Appa is against sending me to work now! He is blaming my job now for all the occurrences... I will try my best again tomorrow morning to talk to him. Let me see if I can make it or not!" she said, pouting with a frown. She was tired and sleepy. It was a long day for her—fighting, yelling, crying—it had drained her physically and mentally. She needed sleep, and she craved Sid's warm hug, which could soothe her soul.

"What? What do you mean? You will not come to work from now on? What, has he gone crazy or what? Sana, I tried my level best to be patient, but this behavior of his, I cannot take!" he growled in anger and frustration.

"I know, Amma and Mama are with me, and they liked you and your family so much. He is just angry with them and showing that to me. When he wakes up tomorrow, I will ask him. He will be cool by then. Today, he was frustrated. It is also taking a toll on him. Bas aur kuch nahi... Tum please naaraz mat ho unse. He is my father, I know him... I will make him understand, but I also need your support. If I could comprehend him, I would meet you... same spot... but if not, I will text you... okay?" she pleaded with him.

"Sana, I want to see you now! I want to hold you... please, I am having this feeling that I am losing you... Please falsify it, mujhe tu chahiye abhi... matlab abhi... Mujhe vishwaas dila ki you are there with me..." He demanded, or rather begged, her to give him the certainty that she was there with him and would not vanish. The fear of losing her was evident in his tone.

"Sidd...." she trembled... "Abhi... Kaise... how?" she thought for any way to fulfill his request. She also craved for the same. They both were on the verge of a mental breakdown, a fatigue which could only be tranquilized in each other's arms.

"I don't know... I am coming there now..." Sid put his slippers on and paced to her community... It was a 10-minute walk which felt like a decade. His long strides and his impatient heart made this walk harder. He reached her flat. "I am here..." he told her.

"Climb up the stairs to the terrace... I am waiting here..." Sana instructed him.

Restless, he bounded up the stairs two at a time, making no sound. It was just 10:45 pm, and still, the lights were on in almost all the houses. He didn't want to cause Sana more problems, but he couldn't help his restless heart. He needed her, and he demanded childishly like a child for his favorite thing in the world, and she also obliged, fulfilling his demands and making way for it—even if it caused her troubles and worries. She didn't care about that at this moment.

He opened the terrace door, and she pulled him into a tight hug, closing the door. The worst day just faded away for both of them in that embrace. Just a simple, tight hug can be so powerful to reduce stress and sadness and have the power to heal wounds. They both had tears in their eyes. Sana kissed his chest near his heart to calm his speedy heartbeat. Sid cupped her face in his palms and kissed his dry lips to her plump ones fervently, passionately! He hunted all the hidden corners in her mouth, hugging her tighter from waist, and she reciprocated the same, hugging him even tighter. Time just stopped for them. They were just enjoying that agonizing bliss of being in love. They were in a state of limerence... yearning for each other with the fear that they might not get each other, making use of every moment they got—even if it meant obsessive thoughts and fantasies. A desire to form and maintain a relationship with the object of love and have one's feelings reciprocated—it was an inexplicable bliss!

Chapter Thirty-Five:
Shadows of Doubt, Lights of Hope

Sid picked her up and made her sit on the cement slab that fenced the water tanks on the terrace. She was in her night suit pajamas, light as a feather and gorgeous in the moonlight. She reached his eye level as he held her tightly by the waist, and she circled her arms around his shoulders, their foreheads touching.

"Sab theek ho jayega na, Sid?" she asked, flustered.

"Pata nahi, I hope so..." he said. Both of them were in a dilemma, thinking about the distress life would bring to their togetherness. He kissed her again, pressing her close to his chest, devouring her presence, not wanting to leave her, wanting to keep her close, taking in each moment to soothe his disturbed heart.

Sana's phone beeped. She parted from him and took her mobile out of her pant pocket, seeing a text from Payal. She had asked her to keep an eye out before she planned to come up to the terrace.

Payal Di:

Sana, jaldi aaja.

"We should leave. Di is texting me to come down..." she said, jumping down and feeling timorous.

"You go first, then I will follow. Keep low when you walk out," she requested.

He hugged her again and said, "Kal aa jaana. I will wait for you... or else I will come here and take you with me. I am telling you, I will do it!"

"No... No... No... I will try for sure. Please shaant ho jao... aur tum aisa kuch nahi karoge. Trust me, please, yaar..." she said, flurried, giving him the assurance and pecking his lips.

"Keep me posted..." Without another word, he left the place, stepping down unobtrusively.

Sana also came down and saw Payal standing in front of her house door.

"Love birds mil liye? Yaar, tum dono Fevicol ka mazboot jod ho gaye ho... Just a few hours ago, you guys met. What happened in between?" she asked, taunting Sana, who sat down on the stairs and gestured for her to sit as well.

"I am tired, Di... It's been a long day," Sana said, leaning her head on Payal's shoulder.

"Go and sleep na, bacha..." she said, tapping Sana's face lightly.

"Appa is not sending me to work starting tomorrow... When I told this to Sid, he got tense and just showed up... Main thak gayi, Di... Kaise samjhau Appa ko?" Feebly, she opened up her perturbed heart to her soul sister—the one who listened without judging, without restricting her.

Friendship is the noblest of all relations, comprising the sweetness of all other bonds yet often stronger than even the closest blood ties.

"Itne main thak gayi? Abhi toh pata nahi kya kya jhelna aur dekhna hai... This is just the beginning, my dear Sanu," Payal said.

"Nahi, aur nahi... Bas ho gaya mera. I cannot take this much stress... I never thought I would face so many consequences just for loving someone! I don't know why he cannot accept the fact that I love him and that I will be happy with him. I thought parents always kept their kids' happiness above everything... But he is more concerned about relatives. 'Log kya sochenge?' Like really??

He is my idol. I wanted my husband to be like him, and Sid is... but thank God he doesn't have this backward thinking of worrying about 'what people will think' like Appa. I want everyone, Di. I want my parents, I want my Anna, I want my Daadi, my uncles, aunts, cousins—my whole family when I step into Sid's world. I can't choose between them and him... Both are important to me, Di. I cannot survive without them all..." She whimpered, covering her face with her palms.

Payal just listened, wanting to comfort her, but she lacked the words to ease her pain.

"And now, another siyappa—Appa stopping me from going to work. I am going to be permanent tomorrow, Di! I love my job, and I want to study more, do my master's, and secure a good managerial position. I have ambitions! Sid is supporting and motivating me for this. He even got me the application form from IMT. And here, my own Appa is adamant about marrying me off to a stranger and ruining my entire life... Why? For his so-called prestige? Unka prestige unka, mera gaya tel lene! Hypocrite!" Sana vented out all her bottled-up frustration.

"I'm sorry, but I am not comparing my Appa with Sid. I love my father, but I had high expectations from him..." She started crying again, tears rolling down her cheeks.

"I hate to cry! I have always been a positive, happy person. Mujhe yeh tension, yeh stress bilkul acha nahi lagta! You know me, Di... My body gets painful, sab jagah dard hota hai... Aaaahhhhhhh..." she yowled, rubbing her face.

Unexpectedly, they heard the front door of Sana's flat open.

"Sana... What are you doing here?" It was Guru.

"Nothing. I am crying, thinking about my fate... my opinionated family, who are so stubborn that they are making my life hell! Bas, pata chal gaya!! Happy? Jaao aur so jao! Sleep well and have sweet dreams, Anna," she scowled, lashing out hurtful words at her brother, who stood astonished at this side of his once-chirpy, fun-loving, and innocent sister.

"Have you gone mad? You're accusing us—your family, who has been with you for 21 years—of that new relationship you have developed? Where are you getting this attitude from? From him? When you were with us, you never acted this way... Is this what you call a good influence?" he retorted.

"Oh, please, Guru... Stop it. I wonder if you are his own brother! She is in a panic, and that's why she is saying all this to you. But instead of being empathetic, you are scolding her and doubting her? Hadd hai, sahi mein!

She has been tying Rakhi to you for years—a promise that you will protect her, love her, and stand by her. But all you ever do is dictate and find faults in her! How is that fair? Can I ask where you are getting this attitude from?" Payal countered, standing up for Sana and making her even more emotional.

He kept quiet, thinking about what Payal had said. It made a little sense—he had never been polite to Sana and had always been strict with her. Maybe it was the responsibility of being a big brother, but he had never been a friend or a confidant to her.

"What do you want me to do then? Agree with what she wants and allow her to marry that guy?"

"He is not 'that guy.' He is Sidesh. He has a name, mind you, Anna. You saw him today—so tell me, from your scrutinizing, critical eye, what fault did you find in him? Haan? Can you point out any? And please, for God's sake, don't castigate him for not being a Tamil Brahmin but a Hindi Brahmin. Is it his fault that he was born in a different geographical part of India as a Brahmin?"

Guru had nothing to counter Payal's argument. She was right. He couldn't find a single reason to reject or chastise Sidesh. He was a perfect man—good-looking, well-educated, financially stable, highly positioned, decent, well-mannered, with a loving family. What was there to criticize?

"There is nothing to criticize. He is perfect. But I don't know if he is perfect for our family, Sana," he said, much calmer now, his demeanor subdued.

"Can you guarantee that the person Appa chooses for me will be perfect for this family? Just because he will be part of our caste will make him the best for our family. What about me? Will he love me, respect me, understand and care for me the way Sid does? Will he respect our family, Anna? Can you promise me that?" she questioned him.

Once again, he had no answer. How could he? He had seen too many examples among their relatives of dominating partners destroying the lives of their spouses.

"I cannot," he admitted, realizing Sana's point.

"Guru, as a brother, supports her. Stand with her. Don't be a tail to your father. Put your voice out to him. You know what's best for her now, right? Be a reinforcing brother to her. Bhaiya, mere rakhi ke bandhan ko nibhaane ka waqt aa gaya hai... Waise bhi, Rakhi is next week. Show her that you mean the promise, will you?" Payal said to Guru, who nodded.

She stood up and pulled Sana to her feet. "Now go and sleep, Sana. You are very tired. Sab theek ho jayega... Your mother and I—and I hope Guru as well—are with you. Appa bhi samajh jayenge. Keep that positivity in you, theek hai?" She patted Sana on her shoulders and gently pushed her toward Guru.

He held her and hugged her tight.

"Sorry, Sana. I didn't know I had hurt you this much. I will be with you—I promise, with all your decisions. Okay?" he said.

Sana couldn't believe his words—she felt like half the battle was already won. She had found a light in the darkness. She felt confident that she could balance the light and the dark, knowing that the darkness did not have to overpower everything in her life. She chose to persevere in what was favorable and not grieve over the challenges that lay ahead.

Chapter Thirty-Six:
Transformation Of The Heart

Sana woke up fresh to a new morning with new hope and enthusiasm. Though she had slept late, she had a good night's sleep as soon as she hit the bed and slept like a baby, the reason being tiredness. She woke up very early, at 5 am, before her father today. She freshened up, took a bath, washed her hair, and wrapped it up in a towel. She wore a long dark blue kurta and black leggings matching the black embroidery in the kurta. She prepared coffee decoction in a filter, pouring hot boiling water over the ground coffee. She put on a tiny blue bindi and kohl in her eyes, went to the puja room, lit the lamp, and applied vibuthi (the sacred ash) by pinching it between her thumb and ring finger, placing it on her forehead just above the bindi and her throat. She prayed for energy and power to be mentally and physically strong, for her vibrancy, and for healing.

Her father woke up next and was surprised to smell the invigorating coffee aroma mixed with the harmonizing scent of incense sticks. He had always been the first person to wake up in the house, boil milk, and make coffee for himself and his sleeping wife. He disliked waking up his sleeping kids, so he found other ways to wake them up—making noise, causing chaos, switching off the fan and cooler, and opening the curtains and windows to let the fresh sunlight in.

Today was different, though. He wondered who chose to do his chores. He was pleased and felt relaxed with the ambiance at home, especially after the eventful day yesterday. He went to freshen up and walked towards the kitchen when he saw Sana coming out with two steel tumblers filled with hot, piping coffee lathered to the top, with a steel cup beneath the tumbler. This was the traditional way of serving filter coffee in South Indian homes.

"Appa, good morning... Coffee?" she asked with a small smile on her face. He is, after all, her father who loves his daughter dearly. He always had a soft corner for her between his two kids. How could she be angry with him? She is like that—never holds a grudge from the previous day. It's always a new day, a new start for her. That's how her father is. He never prolonged any argument or situation for long, and she is greatly influenced by this nature of his. Like father, like daughter!

"Aaj suraj kahan se rise hua hai? How come you got up so early, puja bhi kar li and also made coffee? I think it is my lucky day today! What a great start!" he said in his South Indian accent, taking the coffee from her hand and moving towards the balcony attached to Sana's room, not before saluting God in the puja room with his free right hand.

"Bas, I got up early, so I thought of taking a bath, and after that, I wanted to have coffee. I saw you waking up, so I made some for you as well..." she said, sitting down in one of the plastic chairs placed on the balcony. Her balcony faced East, and her parents' balcony faced west on the backside of the community. They sat down to watch the sunrise, which was about to break, as it was 5:40 am. The sunrise is really very delightful to watch. The darkness of night begins to clear. The stars in the sky begin to grow dim. The sun looks like a ring of fire glowing with orange-colored light spreading around it. The birds wake up in their nests and begin to chirp.

"Appa, I want to go to work. I am getting permanent today. I will have a raise in salary with all benefits and PTO (paid time off). Don't stop me from doing something I like, please, Pa," she requested calmly, looking towards the sun.

He didn't reply to her, and he kept silent. His eyes were just observing the sun while sipping his coffee.

"I am also planning to do an MBA in HR. Sid got me the application form from IMT, and their fee is also very nominal. I will get a student loan from the company," she said in limited words, with no expression or emotion—just her reticent self.

"Good... when is the class starting?" he asked, looking at her.

"Next quarter, which starts in September. I am late with the application submission, but Sid has some jugad (a solution or trick) there, and he will help me out with that and also with the student loan," finishing her coffee, she placed her tumbler down on the floor and curled her foot close to her chest, wrapping her arms around it.

"Acha... Good..." he replied briefly, stating his thoughts in just two words.

"Did you like him, Pa?" she asked him point-blank, looking into his eyes.

He took a deep breath, handed his coffee tumbler to Sana, and she placed it beside hers on the floor.

"There is nothing to not like about him! He is a perfect man any dad would want for his daughter... He has a good family, is well-settled, earns well, has his own house, car, and caring parents and sister, and he's a Hindu. I cannot say anything negative about him, Sana," he replied.

"Then why can't he be your daughter's man?" she asked him very delicately.

"Oh! Please... Don't make me the villain. I am not! I am just a father! Understand?" he said, feeling skeptical.

She chuckled sarcastically, "Nahi, I am not making you the villain; neither can I think of you like that. You are my hero... But here, you are not behaving like a father. Agar Papa ban ke sochte toh haan karte is proposal ko; as you said, there is nothing negative about him. But here, you are thinking more about yourself. You're getting selfish here, Appa... Log kya sochenge? Aapki izzat ka kya hoga? Haina?? Please answer honestly, Pa."

It was a blow for him, her words coming out like a mirror reflecting his own thoughts. He bowed his head, missing the view of the sunrise, and placed his hands on his head, supporting his arm on the chair. She was right, wasn't she? He thought. He was getting selfish about his image and using the excuse of social stratification. He had no answer to her question; he needed time... Time to think, time to talk to himself, time to talk to his brother and his mother. He valued them and their relations a lot, and their thoughts were important.

"You go, wake up your Amma, and make her some coffee; otherwise, she won't get up. She needs to make breakfast and pack lunch for you both. She'll get late otherwise and then blame me for not waking her up on time," he instructed her.

Feeling dejected, Sana got up, taking the tumbler from the floor to wash it, when suddenly she realized what he had just said.

"Lunch for us both? That means I can go to work, Appa?" Overjoyed and exhilarated, her eyes widened in shock as she asked him.

He nodded, smiling... "Go... you don't want to get late, right, on your promotion day?"

She jumped and came forward towards her Appa, giving him a tight hug. "Thank you, Pa, I love you... so much..."

"This is my Appa, I know..." she said happily, running inside to make her mother a fresh, awesome coffee and to share the news that she could go to work.

SS🚗

I'm coming... 😁😁😁

She texted Sid, excited and looking forward to the new day, a fresh, positive day. She changed the name of his contact and wrote... Sid💔, blushing and feeling her cheeks heat up... making herself bold and keeping it open for the world, no more hiding and fabricating her relationship with him to the family.

She dried her hair, combed it straight, parted it in the middle, and applied pink lipstick. She loved flowery fragrances, so she sprayed her favorite rose perfume. She ate her breakfast, packed her lunch, and took the extra lunch box her mom had specially packed for Sid. She never fathomed yesterday that she would be so happy today. She had learned something from this... Positive thinking, or an optimistic attitude, is the practice of focusing on the good in any given situation. It can have a big impact on your physical and mental health... It simply means you approach the good and the bad in life with the expectation that things will go well. It gives one better coping skills and clearer thinking. No matter what situation arises, if one keeps oneself calm and positive, the universe will work in favor of you, and you will find a way out of distress. Again, something she got from her father, and she silently thanked him for transferring this attitude—how to approach life.

"Sana, aaj tera horoscope aa jayega... Appa tera aur Sid ka match karane Guruvayurappan Temple (Krishna Temple) le jayenge, Mayur Vihar main," her amma said, sounding worried.

"Woh bhi ho jayega match, don't worry... Appa job ke liye maan gaye... he will also agree to my marriage with Sid. I am confident," she said with a new zest.

"I hope so, Kanna (Bacha)," her mother said, still doubtful.

She walked out of her community to find Sid's car in the usual spot. Happily, she entered and gave Sid a tight hug, leaving him stunned. He had a big smile on his face, seeing the beauty of the smile on Sana's face.

"What a changeover, Mama..." he said, singing in the same tone as the famous Kolavari song.

"Appa se baat ki subah... and he agreed to come for work... I am confident now that if I explain to him with love, he will understand," she said, animating her face with an eyebrow flicking up and pouting her lips.

"Good... good... I'm happy to hear that... chal, issi khushi mein ek kiss ho jaye..." he said, pulling her towards him, not giving her time to react, and giving her a slow, passionate kiss.

"Ho gaya... bas... chalo ab... Tum kuch zyada nahi intimate ho rahe ho? Kuch shaadi ke baad ke liye bhi rakh lo!" she said, blushing.

"Shaadi ke baad ke liye toh bahut kuch hai... abhi jo mil raha hai, ussi mein khush ho jaye," he said, teasing her.

"Hayee... kitne besharam ho sachi..." she said, painfully shy seeing his bashful nature.

He intertwined his fingers and held her hands tight, bringing them near his lips, kissing them periodically while she chattered nonstop about her talks with her parents.

He was thrilled when he saw her message in the morning, wondering what magic she had done to change his father's decision within a few hours. But he knew she had that aura that could make a stone heart melt, an energy around her that made everyone surrounded by her happy and optimistic, a childlike innocence that was very infectious. He thought about how lucky he was to have a partner like her to cherish for his whole life and thanked his stars for blessing him with Sana...

Chapter Thirty-Seven:
Destiny's Crossroads

Sana was back home after a hectic day at work. She felt tired and sleep-deprived! She slept in the car for all forty minutes of the drive back home. This was the first time she had slept in the car, and Kishore Kumar's music playing in the background felt like a lullaby to her. She didn't realize when her eyes closed, and she went off to sleep. She took a shower, changed into her night suit, and went to the kitchen to get her evening chai from her Amma.

"Amma, did Appa go to check the horoscope? He isn't back yet?" she asked, sitting on the kitchen slab, drinking the chai and eating Mysore Bonda her mom was making, fresh out of the oil and served with coconut chutney.

"No, he didn't go... kuch kaam aa gaya tha unko office mein, so he couldn't make it... Pata nahi, abhi tak wapis bhi nahi aaye! He only asked me to do this. Tere liye bana diye, unke liye aur Guru ke liye baad mein garam garam bana dungi," she said, switching off the stove.

"Hmm... okay," Sana wondered, shrugging her shoulder. Why didn't he go to check the horoscope? But she ignored it, thinking maybe he might really have some urgent office work.

Sid also came back home after dropping Sana off and getting some grocery items his mom had asked him to bring from the supermarket. He had been happy the whole day, seeing the ease Sana reflected today, something that had never happened before. Maybe the burden of keeping something behind her parents' back had been lifted, and now she felt independent and free, unencumbered by her guilt. She felt more confident now about this relationship, and it was evident today, not missed by Sid. He was naturally observant and could guess very well what the other person was thinking and feeling. Sana was an open book to him. He knew what she thought, felt, and believed.

When she slept in the car today, he was surprised. He had been talking about something that happened in the meeting, concentrating on the road and traffic. He realized that she was eerily quiet. When he turned, he saw his beautiful Sana sleeping with her legs crisscrossed, her head slanted toward the window, with a pout and her mouth slightly open. She was in deep sleep, and he, with great affection, admired her. He drove slowly over speed bumps, didn't honk, and lowered the volume of the song as well. He had never seen her sleep like this, and he wanted to capture the moment. He took his phone out and clicked a photo of his sleeping beauty to keep it in his album to treasure.

He reached home and called his mom, "Maa, grocery rakh diye hain... in the kitchen. Please make some chai. I will freshen up and come." He went towards his room and came back to sit in the living room after a few minutes with Kajal and his mom.

"Tu kab jaa rahi hain? How come Dinesh has sent you for so many days?" he asked Kajal teasingly.

"Dinesh is coming tomorrow here, he cannot live without me and Abhi... I will be here till Rakhi and leave the next day," she informed.

"Maa, you take a rest today, we will go and have some chat for dinner. Kya khayal hain Kajal?" he asked, knowing what her reaction would be.

"Oh, wow... yes, yes, yes... I'm in... let's call Sana also na... she will love it too..." Kajal suggested.

"Haan haan, kyun nahi... but she was tired today; I don't know if she will come, but I will ask her. Wait... let me text," he said.

"No... no need, Sid, keep it low for a few days, beta. Abhi Abhi, her parents know about her relationship with you. Give her and them some time, understand? Woh bechari koi bhi bahana bana ke aa jayegi kyunki. She respects you and us, but it will not go well with her father. Don't put her in an odd situation," Sid's mom suggested.

"Ugh... actually, you are right... what will I do without you, maa... Chalo, ready ho jao... I will take the car out," he picked Abhi in his arms and went out for some family time. He hadn't spent good quality time with Kajal since she had arrived, and he had been feeling tense, but today he felt satisfied and relaxed. He wanted to celebrate it, and what's the best way to do that other than a chaat party followed by kulfi and then UP special meetha pan...

It was Thursday, and Sana was back from her job. It was almost dinner time, and she still wondered why her father had not matched the horoscope yet.

"Amma, why is Appa not going to the temple to meet Namboodri (Priest) to match the Jadagam (horoscope)? I see that Sid's horoscope is still in the puja room, kept hidden behind the photo frame," she asked.

"I don't know, don't ask me... ask him only na... Jaldi jaldi haath chala, ab atleast teen roti bana de. Appa is already sitting at the dining table," Amma said, bewildered.

Sid's mom had already matched the horoscope, and it had matched perfectly from their side. It should be the same from her side as well. Somehow, she was relaxed when Sid's mom called her and Sid while they were at the office on Tuesday about their horoscope match... "36 main se 31 gunn mil gaye, abhi abhi Pandit ne bola, what else do we need? You guys are made for each other." She said in an emotional tone that she was happy and blessed them both then.

It felt like a final hurdle overcome by both Sid and Sana. But Sana felt something was fishy with her Appa behaving normally and not asking anything about Sid nor questioning her for anything.

"Appa, did you call Paati (daadi) and Periappa (Tau ji)? What was their reaction about my liking towards Sid and my future with him?" Sana couldn't hold it in anymore and just asked plainly while eating her roti.

"Yes, I have discussed this with them, they were shocked and unhappy," he gave a clipped answer.

"Oh! What are you planning to do, Appa?" Guru asked in between.

"We will see," Appa replied, getting up and walking towards the bathroom to wash his hands.

"What about the Jadagam (horoscope)? Have you matched it? Sid's mom has already matched it, and she said that out of 36 gunn, 31 match, and that it is the best match." She informed proudly to everyone when her Appa sat down on the sofa, switching on the TV.

Her mom and brother were happy to hear that and even congratulated her, but there was no reaction from her dad. It didn't feel right to Sana. No reaction is never a good reaction, according to her. Either a person feels happy or sad, but when someone is passive, it means something is running wild in their mind.

She discussed her turmoil with Sid, telling him about her father's weird, unresponsive behavior. He didn't dwell on it much and told her she was overthinking, asking her to stay cool. But she had a sixth sense warning her to stay alert and figure out what was happening.

I think every woman has that uncanny ability to sense the unsaid, the unknown. They can detect insecurity just by observing actions. Women's intuition is often explained by two factors. First, they tend to use both hemispheres of their brain more efficiently—especially the right side, which is associated with intuitive perception. Two, they are raised to be more in touch with their emotions, allowing them to develop a stronger sense of intuition.

The next day was Saturday—Rakhi day—and also Yajurveda Upakarma, which signifies a ritualistic new beginning and marks the commencement of learning the Vedas. On this day, Brahmins perform the ritualistic changing of their sacred thread (Janeu), a tradition widely practiced in South Indian Brahmin communities.

As was their yearly tradition, Appa and Guru went to the temple to complete the ritual, and once they returned, Sana performed their Aarti and helped her mom with the grand feast. Relatives also joined them for lunch, and Sana tied rakhi to Guru and her two cousins.

She was dressed in an authentic silk half-saree— a deep red skirt with a golden border paired with a matching golden dupatta and blouse. She looked nothing less than a bride adorned with gold jewelry, delicate jhumkas, a red bindi, and jasmine flowers braided into her hair. Her skin glowed, and she blushed with happiness as she teased her cousins and mama. Feeling herself in the moment, she clicked a selfie and sent it to Sid.

Sid💔

"Tu toh bilkul Hema Malini lag rahi hain... wow yaar!! I'm not able to control myself, baby... Bilkul sexy pataka! I want to hold you, kiss you hard... Tu yeh phool pehenke ek baar mujhse mil... I want to see you in this outfit in person! Can I come now? Bol na, main aau? Bas ek baar dekh ke chala jaunga... 😊😁"

Sana

"Are you mad?!!! 😊 Please mujhe pareshaan mat karo… There are already so many people here! I can't meet you anywhere... Aur yeh kya, jab dekho retro logon se compare karte rehte ho! Kabhi Kishore Kumar ke gaane suna lo, kabhi Hema Malini, toh kabhi Madhubala! Kabhi toh bolo ki main Katrina Kaif jaisi lag rahi hoon, ya Deepika Padukone, ya kuch nahi toh Parineeti Chopra jaisi! Hadd hai, sahi main! Main kya karu Ram, mujhe buddha mil gaya! 😄"

Sid💔

"Acha bachu… batao, kitna budha hoon? Ek baar shaadi ho jaaye bas… phir meri poori jawaani dikha dunga! 😊 BTW, tune bhi abhi old gaana gaya… koi naya gaana gati toh maanta main! Old is Gold, baby! Now come to the balcony… jaldi!"

"Hey Ram! Main kahan jaaun iss Majnu ko leke!" she huffed, exhaling a big breath before walking toward the balcony.

Right on cue, he honked his signal—Beep… Beep… beep beep beep! He took three slow rounds around the park, stealing a glimpse of her before driving away, smiling in satisfaction.

She blushed with happiness. It was these small gestures—the way he acted crazily in love—that made her day, made her feel special, and made her fall head over heels for this man. She often thanked God for giving her such a loving partner and felt grateful for her fate—to be cherished by someone who left no stone unturned to show his love. He never said much in words like she did, but his actions spoke volumes about how madly he loved her.

She walked back inside, joining her relatives for more fun banter. It was almost lunchtime—around 1 p.m.—and Amma was in the kitchen frying papadams. Suddenly, the doorbell rang.

Appa was quick to get up and see who it was. All the expected relatives were already present, so Amma, Sana, and Guru wondered who it could be.

They were sitting in the parents' bedroom, enjoying the cooler breeze, when they heard Appa's voice greeting someone and inviting them in.

"Seetha... Guru... come here."

His voice came from the living room.

They both got up and went to him. Sana remained seated, still chatting and gossiping with her mama and cousins, making plans to watch a new movie that had been released last Friday.

Suddenly, Amma came rushing in, panting.

"Ganeshaa (Mama)... dekho na, kya kar rahe hain tumhare Athimber (Jijaji)!" she said in a panicked voice. Then she turned to Sana, her face filled with worry.

"Sana, you stay here! Don't come out until I ask. Lalitha, stay with her!"

Sana frowned. "What happened, Amma? Why are you so hyper? Kya kiya Appa ne? Is he okay? Tell me!" she asked, her voice laced with worry.

"Seetha, kya hua? Why are you so emotional and tense?" Mama asked, his concern evident.

Amma turned to Sana and gently cupped her face, her eyes filled with love, care, and deep worry.

"Sana... listen to me carefully, okay? Don't react to anything. Me, Guru, your mama, mami, and your cousins—we are all with you. We love you, understand? Chollu, kanna (Say it, my child)."

Sana felt her stomach twist in anxiety.

"Yes... yes, I understand, Amma... but you're scaring me. Please, at least tell me what's happening! Why shouldn't I react?

Kya ho gaya?" she pleaded, biting her lip at the sight of her mother's distressed face.

But Amma didn't answer. She simply turned and walked out with Guru, shutting the door loudly behind her. The sound made Sana flinch in fear.

Her gut feeling had been right. Something was terribly wrong.

She turned to her mami and hugged her tightly from the side, her heart racing.

Was Appa up to something?

Chapter Thirty-Eight:
The Price Of Silence

Sana was shocked by what was happening outside. Why was Amma tense, and why did she ask her not to react? But it could only be solved when she came face to face with the situation.

Guru came in, sat near her, held her hand, and said, "Sana, Appa has invited a boy's family to see you with a marriage proposal."

"WHAT???" Sana yelled in shock, her eyes wide open, puzzled.

"He is just a prospective boy, not fixed or anything. Now listen, he has asked me to bring you there. I am with you in whatever decision you make. I am on your side, okay? No one—I say, no one—can force you to do anything. Just come with me. Take some time if you want..." he said, speaking calmly, not wanting to stress Sana out.

But she was aghast, appalled, offended by what her Appa had done behind her back. He had just broken her trust… deceived her… her Appa… her hero… her superstar… had just broken her heart. How could he do that? She wanted to forsake him, run from this situation into Sid's arms, and never come back to him. She didn't cry—she was in shock—her eyes dry, wide open, her eyeballs moving rapidly as she tried to make an impulsive decision on how to escape from her home!

Her home… which didn't feel like hers right now. Even with the other family members around her, he had a special place in her heart… her father!

She loved her father. The relationship she had with him was simply magical! A special bond where she saw him as the strongest man in the family, a protective guide for her, making her strong and courageous. He was the one who let her do everything her heart desired and pampered her like a princess. She couldn't believe he could hurt her like this.

She started to have self-doubt. Had she done something so bad that he had to secretly fix this meeting without even letting his wife or son know? Why? What must have happened since Monday that made him do this? She wanted to know! She didn't want to run or elude this situation. She would face it and ask him for the answers to her WHYs, to her WHATs. Umpteen theories ran through her mind.

"Sana… tere saath koi zabardasti nahi kar sakta. Bas unke liye aa ja, aur baad mein mana kar dena… I don't know what he wants to prove by pulling this stunt!!" Guru heaved, getting irritated.

After spending a good ten minutes in self-talk, Sana took a deep breath and prepared herself for the show, calming her heart and strengthening her mind. As her father always said, she was the prestige of the family, and she would uphold his dignity and respect, not taint the image he valued the most.

"This too shall pass, Sana," she told herself.

Sana walked into the living room with Guru and Mami, her eyes looking down, expressionless. Her eyes darted up when she heard her father's voice.

"Sana, he is Hari... Hari Narayanan... Hari, she is my daughter, Sanaya."

She didn't look at him but first turned to her Appa on her left, her eyes questioning. He was unable to meet her gaze, guilt very evident on his face. She looked down again, folded her palms in a namaste, and then finally looked at the boy her father had chosen for her.

He was sitting on the three-seater sofa with his parents—right where Sid used to sit. It pinched her heart. Just a week ago, she was so happy and excited, but what a change of scene. Life unfolds unpredictably—elation can turn into sadness in an instant.

"Hello, Sanaya. Nice to meet you," he said.

Sana wanted to say, I can't say the same... but she didn't. She simply gave a faint smile, just slightly lifting the corners of her lips, keeping herself calm and resisting the frustration building inside her.

He was a good-looking man—tall, fair, wearing glasses, and seeming decent.

"Sanaya, I am Hari's mother, and this is his dad," the lady in a yellow silk saree sitting next to the boy said. Sana again folded her palms and greeted them with a namaste.

"Did you tell her about us? About Hari? I mean, does she know where he works? Everyone seems to be surprised seeing us, Bala Mama," the lady asked Sana's father in a very dominating and authoritative way. Both men beside her remained submissively quiet in front of her. She had a bossy, intimidating personality.

"No... uhmm... actually, we just got busy. I... I... was not able to tell her, but you can tell her yourself, Mami. That will be much better, I think," he said hesitantly.

(NOTE: In the Tamil Brahmin community, everyone calls each other Mama & Mami, just like in the North, they say Bhaiya and Bhabhi.)

"Oh!! I did not expect that! We had to complete the Upakarma rituals early in the morning just to come here. Anyway, we came because my friend—who is your brother's friend as well—highly recommended your family, and also, their Jadagam (horoscope) matched. We are a very well-to-do family. My son works in Dubai in an accomplished MNC, earning a six-digit salary.

We have our own house here in NCR—a bungalow with centralized air conditioning," she said, glancing up at the ceiling fan with a humiliating look.

"It's just that when he saw your daughter's photo, he was adamant about meeting her. Also, he wanted a wife who was from our community but had grown up in the North. You know how kids are… they have studied here and want the same mindset in their life partners." Then she laughed as if she had cracked a joke.

No one reacted.

Except Sana's father and her husband.

"Ya ya... I know," Appa said.

Everyone else around was making faces at the dramatic lady.

"So now you know about him, Sanaya. What do you do? I was told you did B.Com from DU and are now working?" she asked.

Sana just nodded her head, not uttering a word.

"I think she is feeling shy," the lady said. "Do you both want to talk to each other?" she asked her son.

"Yes, sure, if you don't mind," the boy said, looking toward Sana's father.

"Yes, sure. Sana, take him to your room," Appa asked her.

"Woh... Appa, my room is dirty. He can talk to me here only. What do you want to ask?" she asked the boy in a serious tone.

But before he could reply—

"You keep your room dirty, girl? That's not good. You should always keep your surroundings clean. I cannot tolerate messy rooms. If this alliance works, you will go to Dubai with him, and there are no maids there. You will need to do all the work while he is earning. Purinjidha (Samjhi)?" the lady said strictly.

"She is a very clean girl. It's just that today, with her cousins coming over, they were bantering around," Appa said, clarifying for Sana.

Sana chuckled, seeing his condition and the whole scenario. What a difference, she thought, between this family and Sid's family…

"Sana, take him to the balcony," Appa said again.

Sana nodded and walked him to the balcony—just the place where, not long ago, she was happy seeing her crazy admirer, who loved her hopelessly. What an irony it was. Now, she felt disgusted being here with this man—shorter than Sid, no muscles, just fat. Why am I even comparing him with Sid? she thought.

"You look even prettier than in the photo," he said.

Sana had no interest, so she didn't respond.

He sat down on the plastic chair while she stood near the door.

"Come, sit," he said.

"No, it's okay," she replied.

"Oh wow, what a sweet voice. Do you sing?" he asked.

"No," she said.

"You work?" he asked.

"Yes," she answered.

"I wouldn't like you to work after marriage. I earn enough. You can chill, be a housewife, and enjoy the luxuries," he said, sounding just like his mother.

She again didn't respond. In your dreams, asshole, she thought.

"I like it when girls don't talk much. I would want my wife to be more of a listener than a talker. I like this quality in you. I think I will say yes to you," he declared as if he had made a great decision.

"Let's go," she said, unable to tolerate his presence any longer.

"Yes, yes. It's good that you don't have anything to ask... you'll get to know me after marriage. We'll have all the time in Dubai... actually, we don't even need to go on a honeymoon. Dubai, my home—there itself, we can have our honeymoon… hahaha..." he laughed devilishly, idiotically.

Sana suddenly saw ten heads around him, imagining Raavan standing in front of her. She shook her head, shaking off the obscure vision, and walked faster inside to escape his presence.

"What? You guys came back so fast?" that lady asked again.

Her husband was just a namesake husband, sitting quietly without uttering a word.

"We are good, Amma," the boy said with a grin.

"Ohh... I am so happy to see you smile, Kanna (Bacha). Did you tell her that she cannot work and all the other things?" the lady asked.

"Yes, I did... don't worry. She is very nice and quiet—didn't even utter a word," the boy said.

"He is here for a week more. We will call you with our decision by evening, and then we can make plans for Nischidartam (Engagement)," that autocratic lady said.

"I hope you know how to cook. My son is a foodie; he loves all South Indian and North Indian dishes. Learn them well before marriage—he hates going to hotels. Choliten (bata diya). And also, no western clothes after marriage—only Indian wear, okay?"

She came close to Sana, who was standing behind her father's sofa. Holding her chin, she turned her face left and right.

"She looks so fragile, and her skin is so soft... so beautiful. I will have a beautiful Peran (grandson)," she said.

Everyone in the room felt disgusted with what the family was doing to Sana. Her mother couldn't bear it anymore and walked to the Puja room. Mama had already gone out for a smoke. Guru stood there, watching how they were treating Sana, exchanging looks with his father.

"Bas ho gaya aapka! I am not interested in this alliance. I have already made my decision... Sorry for wasting your precious time. My daughter is not a maid for your son! How are you behaving with her? Obnoxious! I wanted my daughter to be happy and to see a boy from our community, but I guess I was wrong. You people don't deserve my Ponn (daughter). She has been quiet for me, for my dignity and respect... You all can leave, please!" Appa shouted, showing them the way out, completely baffling them.

Guru also stepped in. "Mummy ke chamche... get out! Disgusting people! My sister has been loved and taken care of by us like a princess, and you want her to cook and be a maid for your son? No talking, no job, no studies, no western wear... What the heck?! Why? This isn't marriage—it's a punishment! A life sentence!"

"And you, Mama... you have no voice in front of your wife. She is continuously judging and degrading my sister. Isn't she a woman herself? She can talk and dictate, but not her daughter-in-law? And what is this obsession with a Peran (grandson)? What if a Pethi (granddaughter) is born? Aiyoo Rama! What am I going to do? May God bless the girl who comes into your house as one!"

Appa sat down, slumped on the sofa, his head buried in his palms.

The boy's family shouted and argued.

"Guru, please ask them to go..." Appa said in a sad tone.

Sana walked past him, tired, hungry, drained, and went to her room. She didn't have to do anything rebellious or pugnacious—the universe will work for the things destined for you.

She finally cried, lying down on the bed, wetting her pillow, and letting out all the emotions she had bottled up for her father.

Sometimes, it's okay to cry your heart out... Acting strong is hard.

Chapter Thirty-Nine:
Love's Test

"Sana, kanna (bacha), don't cry, ma pattu (dear)... Chalo utto, have lunch. You must be hungry, na? Endhre ma kanna (get up, bacha)," Amma said, tapping Sana gently to get up as she lay there, wetting her pillow with sobs.

Amma sat next to her pillow, and Sana, leaving the pillow, laid her head in her mother's lap, hugging her waist tightly.

"Ho gaya na baba? See, God does everything for a reason. Now, your Appa will realize how my daughter has chosen a gem of a person as her life partner. Agar nahi samjhe na, Durga Mata ka roop le loongi main... aur unhe pata hai woh kitna dangerous roop hai!" she said, animating her posture like the goddess, trying to make Sana smile.

Sana chuckled at that and wiped away her tears, but she still kept her head in her mother's lap. Amma caressed her face and said, "I am proud of you, Sana. Kitni maturely tune behave kiya. Koi aur hota toh chilla ke bhaag jaata, but you calmly handled the storm inside you. Appa ko izzat di, samaan kiya... Tune unke upar gussa bhi nahi kiya! I am proud to say that we have brought you up well. You know the value of family and how to respect elders. Toh ab hamara bhi kartavya hota hai ki, we value your choice and respect what gives you happiness... Haina?"

"Matlab?" Sana sat up suddenly from her mother's lap, sitting cross-legged on her left side.

Her mother took a plate filled with rice, sambhar, and vegetable curry, mixed it with her hand, and held a small portion towards Sana's mouth.

"Aaaahhh kar..." she gestured for Sana to open her mouth and started feeding her with her hands.

"Matlab ki ab Appa ko mere haath main chhod de... I will handle him and make him understand. Unki himmat kaise hui mere se chhupa ke uss bakwaas family ko yahaan bula ke meri beti ki insult karne ki? Ab mere andar Mother India jaag gayi hai... and that too, a bad one!" she said, successfully shifting Sana's sullen and sad mood to a more relaxed one.

That's how she is—a child at heart, innocent, sometimes oversensitive. But just by acknowledging her feelings and being empathetic towards her, one could do wonders. Her mother's words gave her confidence and comfort, but she was still broken.

Her father had not come up to her yet. Mama and Mami had visited and left. Guru had come and talked to her. But her father... he stayed in his room the whole day and night, not coming out for chai, avoiding her when she asked him to have dinner.

Even all of Sunday passed without him being around. He excused himself, saying he wasn't feeling well, and remained in bed the whole day. Sana overheard Amma's voice arguing with him in their room, but her father didn't respond to any of her allegations or arguments. He chose to remain quiet.

And that silence gave her jitters.

His acting quiet again brought back memories from last week, making her doubt his intentions once more.

She never kept grudges in her heart—she was forgiving. And this was about her Appa, whom she loved with all her heart.

She wondered about the reason for his aloofness. Was he upset? Apologetic? Guilt-ridden? Or... was he planning something again?

No... no... That was the last thing she wanted to think. I'm not wrong, right? she questioned herself.

But what if this time he did something even more alarming?

"Is this how it feels when someone breaks your trust? Did I make my Appa feel this way when I told him about Sid?" she whispered to herself, lost in thought.

She was confused and emotionally drained. Sid was also busy since Kajal Didi and his Jiju were leaving today. She didn't want to bug him and stress him out. If he found out about everything that happened on Saturday, he would get hyper, and Sana didn't have the energy to handle him right now. She just called him briefly to say goodbye to Kajal Didi.

Even Payal Didi was gone—she had started a beautician course in Delhi.

Tonight, all she had were the stars and the moon to talk to, pouring her heart out as she gazed through her bedroom window.

"Why did Appa change so much? Why isn't he talking to me?" she asked the moon.

It didn't reply, of course. But it gave her the peace she was seeking.

"Even when the moon looks like it's ebbing... it's actually never changing shape. Appa will be the same, too, right? Right now, he's like Amavasya (new moon), hiding away. But he'll return, like you... full and bright, like before... with whom I can talk about anything... haina?" she murmured.

With heavy eyes, she drifted off to sleep.

Sid was waiting for Sana at their usual spot to pick her up.

She was late today—a rare thing. She was always punctual, just like him. And he loved that about her—how she valued time.

But today... she was already ten minutes late.

He texted her.

"I'm coming!" she replied.

Sid hated waiting games.

He was eager to see her, to hold her—especially after that day when he had seen her in her South Indian attire. She looked sensual, breathtaking, her curves accentuated, the jasmine flowers in her hair making him weak. He could barely control his emotions that day.

The car radio was playing one of his favorite Kishore Kumar songs, bringing a small grin to his face...

Ho, aaja meri saanson mein mahek raha re tera gajra

Ho, aaja meri raaton mein lahek raha re tera kajra

O hansini meri hansini, kahan ud chali

Mere armaanon ke pankh lagaake kahan ud chali

Lost in his thoughts, he didn't notice when the passenger door opened.

Sana stepped in.

Her authentic rose fragrance instantly filled the car.

She was wearing a new churidar today, looking absolutely gorgeous.

"Wow... tu din ba din khoobsurat hote ja rahi hai, Moti... mere pyaar ka rang accha chadh raha hai tere pe!" Sid teased with a smirk.

"Kya hai Sid?! Khoobsurat bhi bol rahe ho aur moti bhi… ab khush hoon ya dukhi?" she asked, pouting, her eyebrows colliding in a frown.

"Acha, khush ho jaa... You're looking breathtakingly beautiful. Yeh, naya suit hai?" he asked, his eyes full of admiration.

"Thanks… yes. This was my mom's saree… a net one. I had my eye on it since I was a child. She doesn't wear it anymore, so I got it altered into a suit," Sana said with a hint of nostalgia.

"Net wali? Uhmm… sahi hai! Teri Amma net wali saree bhi pehenti thi? Good, good," Sid teased, raising his left eyebrow with a cheeky smile.

It was a skin-colored net churidar with a lining inside, short sleeves that exposed her fair arms, a deep round neckline, and a delicate net dupatta draped around her neck. The outfit hugged her curves perfectly. With her long hair open and glossy nude lipstick, she looked absolutely mesmerizing.

Sid couldn't take his eyes off her.

"Sid, mujhe aaj office nahi jaana... I'm in no mood to work," she said in a gloomy tone.

"Kya hua baby ko? Why don't you want to go? May I know?" he asked, concern flickering in his eyes.

"I'm tired. I didn't sleep well... I feel dull today," she sighed.

"But you look sexy today," he said, smirking.

"Subah-subah pee ke aaye ho kya?" she scowled.

"Nahi… bas tere pyaar ka nasha ho gaya hai," he grinned. "Chal, let's go home then."

"Haan, Maa se bhi mile hue kaafi din ho gaye," she said, brightening up at the thought.

"Maa isn't home, sweetheart. She went with Kajal to Kanpur yesterday. They didn't even bother to tell me until the last minute because they knew I wouldn't let her go," he said, frowning.

"Oh! That's sad… but it's good for her, na? At least she'll get a change of environment. Otherwise, she gets bored sitting at home all the time," Sana reasoned.

"Hmm... maybe," he nodded, still annoyed at his mother's sudden departure.

"But what about your meetings? What will you do?" she asked, worried.

"Don't worry. I'll call Raj and cancel all of them," he assured her.

When they reached Sid's house, he parked the car in the garage, opened the door, and stretched.

"Ek chai bana degi? Subah se nahi pee… late ho gaya uthne mein. Just got dressed and had no time to make it," he requested.

"Haan, Amma packed Idli and chutney for you. Tumne breakfast bhi nahi kiya hoga!" she said knowingly.

"Amma ki jai ho!" he grinned, quickly opening the lunchbox and devouring the idlis.

Sana went to the kitchen to make tea. A few minutes later, they sat on the sofa, sipping chai and chatting.

Sid studied her carefully. She wasn't her usual chirpy self. She looked lost.

"Why are you so dull today? Itni dukhi dukhi kyun hai re, be?" he asked, sensing something was wrong.

"Nothing," she replied shortly, avoiding his gaze.

"Bol rahi hai ya bulwau?" Sid asked, his voice firm.

"Kuch nahi na, Sid. Ab tum irritate mat karo mujhe," she said, brushing him off as she stood up, gathering the empty cups and heading toward the kitchen.

Sid watched her, his sharp eyes noticing the absence of her usual blush. She always turned pink at his teasing, but today... Her face was pale, and her energy dull. He knew her too well—her emotions were like an open book, written all over her face. Something was definitely wrong.

He followed her into the kitchen. She stood by the sink, washing her hands. Without a word, he came up behind her, wrapping his arms around her waist. His lips brushed against her cheek in a soft kiss.

"Something happened—I know it. If you want to talk, I'm here. But whatever it is, don't be sad, okay? I'm with you... always," he murmured.

She turned in his arms, her teary eyes searching his.

"Promise?" she whispered, her voice fragile.

He leaned down, pressing a soft kiss to her lips.

"Promise. And sealed with this kiss," he assured.

She didn't smile, just rested her head against his chest. One hand clutched his shirt, the other wrapped around his waist.

"Sid..." she called him in a sorrowful voice.

"Hmm?" he hummed, his eyes closing in thought. His mind raced, trying to piece together what could've changed since Saturday. She had seemed fine when he last spoke to her. He had barely seen her on Sunday... had something happened in between?

Her voice, barely above a whisper, broke his thoughts.

"Love me."

At first, he didn't quite register her words.

"Hmm?"

She lifted her head, her small hand cupping his face, making him look at her.

"Love me, Sid." This time, her voice was stronger.

A flicker of confusion and worry crossed his face.

"Sana… you're scaring me. Kya hua, jaan? Why are you acting like this?" he asked, tension in his voice.

"I love you with all my heart and mind. And now, I want to love you with my body, too. Did I say something wrong?" she asked, her voice laced with frustration.

Sid exhaled deeply, stepping closer and holding her face gently in his large palms.

"I love you too, Sana. You have no idea how much I have to control myself when I'm around you. But I respect you. I always have, and I always will. I know what this means to you, and I won't let you do something you might regret later."

Tears spilled down her cheeks.

"No one loves me… not you, not Appa. Everyone just says it, but when it's time to show it, they back away." Her voice broke as she sobbed.

Sid frowned.

"How did Appa come into this now?" he asked gently.

"Prove it, Sid. Prove that you love me. Prove your promise. Prove that you'll never leave me. Prove that you'll stand by me through everything!" she wailed, her emotions crashing over her like waves in a storm.

Sid's jaw clenched, his eyes darkening with intensity.

"I don't have to prove anything, Sana. You know it. You know how much I love you. But listen to me, and listen carefully—" he took a breath, his voice deep and unwavering, "I will never—never, till my last breath—leave your side. You are the love of my life, and I will cherish that forever."

With that, he swept her into his arms, carrying her bridal style toward his room…

Chapter Forty:
Silent Confessions

Sana was weak at that time, and Sid knew that he had to deal with her very sensitively. Vulnerability can make a person susceptible to a negative outcome or bring them to a state of being unprotected from some type of danger or harmful experience. Sid was pondering what might have happened to make Sana so weak. Was it leading her toward showing her love for him in a physical way? Or did she want security from him, seeking the trust that he would be there and would never dream of leaving her if he made love to her? He was in a dilemma!

People who are vulnerable experience feelings of anxiety, fear, and apprehension due to the risk they face of some type of harm. But what harm was Sana facing? He had to dig that out from her, and for that, he decided to play along with what she demanded.

Sometimes, to acknowledge one's emotions, you have to run to blow off the steam… You have to remind yourself of the good things in life… You have to have someone to tell you, to reassure you that things will be okay. Sid had a huge task ahead of him. He was a mature man, experienced enough to deal with this beautiful, innocent girl in his arms—someone who just needed to see how worthy she was and rebuild her trust in herself, in him, and in her beliefs.

He entered his room with her in his arms and made her stand near the door, closing it. He switched on the air conditioner, turned on the light in the room, and pulled her closer. Removing her dupatta from around her neck, he threw it far away onto the floor. He admired her shamelessly from head to toe, his gaze sweeping over all her curves while maintaining a distance but keeping his palm on her waist.

"So beautiful!" he said in a smoky voice.

Sana was neither shy nor blushing. Instead, she followed his actions, his eyes trembling, her hands getting sweaty and shaking as they held onto his veiny arms.

"Relax, baby. Be calm," he said sensually, turning her around and pulling her back against his chest. He pushed her hair from one shoulder to the other side. He kissed her very lightly on her neck, then pulled the neckline of her suit down from her shoulder, baring her soft skin.

Goosebumps rose on her skin from his touch, something Sid noticed instantly. He kissed her there again, this time harder, sucking on the skin, making her hiss at the tingling pain and tilt her neck to the other side. He ran his tongue over the spot to soothe the sensation.

He rolled down his big palms, smoothly touching her milky bare arms. Holding her palms, he lifted them up toward his neck, guiding her fingers to lock behind it. His hands traced the curve of her arms, moving down under them to her waist and then back up again. Finally, he hugged her softly around her stomach, holding her close.

Her eyes were closed throughout, and she just felt what he was doing to her. Sweating in the cool room, her hands holding his neck from behind, goosebumps not leaving her skin.

"You look so sexy, Sana. It is so beautiful. This is the most captivating image I have seen. Look..." he asked her to open her eyes and look at their image in the mirror.

She opened her eyes to see the posture they were in, it was enticing, captivating, alluring. Her lips curved a bit, blush creeping up her cheeks which was missing all through the day.

Sid leaned his chin on her bare shoulder, smiling gorgeously, leaning down to her height. His face was peeping out between her arms, holding his neck... His arms wrapped around her waist. They looked enchanting!

"You know I am the luckiest man in this Universe" he said pecking her pouted lips when she turned her face on to his side to ask, "Kyun?"

He gestured to her again from his eyebrow to look at the mirror, and she obliged.

"Iss duniya ki Param Sundari jo mere bahoo main hain," he said, adoring themselves in the mirror with a smile and crinkle in his eyes.

She smiled shyly bending her head down and bringing down her hands to rest just above his arms which still wrapped her waist tightly.

He turned her around to face him and kissed her passionately, exploring her curves starting from her arms, waist, hip, and back. His hands reached the zip on her suit on the back and started to pull it down slowly. She didn't realize that he was opening the zip till he touched his hot palms on her naked back and caressed it softly.

She gasped with a sigh, taking a breath and parting him, eyes wide open, looking at him. Her lips felt swollen, hot, and scented like him.

He turned her again and held her tight, his member poking her back, and she could feel him hard for her. "Do you want this? Look at the mirror and tell me," he commanded, kissing her open back, neck, ear... eyes fixed on the mirror, looking at her attentively.

She didn't respond; she looked puzzled. Her eyes fixed on the mirror, watching him loving her body, giving attention to each part open bare in front of him. Her deep neck showed most part of her bulging bosom.

His hand came up and fondled her bosom, cupping it whole in his palm. She moaned out a rapture. He took her right palm in his and brought it behind to touch his member above his pants. She gulped, touching it!

"This is to show you how ready I am for you, Sana; you don't know how much I yearn for you, how much I crave for you... You are exotic, glamorous, so beautiful not just from the exterior but also from here..." he left her taut bosom and touched her heart, just above her cleavage, keeping his left palm flat there.

He took her right palm away from his member, still intertwined with his finger to his lips, and kissed it softly.

"Do you still have any doubts? If so, tell me. I will comply with what you ask, but remember, this is something divine for me... I want it to be special... This experience will be the first one for both of us... I... I want an alive, sorted, and happy you when we become one. I have always respected your preference. Will you be able to respect mine?" he asked.

She hastily turned around and embraced him, leaping up to his neck and crying, releasing her inhibitions, complexities, and barriers.

"I am sorry... sorry for behaving so crudely with you... Sid... I didn't mean to... but... I am in this situation where I wanted to know if I am important to the people in my life whom I value..." she said, wailing out her sorrows to him, slowly opening herself up.

He picked her up in his arms and laid down on the bed with her above him. He kissed her, closing the zip behind.

"Kya hua hai? Batayegi? Please don't cry, na yaar... I like my happy, talkative, chirpy, jumpy Sana, not this rothudu baby..." he said, making crying faces to lighten the heavy atmosphere.

She giggled, wiping her tears, and pouted, sliding down to his left side on the bed, still half on top of him, keeping her head and hand on his chest, playing with the chest hair peeking out from his open shirt buttons. He wrapped his left arm around her waist, holding her in a tight grip.

"Aur khol du buttons… ache se khel le baalon se?" he teased, opening all the buttons of his shirt and giving her full access to his chest.

She happily caressed his chest and the little hair around it. This was calming her nerves. She was seeing this much of his bare skin for the first time, and she loved what she saw—the tight abs. He didn't have a six-pack, but he was well-toned. His manly fragrance wafted from his shirt and arms. He was a sight to behold.

He didn't say anything further, giving her time to open up. He didn't want to pester her anymore, just appreciating the silent moment they were sharing. At this moment, in each other's arms, everything felt right. This was the best time he had spent with her—so close, so bare, so open, so comfortable. Her touch, her coziness, and her ease of physical proximity with him encouraged a serenity and contentment within him. He was the happiest man in the world at this moment, in this position and in her presence.

"Remember, I told you that Appa was acting weird last week?" she said slowly in a low voice.

"Hmm… yeah, I remember," he responded attentively.

"On Saturday, he called some boy's family to see me… for marriage," she said, her hands still playing with his chest.

He tightened his arms around her waist. Lifting his head, he said in a loud voice, "What??? What the heck??? And you're telling me this now? Has he gone mad or what??? Sana, you are staying with me here from now on. I will not send you back there anymore. This is the limit!"

Tensed, he ran his fingers through his hair in frustration.

"Kuch nahi hua... suno toh sahi puri baat," she said, hugging him tighter, kissing his chest, and gently pulling his head down.

He didn't say anything, anger surging through him, but he knew she needed him to listen more than anything right now. He had to be patient. Keeping both his hands under his head for support, he focused on her words.

"They showed how worthless, judgmental, and overly critical they were. No one liked them... they treated me like shit! Appa couldn't bear it, and he threw them out of the house!" she said, calming his racing heartbeat.

"But after that, he's silent again, Sid. He's not talking to me; he's ignoring me... You know I cannot tolerate it when someone close to me does that. When you ignored me, I was broken; it pained me... and now it feels the same... I am broken. He is my Appa... my hero... my first love... Why is he doing this? Is he planning something again? I am scared, Sid!!" she cried, clinging to him tighter, wetting his chest with her tears.

Sid held her close, wiping her tears with his shirt.

"Mujhse tum aaj hi shaadi kar lo... haan, wohi sahi hoga... Then he can't do anything..." she said desperately, sitting up slightly, slanting toward him.

"Isiliye maine aaj woh sab kaha tumse... not because I have any doubts about you, but to reassure myself that after this, he cannot hand me over to any stranger. I will be all yours... I cannot breathe without you, Sid... Tum mere sab kuch ho. I cannot imagine my life without you... Why is he doing this? He is avoiding me, Sid... baat nahi kar rahe, aankhein nahi mila rahe! Kyun?" she asked, searching for answers, needing his reassurance to calm her restless mind.

As she shared everything with him, her agitation slowly faded. Laying back down in his arms, she found the peace she had been seeking. Holding onto him, she once again played with the hair on his chest as if it provided her a sensory calmness. The emotional similarity is important, and for Sana, only Sid could give her the assurance she needed.

Chapter Forty-One:
When Hearts Speak

"You need to talk to him, Sana... Communication can solve any problem. You can cook up whatever stories are in your mind, run your imagination wild, assume anything... but the reality might be different. His reasoning might be a contrast to what you have thought. Jab maine phone nahi utaya, tere messages ka reply nahi kiya, toh tune kya kya imagine kiya... but reality was different, right? My phone was switched off... I didn't check that... my mistake, I agree, but it was different, right? Not bitter like you thought. It might be the same with him... Avoid assumptions!" Sid said, making Sana understand. Though he was furious, his love for her made his enraged temper take a back seat. Right now, he had to deal with sensitive Sana, and that too very tactfully.

"Par... he is ignoring me!" Sana said, whining.

"Fight past the wall and break it down na... hain toh tere Papa hi na... Woh nahi kar rahe toh tu jaa unse baat kar... Choti nahi ho jayegi agar tu initiate karegi talk toh. Clear it up, ask him all the questions that are bugging you... find the issue and try to solve it," he said very softly, fondling her long, silky, straight hair and massaging her scalp.

"Hmm... you are right... When he was ignoring me, I just brooded over that and made a barrier around myself and doubted me and everyone... I will talk to him..." she mumbled, yawning, closing her eyes, listening to his heartbeat... *dhak dhak... dhak dhak...* and his stroking her hair was making her sleepy, and she drifted off to sleep... with eyebrows brought together, pouted lips slightly open... she crashed out, just like that!!!

Sid was astonished to see the girl in his arms just sleeping like a baby. The girl who, just a few moments ago, was in a different zone, on an emotional roller coaster ride, was now calm and flaked out in a blur! He chuckled and admired the sleeping beauty, who, without any inhibition, reservation, shyness, nervousness, boundaries, or awkwardness, just slept hugging him against his chest.

He felt proud at that moment. A smile crept onto his face. She was so close to him, a closeness he had always dreamt of, and reality seemed so much better. He never thought he would experience this euphoria of holding her in his arms like this in his bed, this soon, before their nuptial.

He admired her face, her hair, her nose, her plump lips—a little swollen from the kiss—her neck, her shoulders, and the hickey on them. His gaze drifted down to her bosom, peeking from her deep-neck top, revealing most of her fair, milky, bulging skin, pressing against his bare chest... making him hard again. This was way too erotic for him.

He distracted his eyes from that and looked down at her waist, where her suit had ridden up slightly, exposing a bit of her skin. He caressed the naked skin there with his hands, which were holding her lightly.

Her legs, covered by skin-colored tight leggings matching the color of her top, hugged his thighs. Her small feet, adorned with pink nail paint, peeked out. He was fascinated by her feet. He wanted to hold them in his hands and feel them. He never missed a chance to do so when they were in the car, where she usually sat cross-legged, and he would hold her feet, massaging them and feeling them. But right now, he dared not move and disturb this sleeping beauty snuggling into him and snoozing.

He too drifted off to sleep, but not before taking a selfie of them in this position. He had an album filled with these stolen moments of Sana and himself, which he checked every night before going to sleep.

Sana woke up first, feeling the cold air from the air conditioner. She was not used to this chilly temperature and always felt colder compared to her family members. She flinched, opening her eyes against the room's bright light. She wheezed as she realized she was snugged into Sid's chest, hugging him and sleeping almost above him. She wondered how she had drifted off to sleep when they were talking so seriously, but she felt relaxed, fresh, and energized after this nap.

Sid was in a deep sleep, snoring very lightly, his mouth open and facing her near her head. A smile formed on her face as she looked at this gorgeous, ravishing, perfect man beneath her. All her blurred thoughts filled with doubts and apprehensions had faded just because of this profound man who had handled her with such brilliance... so delicately, as if she were a fragile doll that could break if not handled carefully.

She was so proud of him, knowing that he never lost control and managed his senses when she was vulnerable and open to going to any extent. He had shown her the right path like a guiding angel. She was in awe of him. He was perfect for her... Matured for her childishness... Controlled for her feebleness... Experienced for her ignorance... Logical for her confusion... Fire for her coldness... Sensible for her craziness... They completed each other. His negatives were her positives and vice versa, showing each other the right side of themselves and every situation.

She touched his face, stroking his chin, jaw, and lips. A current ran through her body. She was tempted to kiss him at that moment, and she didn't restrict herself. He was hers and only hers to love. She moved slightly upwards and pecked his open lips, his cheeks, his nose, his forehead, and then came down again to his lips.

"Mera sone ka advantage le rahi hai?" Sid said suddenly, grasping the shocked Sana firmly by her waist and arms.

"Hayee... darra hi diya..." Sana said, panting, holding her chest, and lying back on the pillow away from him, on his left.

He turned and came above her, his left hand still on her bare waist and the other resting on her pillow.

"Kya kar rahi thi?" he asked.

"Kuch nahi..." she blushed, shying away and turning her face, avoiding his prying eyes that were making her flush.

"Main bhi karunga... We need to clear our accounts, right?" he said with a smug look.

She snapped her neck towards him, and with her eyebrows colliding, she said, "Tum so nahi rahe the... Hayee, kitne pappi ho tum... Matlab full maza le rahe the!"

"Toh na lu... Meri sharamilee ka bold roop kaise miss karta?" he said, laughing.

Kissing her forehead, nose, cheeks, and then lips—softly at first and then with a swift gradation of intensity that made her cling to him. His insistent mouth was parting her lips, sending wild tremors along her nerves, evoking sensations she had never known she was capable of feeling. She kissed him back with the same intensity, her hands exploring his chest, hugging him closer. His hands traced all her curves, her neck, igniting sensations deep within her.

His hand gently massaged her breast, erupting a moan from her.

"Sid..." she whispered in between their kiss.

"Can I see it... touch it?" he asked with desperate, expectant eyes.

She nodded her head in agreement, understanding his need. There was no way she was going to deny this golden man who did not take advantage of her during her weakest moment.

They explored each other in that room, not crossing the limit they wanted to keep until after marriage, preserving its holiness and making it special.

*

"Appa... coffee." Sana served his favorite filter coffee in the evening, which was usually family tea time.

He refused to come out of his room and was watching a Tamil news channel, sitting in his wooden recliner chair. He grabbed the coffee and engrossed himself in the news once again.

"You will not talk to me, Pa?" Sana asked, sitting down on the bed beside him.

He didn't reply but bowed his head, breathing heavily.

"Sorry, Appa, if I did anything wrong. I had no intention of hurting you... I cannot tolerate this aloofness from you. Main kya karun jo aap phir se baat karoge mujhse?" she asked, sadness evident on her face, her voice carrying pure honesty.

"Why are you sorry, Kanna (bacha)? I am ashamed of myself, regretting what I put you through in front of those cheap people... My intentions were never to insult you or make you feel low... never... but now I feel low myself! I am not able to face you. I am embarrassed for hiding things from you, from my family, and for putting you all in a situation that even an enemy doesn't deserve... I am sorry... Maaf kar de apne Appa ko..." he said, repenting, his voice and face filled with remorse.

"No... no, Appa... please aisa mat bolo... Aap bade ho... chhote se sorry nahi maangte," she said, holding his hand and coming close to him.

"Bado wali harkatein toh nahi kari na maine... Tu itni si hoke, unke samne, ya baad mein mere saath koi scene nahi create kiya... You kept silent, endured all the pain, insult, and hurt... never uttered a word... You are showing the maturity that I lacked! Abhi bhi mere se fight karne ke bajaye... You are asking for an apology... I think I have taken away your innocence, made you too soft... Don't endure it, Sana. Fight... yell at me... shout at me... for what I did to you. I was waiting for you to come and ask me! But instead, you showed the respect and faith in me that I do not deserve..." he said, guilt-ridden.

"I was hurt. I was in pain when you went behind my back and called someone—a stranger—to see me! For what? For your belief, community, caste, and relatives who don't know me as much as you do, Appa? I never expected this from you... but I learned one thing from it. I now know how it feels to break someone's trust. I now know how you must have felt when I told you about Sid... I now understand how painful it must have been for you.

But, Appa, I did not do it on purpose. I just fell for him unconsciously. That is why I did not revolt against you, did not rebel—because I did the same thing. But my intentions were never wrong... so how can I question you?" she said, tears rolling down her cheeks, her eyes reflecting deep, intense sorrow.

"Don't cry... Yes, you did hurt me... but I did too... and I should not have called them here without enquiring, without knowing the family—just hastily fixing everything, getting influenced by Anna (Bhaiya). I should not have listened to him..." he said, repenting again.

"Listen to your heart, Appa... That is what you have taught me, right? To do what feels right to me, that my conscience will show me the right path. Remember, I wanted to do B.Com when everyone told me to do BCA? I wanted to learn dance when everyone said to learn classical singing... I wanted to learn to ride a scooter when everyone said to learn to drive a car... You told me to listen to what my heart said; you guided me. Then why are you not listening to your heart... your conscience?

I know my Appa... He is the best in this world, so pure and honest, and he will do the best for me and also respect me," she said, hugging him from his side as he caressed her head.

Both father and daughter communicated and removed the barrier of misunderstandings. They talked, spending the lost time with each other, returning to their natural selves. When we listen to understand, most of our problems get resolved, and hidden issues come to light. A heart-to-heart talk—open and honest communication—can solve even the biggest of issues.

Chapter Forty-Two:
Written In The Stars

It was Thursday evening. Sana came back from work exhausted after a hectic day and a tiring bus ride. Sid had an important meeting that clashed with their usual schedule, and he had to leave early for Delhi, missing their evening drive back home.

The entire week, she had been going home with him, making chai, spending time together, and cooking light and healthy dinners for him. He would chop the vegetables while she cooked effortlessly in his kitchen, all the while stealing romantic moments between tasks. Tonight was different. Sid had a dinner meeting with his clients, so Sana didn't have to worry about preparing his meal. His breakfast and lunch were taken care of by her Amma's kitchen, and she also made it a habit to keep Sid's mom updated about everything happening around them.

They had grown closer than ever. Sid, who once hated when his mother left him alone, now found himself grateful—this time, it was Sana filling that space. She was getting increasingly comfortable with their physical proximity. Sid would drive fast just to get home sooner, eager to have uninterrupted time with her before she had to leave. Yet, she would end up staying late each day.

But today was different. She returned home on time, only to find her parents missing. She picked up the spare house keys from Payal Di's place, freshened up, lit the diya, made herself a cup of chai, and sat on the balcony, scrolling through her phone.

She texted her Appa, asking about their whereabouts, but he didn't reply. Growing restless, she tried her mother's phone, but there was no answer. As time passed, worry crept in. It was already 8 p.m., and they hadn't returned, nor had they sent any message. To distract herself, she began preparing dinner.

Just then, Guru walked in after work.

"Anna, where are Appa and Amma? They're not answering my calls or picking up their phones. Do you know anything?" she asked, concern evident in her voice as he removed his shoes.

"Oh yeah, Appa mentioned this morning that they were going to Delhi for some work. They'll be back soon—you know how bad the traffic is. Appa has the car, so he'll manage. But my day was hell—I'm dead tired from taking the bus!" he groaned. "Let me shower first... I'm starving! Did you cook something?"

"Yeah, I made baingan ka bharta and dal. I'll make fresh rotis now," she replied, heading towards the kitchen.

They ate dinner together when the doorbell rang. Guru got up to answer it.

"Appa, where did you both go? I was so worried! And why weren't you answering your phones?" Sana complained as her parents walked in. "Amma, a phone is not just meant to sit in your purse! You're supposed to answer calls!"

But instead of responding, they just smiled at her—strangely, almost mischievously.

"I'm so mad at you both, and you're smiling? Seriously?!" she frowned, stomping off to the kitchen to get them some water.

As she returned, they gestured for her to sit with them.

"Sana, sit down. We need to talk," Appa said firmly. "Guru, you too."

Confused, she did as told. Amma moved closer and pulled Sana into a tight hug.

"What's going on? What's with all this extra love?" she asked, her brows knitting together.

"Because the news is that good!" Amma said excitedly. "We went to the Guruvayurappan Temple in Mayur Vihar today to match your and Sid's jadagam (horoscope)… and it matched, Sana!"

Her mother's face lit up with exhilaration.

Sana gasped, her eyes widening in disbelief. She turned to her Appa, silently asking for confirmation. When he smiled and nodded, the reality of the moment hit her like a tidal wave.

"We also asked the astrologer to suggest a good date for Nichyathartham (engagement), and he said September 10th would be very auspicious!" Amma added eagerly, pouring out all the details of their temple visit and the astrologer's words.

Sana sat frozen, her mind spinning in a euphoric haze. Her vision blurred, and her mother's face appeared foggy as emotions overwhelmed her. The sheer joy on her face was unmistakable—animated yet paralyzed in disbelief. She darted her gaze between her mother and father, still trying to absorb the news.

She was pulled back to reality when Amma shook her lightly. "Kahan kho gayi? Are you even listening? Sid ki maa ka number de… we want to talk to her!"

Still wordless, Sana suddenly sprang from the sofa and launched herself into her father's arms, embracing him tightly.

"Appa… ooohhhh Appaaa!" she cried, her emotions pouring out in silent gratitude. No words were needed—her hug spoke volumes.

Her father, eyes brimming with unshed tears, held his precious daughter just as tightly. "Khush raho beta," he whispered, his blessing carrying the weight of his love.

Watching the touching moment, Amma chuckled. "Baap-beti ka milaap ho gaya? Guru, aaja beta. Why should you be left out? Gale mil le mujhse—these two have already formed their team!"

Guru laughed and happily embraced his mother, completing the family moment.

"September 10th... haan!" Sana finally said aloud, as if saying it would make it more real.

"Haan, and now we need to inform Priya Behen and Sid as well. Call them if you think this is the right time," Appa said.

"Woh Appa... Maa is in Kanpur. She'll be back Sunday evening... but I can call her now, and you can speak to her. Should I tell Sid first? Then you can share the details with him later?" she hesitated.

"Yes, yes, of course—whatever you feel is right," he agreed.

She took Appa's phone, added Sid's mom's number to his contacts, and made the call. When Maa answered, the conversation flowed naturally, full of joy and relief. She was elated, knowing that Sana's father had finally accepted Sid as his son-in-law.

"Sana, I am so happy, bacha! Finally, we are one step closer to bringing you to your second home. My sweet girl, you melted your father's heart—just as I knew you would. You're so precious; no one can resist you or refuse you anything," Sid's mother gushed, showering her with love.

Sana giggled. "Hayee Maa... bahut mehnat karni padi! But koi na—der aaye, durust aaye!" she laughed, feeling the warmth of a second mother who loved her just as dearly as her own.

"Maa, I have a request..." she said softly.

"Haan, bol na," Maa encouraged.

"Can I be the one to tell Sid first? Then you can tell him later?" she asked hesitantly.

"Arre, yeh bhi koi puchne ki baat hai? Of course, beta! You should be the first to tell him. He'll go crazy with excitement—only you can handle him! I'll call him tomorrow morning, okay? Right now, go tell Kajal too. I need to handle her excitement, and you... you take care of your pati," she teased, laughing.

Sana blushed deeply. Pati. The word sent a warm, fluttery feeling through her.

She spent some more time with her parents, chatting and sharing dinner. Then, finally, she went up to the terrace, feeling a deep sense of liberation. For the first time, she didn't have to hide anything. She could tell the truth openly that she was going to call Sid to her parents, no more secrets, no more fears.

Tonight, everything had changed.

Sid got home by 9 p.m., exhausted from the day. After a quick shower, he slumped onto the sofa, mindlessly flipping through news channels while scrolling through his phone. His thoughts kept drifting to Sana. Her last message was at 6 p.m., letting him know she had reached home. But after that—silence.

Usually, she would text, prod him with questions, or demand updates on his whereabouts. But today, nothing. His phone hadn't buzzed with her name all evening.

He frowned, picked up his phone from the charger, and called her. She disconnected. His heart skipped a beat. He sent her a message—she saw it but didn't reply.

His pulse quickened with uneasy thoughts. Without thinking, his body moved on its own—he grabbed his keys and walked out, heading straight for her community. He didn't have a plan, just a desperate need to see her, to know she was okay. He was exhausted, but more than anything, he missed her—her voice, their car rides, her face.

Just as he was about to enter her complex, his phone rang. Sana's name flashed on the screen. He picked up instantly.

"Kahan hai tu? Phone kyun kata? Message ka reply kyun nahi kar rahi? Teek hai tu? I'm coming—I'm almost at your gate. Bahar aa—I want to see you!" He blurted everything in one breath, his voice laced with worry.

"Hey Ram... kaan phat gaye! Why are you shouting? Saare community wale bahar aa jayenge. Mere saath-saath unki bhi shakale dekh lena," she teased, giggling.

"Sana, this isn't funny! I was worried. Where are you? Come outside—meet me in the park, the same spot," he said, his eyes scanning her balcony.

"Pata hai... I'm watching you," she said, amusement in her voice.

He frowned. "Then why can't I see you? Mazak mat kar, jaldi aa jaa—better if you come down for a walk and meet me properly." He ran a hand through his hair, wiping the sweat off his forehead.

"Mr. Sharma, you're looking hot even when you're sweating... hayeee garmi!" she teased, making his irritation melt into a smirk.

"Ab bas, bohot ho raha hai tera. Irritate mat kar—where are you?"

"Thodi apni nazrein upar uthao, jaanemann," she whispered.

He tilted his head up toward the terrace—and there she was. Standing like a vision against the night sky, her bunny teeth flashed in a radiant smile as she waved down at him.

He exhaled, smiling despite himself, and waved back. "Wahan kya kar rahi ho?"

"Tumhara intezaar," she said, her cheeks glowing pink even from a distance.

His heart clenched.

"Main aaun? Please... aaun?" His voice dipped into the pleading, excited tone he always used when begging to come over.

She giggled. "Hmmm... but mujhe chocolate chahiye. Pehle Chacha ki dukaan se Dairy Milk leke aao, then you can come up. Okay?"

He raised a brow. "Kya baat hai, aaj meri Moti baby ne khud se kuch maanga mujhse... I will get it. Wait."

Disconnecting the call, he made a quick stop at the shop, bought the chocolate, and hurried to her building. Sneaking up the stairs without making a sound, he pushed open the terrace door.

And there she was.

The dim moonlight bathed her in an ethereal glow, her hair wild and flowing with the cool, pre-rain breeze. She was breathtakingly beautiful—gloriously, heartbreakingly attractive.

Before he could react, she ran into him, throwing her arms around his shoulders. The force made him stumble back a few steps, but he caught himself, gripping the doorframe—and her. He held her tight, his arms locked around her waist.

Her feet left the floor as she clung to him, her fingers curling around his neck. Without hesitation, she kissed him.

Time stilled.

Sid's breath hitched. The world disappeared, leaving only the addictive warmth of her lips, the intoxicating way she invaded all his senses. The raw emotion poured into her kiss, stealing his every thought. His grip on her waist tightened, drawing her impossibly closer.

His eyes fluttered open for a moment, just to make sure she was real—not a dream. She was there, eyes shut, lost in him.

And then, between breaths, she whispered—

"September 10th."

His brows furrowed, confused. "What?"

She pulled back just enough to look into his eyes, her lips brushing against his as she smiled.

"September 10th, Sid," she repeated, this time slower, still in his arms, smiling wide, surer, watching his face intently.

 Sid frowned slightly, not quite understanding. "What?"

She gently slid down from his hold, her fingers never leaving his. Pulling him along, she perched on the cement slab, her legs dangling. He instinctively stood between them, his hands resting on her waist, his thumbs absently stroking the fabric of her kurti.

"Give me the Chocolate," she demanded softly, her eyes twinkling.

He narrowed his eyes. "Tu aaj weird behave nahi kar rahi? Pehle bina baat ke kiss kar liya, ab yeh date bola, aur chocolate ki craving kyun ho rahi hai tujhe?" He tilted his head, scrutinizing her.

She bit her lip, then grinned, blushing. "Hamari engagement date... September 10th."

His breath hitched. His heartbeat slammed against his ribs.

Realization dawned. His body stiffened. His breath hitched. His eyes—once hazy with passion—went wide.

He blinked.

He had waited so long for this moment.

And now, it was real.

"Congratulations to us," she giggled, breaking off a piece of the chocolate bar and slipping it into his mouth. Before he could even chew, she leaned forward and bit the other half straight from his lips, savoring it as she met his stunned gaze.

Sid was frozen. Staring at her. Processing.

His mind struggled to keep up. Engagement? September 10th? Her father agreed.

His heart pounded so loud he could hear it in his ears. His lips, still tingling from her touch, parted in disbelief.

"Sid... kuch toh bolo," she whispered, nudging his arm.

Nothing.

She chuckled, patting his chest lightly. "Tum toh shock mein chale gaye!"

Suddenly, he inhaled sharply, eyes wide, realization hitting him like a lightning bolt.

"Kya bola tune? Engagement? Tere Papa maan gaye?" His voice cracked with overwhelming emotion. "Oh my God, Sana... I—" He exhaled shakily, his hands tightening around her waist. "I am so happy... this is like a dream... majak toh nahi kar rahi na?"

His voice, raw with joy, trembled as his eyes shimmered—tears threatening to spill, but his lips stretched into an uncontainable smile.

She shook her head, her own eyes glistening.

And then, before she could say anything more, he crushed her to him, spinning her around, his laughter echoing into the night.

Their foreheads touched, breaths mingling in the crisp night air. Just then, the sky rumbled, and soft droplets fell, kissing their skin.

Rain poured down in a sudden blessing, drenching them in its embrace. The universe itself seemed to celebrate their love.

Drenched, breathless, overjoyed—Sid cupped her face.

No words were needed.

Flabbergasted with satisfaction, joy, and the weight of fulfillment, he pulled her in, capturing her lips once more—this time, sealing the promise of forever.

Chapter Forty-Three:
A Union of Hearts And Cultures

In Tamil Brahmin Iyer weddings, horoscope matching is a sacred step. Once the stars align and the families agree, the Nichayathartham (Engagement) is held—a ceremony where both families formally unite, choose the Muhurtham (auspicious wedding date), and kickstart the wedding preparations. Traditionally, this ritual takes place at the groom's house, and today was no different.

However, Sid's mother, with her boundless grace, had one heartfelt wish.

"Bhaisaab," she had told Sana's father, "I know that as a mother, I have dreams for my son's wedding, just like you have for your daughter's. I was blessed to fulfill mine during Kajal's wedding. Now, I want you to fulfill all your wishes for Sana's wedding, in your traditions, just as you envisioned."

Her words struck a deep chord. Sana's parents, who had assumed the ceremonies would follow a North Indian style, were overwhelmed with emotion. Gratitude swelled in their hearts for this dignified woman, who, despite cultural differences, embraced their traditions as her own.

The Engagement Day

Sid's house gleamed under the soft glow of marigold garlands and fairy lights—simple yet elegant, befitting an afternoon Muhurtham. The house was alive with energy, bustling with the sounds of laughter, chatter, and last-minute preparations.

Kajal, Sid's ever-enthusiastic sister, had arrived with her in-laws, bubbling with excitement. She took charge of nearly everything, running errands, coordinating with the caterers, and ensuring everything was picture-perfect for her brother's Sagai.

A Tamil priest, arranged by Sana's father, had already arrived to oversee the rituals. He examined the setup, making sure all the essentials were in place. Meanwhile, Sid's closest friends—Rahul, Sumit, and Vishal—busied themselves, assisting Sid and his mother, ensuring every detail was just right.

Children dashed around playfully while elders gathered on the porch, engrossed in nostalgic conversations. The aroma of delicious food from the caterers lingered in the air, adding to the festivities.

And in the heart of it all, Maa—Sid's mother—radiated unparalleled joy. Draped in an exquisite maroon saree with a golden border, she glowed with happiness, personally overseeing every aspect of the event.

The wait was almost over.

Meanwhile…

Sana💖

Ready, Mr. Sharma? 💕💕

Sid💖

Bas Mrs. Sharma ka intezaar hai! ☺️💋

Sana💖

Intezaar ka phal meetha hota hai! Have patience, my dear! ☐💋

Sid💖

Kab aa rahe ho yaar? Aur nahi hota wait… aur tune apni pic bhi nahi bheji. Come fast!

Sana💖

Samne hi dekh lena… ab hamara swagat nahi karoge? We just entered your street! ☺

Sid's face broke into an uncontrollable smile as he read the message. His heart raced with anticipation. He turned to Sumit and said, "Bhai, Sana's family is here! Let everyone know—it's time!

Excitement rippled through the house.

She was finally here.

The moment they had all been waiting for had arrived.

Sid stood in front of the mirror one last time, checking his reflection. The blue kurta with golden embroidery fit him perfectly, and the golden pajama added just the right touch of elegance. His hair, freshly trimmed and set with gel, looked sharp. Kajal had helped him with a little makeup, just enough to give him that natural glow. He couldn't help but smile at himself. "All the best to me… Bless me, Papa. I know you're here with me. You would have loved Sana. Give us your blessings." With a soft sigh and a smile, he left the room, his heart fluttering with excitement. He couldn't wait to meet her, to see her and her parents for the first time in his house.

But just as he stepped out, Sumit and Rahul intercepted him, dragging him back to the room with a grin. "Stay here, man. We'll call you when it's time." Sid felt a flicker of frustration, but he calmed himself. *It's worth the wait, Sid. It's worth the wait.* He sank back into the chair, his mind already racing ahead to the moment when he would finally see her.

Sana, radiant as ever, stepped out of the car with Guru and her parents trailing behind her. Her cousins, Payal di, and a few close friends, including Neelima and Chetna, joined the procession. A distant relative from her father's side, who was visiting from Delhi, also made his way to Sid's house. The gathering at the entrance grew larger, with cars lining the street, everyone eager to enter Sid's home.

Sana stood tall in the center, feeling the warmth of the day, but even more, feeling the weight of what was about to happen. The priest, ready for the rituals, signaled to Kajal, asking her to perform the Aarthi to welcome her into Sid's family. She smiled, grateful to be part of such a momentous occasion, and walked toward Sana, carrying the flame in her hands.

Inside, Sid's heart raced. He'd been waiting for what felt like an eternity, and the anticipation was getting the best of him. His patience was thin, and he could feel his nerves buzzing with every passing second. Finally, unable to wait any longer, he stood up, opened the door, and walked into the living room.

The room, bustling with activity, fell into a brief silence as everyone turned to greet him. But Sid's gaze was locked on one person. He scanned the room frantically, trying to get a glimpse of her. There she was—standing in the middle of the room, surrounded by friends and family, her back to him. He could see the blue saree perfectly pleated and her hair elegantly braided, adorned with jasmine flowers. He couldn't yet see her face, but he could feel her presence like a magnetic pull.

Her parents, his mother, and others were speaking to him, but he couldn't focus on anything but her. And then, like a moment frozen in time, the noise around him faded as he heard his name being called. Sana turned.

It was as though the entire world stopped for a moment. The spark between them was undeniable. The chemistry, the connection, all of it intensified as their eyes met. Sid's heart thundered with joy as he took in the sight of her—simple yet breathtakingly beautiful. The blue Kanchipuram silk saree she wore matched his outfit perfectly, their plan coming to life in the most beautiful way. The fine gold necklace, the matching Jhumkas, the delicate bindi—it was all so stunning, but it was the smile on her face that took his breath away.

And in that moment, it wasn't just the day that mattered. It was this moment with her. Their future, their love, it all felt so right. The happiness radiating from both of them was unmistakable, a silent acknowledgment that this was just the beginning. This moment, this day—was the first step toward forever.

Sid had always believed in the power of prayers, and the visit to the Shiva temple just days ago had solidified that belief. Together, they had prayed for this day to go smoothly. And as their eyes met, everything seemed to fall into place, just as it was meant to be.

The atmosphere in Sid's house was filled with warmth and excitement as the engagement ceremony continued. Sid and Sana sat together on the mat near the *havan kund*, as instructed by the priest. The quiet serenity of the moment contrasted with the bustling crowd around them. Sana, always a little shy and reserved, felt her cheeks heat up as Sid complimented her.

"Beautiful... you are looking so gorgeous, Sana," Sid said, his voice soft and sincere.

"Tum bhi, very handsome," Sana replied, her gaze lowered, clearly flustered by the attention. Sid knew how self-conscious she could get, especially in front of so many people. But he loved how she seemed to shine despite her shyness.

As the priest began chanting mantras and performing the *Ganesh puja* to clear any obstacles, Sid couldn't help but steal glances at Sana. Her hands, freshly adorned with dark, intricate henna, looked even more beautiful as the gold and glass bangles on her wrists sparkled. Sid found himself captivated by the delicate beauty of her hands, barely able to tear his gaze away. When the priest asked him to hold her hand, Sid eagerly complied, his fingers gently wrapping around hers. The sudden reaction from everyone around them—laughter and playful teasing—made Sana blush furiously.

"Kya hain sab majak bana rahe hain, Sid? Thoda aaram se..." Sana whispered, only loud enough for Sid to hear. She looked so adorable in her bashfulness, but Sid couldn't help but smile and tighten his grip on her hand. He didn't want to let go. For a moment, the world seemed to shrink around them, just the two of them.

The family exchanged *Thamboola*—plates filled with betel leaves, coconut, and fruits—symbolizing the consent of the elders for the marriage. It was a simple but meaningful exchange, and Sid and Sana were then asked to stand up for the final ritual: the exchange of rings. Together, they had chosen the rings, and they were simple yet elegant—golden rings with delicate engraving, a larger one for Sid and a smaller one for Sana. As the rings slid onto each other's fingers, a sense of contentment washed over them, and the room erupted in joyous cheers. Flowers rained down on them, and everyone clapped and celebrated the occasion with loud shouts of happiness.

The priest then reads the *Lagna Patrika*—the official announcement of the marriage date and time. The wedding was officially set for December 13th. Sid leaned toward Sana, a smile of pure joy on his face.

"3 months from today," Sid said, his voice filled with excitement, nudging her with his elbow.

Sana, still smiling blissfully, let out a soft sigh. "Hmm... imagine, 3 months ago I saw you, and in the next 3 months, we are getting married. It feels surreal!" she whispered, almost as if in disbelief.

"We'll make these 3 months unforgettable," Sid said, his voice full of promise. "We'll fill them with memories to cherish, especially after we get married."

Sana nodded, her heart at ease, her peace settling deeper within her now that everyone had officially acknowledged their relationship. It felt real—so real that the emotions that had been building inside her since the beginning of this journey now flooded out like a gentle river.

Sid's family showered Sana with beautiful gifts—cosmetics, dresses, and a stunning white stone gold necklace set. In return, Sana's family offered Sid clothes, a gold chain, and other thoughtful gifts. The exchange of these items symbolized the coming together of their two worlds, and with each gift, their connection grew deeper.

Later, as the couple changed into their new clothes—Sana in a vibrant yellow saree with a golden border, the jewelry she received from Sid's family now adorning her—Sid dressed in a traditional Kerala silk shirt that had been specially purchased for him by Sana's father, and helped by Guru as he donned the gold chain given to him by Sana's family—they looked even more perfect together.

Once they were dressed, they gathered again for more rituals. Sid and Sana's foreheads were decorated with *Tikka* as blessings were showered upon them. In the presence of family and friends, they received *Kumkum*, turmeric, fruits, and coconut in the pallu of Sana's saree from her Amma, Kajal, and the other ladies. A beautiful *Aarti* was performed to ward off any evil eye and negativity.

The final rituals concluded, and everyone moved to the terrace, where a grand food setup had been arranged under a *Shamiyana* tent. Servers brought out a delicious lunch for everyone, and the air was filled with chatter and laughter. Sid and Sana's friends gathered around them, playfully urging them to feed each other sweets. Without hesitation, they happily complied, sharing a plate of sweets, their joy palpable.

As they fed each other, the world seemed to disappear. They were in their own bubble, savoring each moment, each bite, each smile. The photographer captured the moments, but nothing could compare to the bliss they were experiencing, a joy too pure to be captured by any camera. It was a day they would never forget—a day that marked the beginning of their journey together.

Sid and Sana were lost in the magic of the moment, not needing anything else but each other. Their hearts were intertwined, and the day, their love, and the journey ahead felt like a dream come true.

"Maa, Appa, and Amma... we have a request to make," Sana said after they finished their lunch and were sitting in the living room, chatting around with family and friends.

Everyone stopped when Sana, in a firm voice, grabbed their attention. All of them looked at both Sid and Sana, asking in gestures what had happened.

"Enna Kanna (what, my child)? What happened? You want something?" her Amma asked.

"Uncle, we have a request, and this is regarding our marriage," Sid said, holding Sana's hand while looking at her father.

"Haan, bolo beta... waise, you can call me Appa when you're calling Seetha Amma... then why this partiality?" he asked, laughing, his belly shaking with the laughter. He was happy and relaxed, seeing his daughter so happy and seeing how close Sid's family was and their beautiful house. A father always has the wish that his daughter should go to a family that is better off than he is. Seeing all the amenities, as a father, he felt peaceful, knowing he need not worry about his daughter's future.

"Sahi baat hain Sid, call him Papa or Appa... whatever you want," Maa said, instructing him.

"Haan... haan, teek hain... Appa... we had a wish regarding our marriage... can we say it?" Sid said, coming back to the topic.

"Of course, beta, anything. Bolo... if I am capable, I will definitely try to fulfill your wish. I promise that," Appa said, worried that Sid might be talking about something he couldn't afford to do. Wild thoughts started running through his mind about arranging finances. His face fell a bit with worry.

Chapter Forty-Four:
Sun And Moon Vows

"Appa, I know Maa has said that we will do the marriage rituals as per your tradition, and we love that decision. But... our marriage is between two families here, two cultures... and we want to merge both the rituals together, if you don't mind, like Sangeet, Haldi, Mehendi... In the morning, we can get married as per your customs in the temple, as per your wish, and then lunch... like you have planned. At night, on the same day, after the reception, can we marry again as per our customs!" Sid said hesitantly, a little doubtful of his suggestion.

"But Beta, why do you want that?" Maa asked, worried, thinking about why Sid, without any discussion with her, had put forth this idea!

"Maa, I know your wish... you have always dreamt about my marriage, worried about it. I know I have delayed my marriage. I am 35, and you have waited for long! But when I saw Sana, I knew she is the one. I want to fulfill your dreams about my marriage as well, Maa... and besides this, I heard you and Kajal talking..." Sid said, remembering the conversation he overheard when he was about to enter his mom's room after dinner two days ago.

Flashback

"Maa... mera dream bhaiya ki Barath main nach ne ka reh gaya... aap ne kyun bola to have marriage as per their rituals?" Kajal whined, saying it to Maa, lying down in her lap.

"Arre toh hum nachenge na... they also have some ritual like this... Bas Sid will not be in Godi but in the car... Unka marriage subah ke time hota hain, so you will dance in the morning..." Maa said, smiling, stroking Kajal's hair.

"Subah? Oh, I didn't know that... weird haina, but what about your dreams, Maa... apne itne sapne dekhe the... Sid ki shaadi main yeh karungi, woh karungi..." Kajal said, slacking her hands.

"Koi baat nahi... you know... beti ke maa-baap bahut sapne dekhte hain... Maine teri shaadi main sab armaan pure kiya na... they must also have it, right? And Sana ke parents itni muskil se agree hue hain for this marriage... This is the least I could do from our side..." she said.

"Phir bhi maa... You were all worried and exhausted during my time... Sid ki shaadi main, you would have enjoyed the rituals without tension and stress... sab reh gaya..." Kajal pestered her.

"Hmm..." Maa sighed and said, "For me, Sid's happiness is more important than anything else, Kajal... woh khush toh main khush huin... already itna late kar diya isne shaadi karne main, I just want to see him happily married to Sana. Bahut responsibility le hain bechare ne choti si umar main... I see him happy now, with her... It doesn't matter in which way he does... bas shaadi honi chahiye... agni ke saath phere le ke... agni ko sakshi maan ke, bade logo ke aashirwad se... and that will be achieved in their way of marriage rituals... right? Ab zyada mat soch." Patting Kajal's head, she laid down with a sulken face, which was noticed by Sid.

"We can do pre-marriage rituals, na Maa, at least... Sangeet, Haldi, Mehendi... I want to see Sana wearing the Lehenga given by us..." Kajal said, lying down near the sleeping Abhi.

"She will wear our Lehenga in the reception... we will have that after marriage at night... That is what Bala Bhaisaab said... Let's see... Pehle engagement toh jaye, Kajal... Tu kahan abhi se shaadi ke plans kar rahi hain... So jaa... I am tired," Maa said, shutting Kajal down and turning to the other side.

Brooding, Kajal turned and said, "Right... Pehle Sagai toh ho jaye... Good night, Maa..."

**

"You don't have to sacrifice your dreams for my happiness, Maa..." Sid said, holding his mom's hand.

She had tears in her eyes, welling up, seeing her loving son who never stops showing how adorable, responsible, and understanding he is.

"Appa, when Sid asked me about this, I was so excited and felt this was the right way... Imagine, we will be tied together, witnessed by the Sun and then by the moon & stars as well... I am so thrilled. We have always valued our families in our relationship and always kept them ahead of us... Even now, I want you, Maa, everyone to be happy and satisfied and not compromise with any of their dreams," Sana said, hugging Appa's arm sideways.

"Priya behen, we have already been indebted by your kindness. I have no problem at all with this idea... You could have told me before; I would have happily agreed for your side ritual wedding," Appa said with a little smile.

"Appa, so here's the plan..." Sid said with full enthusiasm.

"We will have Sangeet, Haldi, and Mehendi, followed by Tamil-style rituals on the morning of the wedding day. Then, in the evening, we have the reception planned, and we can do the North Indian Hindu style at night. I know it can be a bit tiring... but if we are together, we can figure it out, right?" he asked.

"Bilkul beta, I will take care of everything. Don't worry," Appa said with his chest broad.

"No... no... You will not take care of everything... not at all... This marriage is just not your responsibility... I will be taking care of half of the responsibility. The morning will be taken care of by you... the evening by me... expenses, caterers, guests, venue... everything," Sid said in a firm, strong voice.

"Arree... aise kaise... We, as the daughter's family, will do it... It is our duty... Beta... we won't want anything to be shared. I have saved enough for Sana's marriage and I am also taking a loan for it... Guru is also helping me out... You don't have to worry about it. It's all planned and sorted. No more discussions about this," Appa said forcefully, with furrowed brows, but in a healthy way.

Sid went towards him. Everyone in the living room was witnessing the scene—silent murmurs, just gesturing at each other. Some with adoration, some questioning, some surprised. Various prying eyes were waiting to see what was ahead.

"Appa... I call you that. Do you consider me your son?" Sid asked.

"Yes... yes... no doubt... you... you are my second son," Appa said, stammering as he saw Sid so close to him. He was sitting on the sofa, and Sid sat next to him on the right, with Sana on the left armrest. Appa was hesitant being so close to him, as Sid was his son-in-law, and he had to give him the respect. He sat up straight, getting up from his relaxed posture, his spine straight, shoulders stiff.

"This marriage is not just about me and your daughter; it's two families coming together. Like this house is getting a daughter, your house will get a son in me. I am also getting married in this, and I have the full right to spend my savings on my marriage. I want to equally participate in it. Agar mere Papa hote toh, he would have done the same... haina, Maa? Traditionally, the bride's family is responsible for paying for all wedding expenses. But I want to break that stereotype, Appa... Our marriage has already managed to break your beliefs and customary thoughts about religion and caste, right? You valued people more than your beliefs, didn't you? So I want to break this traditional way as well... Please honor my decision, Appa," Sid requested with a firm, tenacious voice.

"Appa, Amma... aapko jaise dhoom dham se meri shaadi karni ho, karo... We are not asking you to compromise on anything you desire. But Sid, Maa, Kajal Di... also have desires, and I think we should respect that, haina Pa? Even the Dharma Shastra doesn't have a stipulation about who should defray the expenses of the wedding," Sana said, explaining her point of view.

Both parents couldn't say anything. Their eyes were brimming with tears, overwhelmed with pride at the maturity their children were showing.

"Ab chup hi rahoge, Appa? Kuch bolo na... Otherwise, we will just do court marriage... koi siyappa hi nahi... done dana done," Sana said with a frown, pouting.

"Chup... Pagal... kuch bhi bolti hain..." her Amma said, wiping her tears.

"Sid beta, what do I say... I don't know what good deed I did to get a Mappilai (Damad) like you... You are showing us an example of how a son should be and what I will also do in Guru's marriage. I totally respect your decision and honor it. We will do as you please. Priya Behen... aap khush hain na? You have raised a good son; you must be a proud mother, I must say. Kush raho..." Appa said, joining his palms and bowing down his head, with tears coming down his eyes.

"Arre Appa, endique aruverel? (Why are you crying?)" Sana asked, coming down and wiping his tears.

"Tears for contentment, Kanna (Bacha)..." he replied, hugging her.

Sid was happy. He hugged his mom and Kajal, and everyone congratulated him, praising him for his thoughts. Some elderly ladies of his family were critical, but he didn't care about them. He always did what he felt was right, not bothering about people, except what his mother thought, and she was proud of him, and that was what mattered to him.

When he listened to Kajal and Mom's talks the other day, he immediately called Sana and discussed what needed to be done. It was Sana's idea to make his mother's dream possible by getting married in both rituals. He smiled thinking of her exact words...

"Sid... we will do 14 Phere... imagine... our bond will be the strongest... Suraj ke saath saath... Chand aur Taare bhi gawah honge hamari shaadi ke..."

He might be shining right now in front of everyone like a star, but the light he was producing came from the Sun—his Sana, who was behind him, giving ideas and suggestions, supporting him like a life partner, like a companion, like a teammate.

Both of them gave a satisfactory smile, eyes fixed on each other, thanking each other, their faces emitting gratitude and love for one another...

Chapter Forty-Five:
The Rhythm of Us

Things do not need to be perfect to make us happy, and pursuing perfection in our lives can actually make us less happy. Happiness is more of a skill that we can work on every day by actively choosing thoughts, connections, and beliefs that make us feel good. Sana and Sid were reflecting every part of themselves with felicity and aptness.

Sana had started her MBA evening classes. Sid would drop her off every day after work and also pick her up at night. Sometimes, when he couldn't, he would ask Guru to pick her up. They were getting into a flow of their routine. Sana didn't have to give false excuses to meet Sid anymore; she would just ask her parents genuinely and meet him. He would now come to her flat to pick her up, not hiding behind the entrance gate to pick and drop. At night, while dropping her off, Amma would almost every day call him up, feed him with her special snacks and food, and also pack some for his mom.

Sid had come very close to Sana's parents. He bonded very well with Appa, talking about current affairs, news, sports, financial tips... everything that came to their minds. Appa had been a cricket buff, and Sid, being a cricket player in his early years, would spend most of his time talking and watching the game. Guru would join them both, and it was a trio team hooting and shouting at each ball and scoring. This made Sana and Amma frustrated as they missed all the serials and movies during that time, while the boys demanded snacks and drinks, keeping them busy in the kitchen.

Sana had also fought with Sid once, as she felt he wasn't giving her the proper attention.

"Tum jab dekho yeh cricket... cricket... dekhte rehte ho... Appa and Anna kam the jo tum bhi join ho gaye pareshan karne?"

she frowned, pouting her lips while coming back from her evening class in the car.

"Important match hain aaj... yaar Sana, please ab doobara mat shuru kar... Just a few more days, uske baad yeh league khatam ho jayega. After that, all my time is yours, baby. Tere ko full attention dunga. I promise," he said, parking the car in front of Sana's flat and hastily getting out of the car.

Sana came out as well, taking her belongings. "Teek hain, then I will not talk to you till then. Baitho apna cricket le ke... Hugh," she shrugged her neck and followed him upstairs.

Sid didn't take any heed of her words and rushed inside as the match had already started, and it was a crucial one. He decided to deal with her later since she was very easy to crack and could be easily diverted with a click of his fingers now. He knew her too well! She was an open book—young, naïve, and innocent, which, at her age, was exactly how one should be.

"Amma... coffee milega, please?" Sid asked casually, as though he were asking his own mom. It had been more than a month since their engagement, and he had been regularly coming to her place almost every day. Watching matches with her dad and brother had made their bond even stronger. He missed the days when he used to watch the match with his dad, who was always critical of his comments. Now, he either watched it alone in the confinement of his house, where Maa was least interested, or at the club with friends, which had become increasingly rare as most of them were married and had family responsibilities.

"It's late, Sid. Dinner time ho gaya hain... I am making Masala Dosa today with sambhar. First, have that, and then I will make coffee after that, okay?" Amma said, smiling. She knew he loved dosa and any South Indian cuisine. He loved simple, plain food and South Indian cuisine, mostly sane of masalas and oils, which was perfect for him—healthy and tasty. Amma didn't feel the hesitation with him anymore that she once did. Now, as her son-in-law, she treated him with respect, sometimes even more than needed. Sid had a way of making everyone feel comfortable around him; his friendly and inclusive attitude made him approachable and likable.

"Wow, Dosa... ya ya... I will eat that first, then. Kitna hua score, Guru?" Sid said, sitting down on the couch and pushing Guru in the middle next to Appa.

Sana's mood was volatile. She couldn't handle Sid's negligence towards her anymore. This had gone too far, and she was determined to teach him a lesson and give him a taste of his own medicine. She didn't approach him the entire evening and night. She thought he would miss her, but to her shock, he hadn't even bothered to call or think about her. He was completely engrossed in the match, the whole three hours of the twenty-twenty match.

"Amma, yeh Appa ke saath kaise manage karte ho, when he ignores you and gets glued to this stupid TV and match all the time?" Sana asked, lying down with her mom in her room.

"Aadat pad gayi hain... I know he will come back to me only after his source of distraction. Sometimes, it's okay to have that type of distance, you know. I get my time to do stuff that I always want to do, which otherwise I don't. Jaise ki dekh, aaj maine apna pedicure kar liya... ghar baithe baithe, itne dino se soch rahi thi karne ko," Amma said, smiling and touching her clean, soft foot after the nice warm cleanup, followed by foot cream application, just before lying down on the bed.

"Hmm... but mereko irritation ho rahi hain. Sid is not giving me attention; he is not even glancing at me or missing my presence! Aaahhhh..." Sana expressed her sorrow audibly.

"Pagal, purre din toh tere saath hota hain, subah se leke shaam tak. Tereko pick karna, lunch saath karna, college drop karna, pick karna... yahan soch, hamara Beta jaise ho gaya hain. Sab se kaise gul mil gaya hain. How many ways is he giving you attention?

Kuch der apna mann ka bhi karne de, he is not doing this purposefully na Kanna (bacha). Jab kabhi tera time aayega aur tu kissi cheez mein mast busy ho jayegi, tab he will realize the feeling of being ignored. You both will learn to balance and learn to cope with these situations. Sometimes tereko samajhna padega, sometimes usko," Amma said very simply, offering some wisdom from her 26 years of marriage, teaching Sana how to face this situation in the future.

"Ya... right. Maybe I am expecting too much. I should not complain like this. Kitna karta hain woh," Sana said, yawning, and hugged her mother from behind, dozing off in the bed. Appa had to sleep in Sana's bed after the match. Sid, too, didn't disturb her when he left the house. He surely wanted to say goodnight, but seeing her sleeping, hugging, and cuddling in her mom's arms, he didn't have the heart to wake her up after the tiring day.

**

It was a weekend, and the wedding cards were printed. Guru had gone to Delhi to pick them up with Sid. Sana had chosen a fancy one, a banana leaf style, giving a South Indian touch to the card. Sid left his mom to choose, and he picked from the top three she liked: a simple red wedding invitation.

Just a month left for their wedding, and everyone was excited. Sana and her parents had started shopping for clothes and jewelry. They had booked Guruvayoorapan Temple (Krishna Temple) in Mayur Vihar for the morning South-style Iyer wedding. They had a big dining hall and a banquet hall just for the wedding, with rooms attached for changing. It was a comfortable venue and within Sana's Appa's budget. Caterers were booked, and it was almost a three-day wedding ritual. All the relatives from Chennai and Kerala would be attending the wedding, and they expected a huge gathering. Appa had a large friend circle, having worked in Ghaziabad for more than 15 years, so he had many people to invite to his only daughter's wedding. He wished to make it grand.

Amma and Appa planned to go to Chennai and Kerala to personally invite all the relatives. They asked Sana and Guru to come with them, as they also planned to buy some jewelry, silk sarees, and clothes for Sid and his family from there. Guru couldn't make it, but Sana happily agreed to go with them, though Sid was agitated by her decision.

"I have to go, Sid. Dadi hain and Tau ji hain, they didn't agree on this... pata hain na... Appa ne kaise taise unke against jaa ke agree kiya hain... I need to go with him, to support him and be with him when they question him. I know he can handle them, but phir bhi... samajo na..." Sana said, trying to make him understand.

"Kaise rahunga ek hafte yaar tere bina... Main bhi chalu? I will also be there to support him... koi mayaka lal unhe question karke toh dekhe..." he said, arguing with her.

"No, na Sid... acha nahi lagega, aise shaadi se pehle tumhara humare saath aana... Baad mein le chalungi, I promise... ab jayda gussa mat karo na... I will be in phone all the time, video calling you and messaging you... tumhe hi toh choose karna hain meri shaadi ki saree bhi... You will get bored shopping also... please na, just one week..." she tried to make him comply.

"Hmm... teek hain jaa... kya bolu..." he said with a sullen face. They were sitting in Sana's terrace under the moonlight; it was 11pm at night. Sana's back was on Sid's chest. They were sitting on the floor, Sid's left leg folded up and Sana's face supported on that, her arms around his leg. There was silence after the agreement. Both of them were sad about the upcoming distance. She had to leave the next day on an afternoon flight.

Sana abruptly broke the silence and sang very softly in a melodious voice, watching the crescent moon...

Bade acche lagte hain

Yeh dharti, yeh nadiyaa, yeh rainaa

Aur tum...

Hum tum kitne paas hain

Kitne door hain chaand sitare

Sach poochho to mann ko jhoothe lagte hain yeh saare

Magar sachche lagte hain

Yeh dharti, yeh nadiyaa, yeh rainaa,

Aur tum...

Sid joined as well with her, holding her hand, bringing her close to him, and kissing her gently on her cheek...

Tum in sab ko chhod ke kaise kal subah jaogi

Mere saath inhe bhi to tum yaad bahut aaogi

Bade acche lagte hain

Yeh dharti, yeh nadiyaa, yeh rainaa aur

Aur tum...

Absence makes the heart grow fonder. Absence diminishes mediocre passions and increases great ones, as the wind extinguishes candles and fans fires. Being close gives one physical connectivity to a partner, but sometimes distance makes emotional intimacy stronger. Love knows no distance, it eyes for stars and can travel anywhere.

Sid said, "I will exist in two places: here and where you are."

Sana replied back, "It doesn't matter where I am, I am yours and will stay here... in your heart... and you in mine."

They kissed each other like there was no tomorrow...

Chapter Forty-Six:
A Path of Togetherness

The most important thing in the world is family and love. Nothing is better than going home to family, eating good food, and relaxing in the arms of your loved ones.

Sana's family was able to somehow convince her Paati (Daadi) after a lot of struggle. When she was convinced, all other family members happily embraced Sana's selection to get married to the one she loved. It actually instilled faith in another cousin Sana had, who was in love himself but was scared to disclose it to his parents. But he, too, opened up about his love, considering the apt situation and timing. Though everyone was shocked, they had no choice but to accept his proposal.

"Sid... oh my God... Sid! Tum vishwaas nahi karoge, Appa ne kya jawaab diya Paati ko... I mean, she was stunned by all his counterarguments. Woh toh tumhe mujhse zyada pyaar karte hain ab... I mean, ek word nahi bolne diya unhe tumhare khilaf. Kya jaadu kar diya tumne... Pehle mere saath, then now with Appa and Amma also... Bas shaadi mein sab aayenge aur aise hi apna jaadu bikherte rahna sab pe... Hehehehe..." she giggled, jumping onto the bed to lay down while on a video chat with him.

"Ab hum hain hi aise cheez ki koi pyaar kiye bina reh hi nahi sakta," he laughed along with her.

"You know Appa's cousin bhaiya ka beta, my brother Mani Anna, he is also in love with someone who works in his office. She is from Kerala, a totally different caste and religion. He expressed his wish to marry her in front of Paati... I mean, hum sab yahan already try kar rahe hain for my alliance, but jab unhone bola, toh everyone was shocked... Sab ka attention shifted to him, and that made our acceptance easier. Everything happens for good, haina?" she said, smiling.

A week went by quickly, with wedding cards being distributed personally to all the close relatives in Chennai, Kerala, and also Palakkad City (a border city between Tamil Nadu and Kerala) where their ancestral temple is. They prayed there for Sid and Sana to complete the marriage smoothly, offering the wedding card to the deity as well, seeking blessings. They shopped in Kanchipuram and got authentic silk sarees, silk dhotis, and wedding clothes for Sid, Sana, and their relatives from weavers at wholesale prices.

Guru and Sid both went to Delhi airport to pick them up. They had a lot of luggage coming back, so two cars were needed. Sid was happy to see Sana and her parents after a week of distance. He asked Sana to sit with him in his car, and Appa also nodded in approval. She hurriedly went to sit with him.

They were both waiting to hug each other, which they couldn't do in front of the crowd, but as soon as they saw Guru drive off, they hugged each other in the parking lot itself. Sana had a soulful smile plastered on her face the whole time. Sid squeezed her body, hugging her tightly.

"Sid... I am here..." Sana said, feeling the intensity of his hug. She kissed his shoulder, his neck, and his hair, caressing it softly to calm him down. He, too, loosened his grip to kiss her back on her neck, sniffing her fragrance.

"I missed your smell..." he said.

He softly bit her shoulder, and she hissed a moan.

"Aaahhh... Sid... please... don't bite... kiss me..." she demanded in a soft voice.

Sid chuckled at her and brought his lips close to hers, breathing out warm, heavy breaths.

"I want it too..." he said and sucked her lips passionately, roaming his hands over her neck and all over her curves, feeling her presence, bringing her close to him in the confinements of the car, which he had missed the whole week.

He opened her hair, which was clutched up in a bun, and smelled it.

"I like it open..." he said and kissed her back again.

She touched his chiseled chest, sneaking her fingers inside his T-shirt to feel his bare skin, then snuggled him from the waist.

"We should leave now... Anna must have reached halfway... and we are still at the airport!" she said after 30 minutes of their amorous kissing and caressing.

"Hmm... Maa is going to Kanpur tonight to invite Kajal and her in-laws personally... she will be back the day after..." Sid said.

"Yes, I know... she told me. Kajal Di is very excited," Sana replied.

"Is there anything that you don't know?" Sid asked, smiling.

"Nahi... I know everything. Main roj baat karti thi un dono se... sometimes even video conferencing... I am up to date, you know," Sana said, folding up her legs as usual and increasing the volume of the song, a new number playing on the radio.

Sid took her legs and started massaging them unconsciously as part of their normal routine, and she willingly gave her other leg as well to receive the same attention.

"Kal office skip karte hain... college bhi... we will spend the whole day at my place... okay?" Sid said, eyeing her response.

"I just took off last week... job se nikal denge mujhe itni chhuttiyan loongi toh! Nahi, I don't think it's a good idea..." she simply snubbed him.

"I have everything settled... don't worry. I have arranged time off for you; my meetings are taken care of... aur college mein bhi bol diya hain..." he said, concentrating on the road with a very serious expression.

"Hugh!! Yeh sab kab kiya tumne... You didn't even ask me? Plan kya hain tumhara? Why does it sound fishy to me!" she said, looking at him with raised brows.

"Kiya hain kuch plan... bas... I know just three weeks are left for our marriage... but mere se nahi ho raha!" he said, brushing his hair nervously while waiting at the traffic signal, fearing her reaction to his brief comment.

"Kya plan kiya hain... You are scaring me now... Is it what I am thinking?" she asked curiously, her eyes wide.

"What are you thinking?" he asked with a mischievous smile creeping onto his face.

"Wohi... gandi baat!" she said, her face turning red.

"Gandi baat!! Woh kya hota hai?" he laughed out loud. This girl could turn any serious topic hilarious, he thought.

"Hayee... Sid... mere ko kuch kuch ho raha hain... mat kar... mat kar... mat kar aisa!!" she said, covering her face with her palms, feeling timid and shy.

"Baby, maine kya kiya? Abhi toh kuch kiya bhi nahi... kal ke liye rakh yeh kuch kuch... abhi car chalane de... don't distract me with your red, shining face..." he said, continuously smiling and chuckling as he watched her.

He had been very tense about talking to her about this, but she made it so easy for him. Her innocent talks and gestures could lighten any situation. It was a quality he adored in her.

This distance from her made him impatient. The closer you are to someone, the more intolerable the distance becomes between the two. It is hard to be patient sometimes when your whole body is on fire thinking about someone special and missing their physical proximity. The heart becomes impatient with matters that appear to be superficial and have merely extrinsic value, as it wants to achieve its desires as fast as possible.

Sid and Sana's hearts were fully invested in resources, including time and effort. Theirs was a profound love, and marriage paradise was around the corner. There was no need to rush into anything, but they had endured waiting and had persevered through the difficulties entailed with the beliefs and egos of society. Having a patient heart is an expression of profound love; it involves both excitement and calmness. Hadn't he been that?

The night went by with twisting and turning. Sana's heart was pounding, whooshing, roaring, and rumbling, anticipating the next morning. She had the same passion inside her that Sid had, though she had been less vocal about it. They were both introverts by nature but balanced each other perfectly. She knew and understood him completely. He had been a gentleman throughout, during passionate moments and weak times, never trying to force or intimidate her with any of his wishes or advances.

But now, he had the right to ask for it. They had fought together for this relationship, and the ultimate moment was just around the corner... their marriage in just three weeks.

Yes, her heart told her. She was ready for whatever the day would bring. This man, her love, her polite, calm, and considerate-to-be life partner, had been the most chivalrous, courteous, and respectful towards her. What reason did she have to decline his wish to show his love for her? She had none.

A few weeks back, Amma had shared some wisdom about this with her. She had felt shy hearing it, but now she was grateful as she knew what to expect.

"Sana, see, we as humans have this feeling of sex, and it is very natural."

"Amma... kya hain... why are you saying it so explicitly?" Sana shrieked in shock when her mother talked about something like this, which had never been discussed before.

"Everything has its time to talk. Now I have to tell you about this, and I will discuss it very clearly. You should know... Jab tera khana seekhne ka age hua, toh sikhaya na... Saaf safai rakhna, kapde sambhalna... uss age mein sab time pe, we as parents have to teach kids. Now you are getting married, and you should know about SEX. It's not wrong to say it out loud when you will soon face it," Amma said with authority and confidence.

"I know about it, Ma. School mein education diya tha... aur Payal Di ne bhi bataya hain iske baare mein... I am well aware of it... Please, mujhe sharam aa rahi hain aapke samne iske baare mein baat karne mein... I am going," Sana said, getting up from her parents' bed, where they were both applying nail polish.

Guru and Appa had gone to the market to buy groceries and vegetables, and both mother and daughter were enjoying their girl time.

Amma pulled her hand and made her sit again.

"Chup chap baith jaa... warna maar khayegi mere se... Jab bol rahi hoon toh sunn le bas... tujhe kuch kehne ki zaroorat nahi hain... just listen... Okay."

Sana nodded her head, twisting her lips, and with a blushed face, sat opposite her mom on the bed.

"Sana, like how we get hungry and eat food, right? Humko toilet aata hain toh jaate hain na... Same, this is also a natural phenomenon. Bas hamari society mein iske baare mein baat karo toh taboo hain! Theek bhi hain, sab cheez ka age hota hain, time hota hain... Yeh koi galat cheez nahi hain, jo tu itna weird feel kar rahi hain. This is a way of showing love to your better half. Jaise Appa mere liye subah coffee banake dete hain, I love it... main unke pasand ka khana bana ke deti hoon. We show affection in different forms. This is one of the ways to show your affection and love, and it is pious and should be righteous when you love someone."

She explained everything—the process, what to expect, how to enjoy, how to participate equally, and how to respect the other person in the act. She also emphasized not keeping any affliction towards it. As parents, they have immense experience in teaching their kids properly rather than a friend who may not have experienced it themselves or have limited knowledge about it.

If a parent doesn't do that, they risk their children drowning in erroneous interpretations, feeling vulnerable in a highly sexualized world, and becoming isolated from open communication with them. Sex education at home is not a magic chalice, but it will guide children toward sexual health. What they do with that knowledge is up to them, but providing it is the responsibility of a parent or someone knowledgeable about it.

Chapter Forty-Seven:
Embracing Love

It was an important day for Sana and Sid, the day they were finally going to consummate their love after five months of courtship, struggles, and ups and downs. Both of them were prepared. Sana had thought she would experience this moment after marriage, but she was ready—for the man she loved and who would be her husband in just three weeks.

She was doubtful if she was doing the right thing, having been taught since birth to be careful, honest, and trustworthy. She was nervous about this day, but his face calmed her down. The one she was about to surrender herself to was none other than her comrade, her companion—the one her heart had approved, the one her parents had approved.

She made efforts to prepare herself—cleaned herself well and kept a sanitary pad in her purse. Her mother had told her about the bleeding she might have the first time. She was grateful to her mother because, thanks to her, she knew what to expect. She also kept a painkiller, just in case.

She chose a long red skirt with gold prints that matched a white turtleneck long-sleeved sweater tucked into the skirt. It was getting chilly in Ghaziabad in November. Her freshly washed hair was left open, just the way he liked. A little moisturizer, kohl in her eyes, red lipstick—sans bindi today—red looped jhumka earrings, and a red scarf around her neck completed the look. She didn't need a blush; she was already blushing naturally today. The reflection in the mirror was just for his eyes' delight—only his.

She told her parents she was going to work today—just one last excuse, she thought. It was for him and for herself, too. She didn't feel guilt; she was ecstatic today, anxious, happy, and full of excitement. She headed out on time with her purse and lunch box, just as if she were going to work.

He was waiting for her outside, below her flat entrance.

"Sid, good morning, beta. I have packed breakfast and lunch with Sana—khaa lena, okay? I know Priya Behen nahi hain, you must be hungry. Raat ko aa jana for dinner, okay? Bye... Bye, Sana..." Amma said, waving to them from the balcony.

He just nodded and said bye to her.

They drove to his home in silence. No one uttered a word. Sana just sat stiff, fidgeting with her fingers nervously. It was only a five-minute drive, but he drove fast, at full speed. He couldn't say anything to her—kept silent as well. He was nervous, too.

He parked the car in his garage and closed the gate. She was still sitting inside, praying silently, biting her lips.

He opened the car door. "Bahar aa ja," he said, the first words he had spoken.

She took her bags, stepped out, and followed him.

He looked dashing—fresh from the shower, wet hair, and his gray shirt showing water patches on the back. He was wearing white jeans with it. He smelled glorious—like fresh musk. He looked sexy. The top four buttons of his shirt were undone, revealing his chiseled chest, which she loved to caress, especially the hair on it, which gave her a strange sensory calmness.

She kept her belongings on the sofa and rushed toward the kitchen to drink some water.

"Chai bana de, Sana," he said, opening her lunch box to eat breakfast.

He didn't like the aloofness she was showing towards him. He had had a rough night. In the morning, he had overslept and messed up his schedule—and the plan. He had wanted to prepare the room with candles and flowers. He hadn't been able to do any arrangements. He was upset with himself for being this edgy and hysterical.

"Haan…" That's what she said since she sat down in the car—otherwise chatty, her.

He opened the first lunch box he saw and gobbled down the food. He saw Sana coming inside with a tray in her hand and two cups of chai.

"Arre… kya hain, Sid? This was lunch… breakfast wala box yeh tha! Tum bhi na… Chalo, koi na… ab lunch mein breakfast khana… Aur yeh kya? Tum pura chat kar gaye! Mere liye kuch bhi nahi rakha?" she scowled and glared at him.

"Subah se mute button mein thi, ab kaise chapar-chapar bol rahi hain!" Sid lazed down on the sofa, keeping both hands on the headrest and legs spread on the table.

"Pehle uthho aur haath dho ke aao… Go! Then only you can drink tea. Table pe khaana rakha hain, wahin pe bhi rakh rahe ho… Hato!" she complained, pushing his legs down and pulling his hands up to make him stand.

He came back after washing his hands and gargling his mouth.

"Kya mast poori aur aloo sabzi banati hain teri Amma… Restaurant khol dete hain unke naam ka—just poori and sabzi in mornings… Mast profit aayega," he said, sitting down and sipping the chai, pouting his lips to blow out the steam before drinking.

Sana loved to watch him eat and drink. His mannerisms while consuming food were fascinating. He always appreciated and relished food—a quality she loved about him.

"Hmm… Appa also says the same," Sana said, sitting down facing him on his left.

"Why are you so silent and composed today?" he asked abruptly.

"Why are YOU silent and composed today?" she asked him the same, emphasizing you.

"Pehle maine poocha… Bol!" he asked.

"Nahi, ladies first… First, answer my question," she artifice.

"Same reason that you have," he hoaxed, smiling.

"Acha? What is my reason? Bada pata hain tumhe," she befuddled and sat straight, folding up her legs on the sofa.

He didn't say anything. After a while, he asked, "Sana, let's go to Agra. It's just a three-hour drive. We have a full day today… Aise tension wala tera reserved face nahi hazam ho raha… I want my happy, smiling, full-of-life Sana…"

Sana jerked her face towards him and exclaimed, "Just don't blame me… Look at you! Tum nahi ho tension mein aur reserved se? Warna car mein baithe hi… Huggy do… Kissy do… Haath do… Pair do… ka mantra padte ho! Aaj abhi tak touch bhi nahi kiya! Huggghhh!!! Bade aaye ghar bula kar plan karne waale… 'Kuch kuch kal ke liye rakhna'—huh! Phat khud ki rahi hain aur mujhe kehne waale… 'I want full-of-life Sana!' Full hi hoon! Dekha bhi nahi aaj mujhe, kitne pyaar se ready hoke aayi thi tumhare liye… Ab Shahab ji ko Agra jaana hain… Kkkkk… Mmmm…"

She squealed and tried to mimic him mockingly but was interrupted in the middle by Sid with a tight, fierce kiss—biting her lips, sucking, and devouring each part of her inside.

He couldn't stop himself from embracing this beautiful-hearted girl who made his nervous heart calm just with her spirited talks. He felt the kiss expand beyond their bodies, whirling them around, swirling them into the stars. He picked her up in his arms and walked towards his room. It was messy, with an unfolded comforter and an unmade bed, but that didn't matter to either of them... Their eyes were just hooked into each other, passion burning inside them. Both of them went deep inside, seeing the honest, unspoken, and undiscovered parts of their love.

They explored every part of each other's bodies—foreplaying, stripping down not only their clothes but also their thoughts, perceptions, and inhibitions. Feeling each other, smelling, tasting, and touching with lust and passion. They consummated their love, completing each other, and became one. They felt emotionally and physically gratified.

"Thanks, Sana..." Sid said, cuddling her as she lay above him, the comforter covering their naked bodies. His right hand was intertwined with her left, while his left hand fondled the skin of her waist.

"Love you bolte hain, thanks nahi..." she pouted, spanked his chest, and laid down on it, listening to his calming heartbeat, playing with his thick fingers that gave her an undying pleasure she never knew before.

He chuckled. "Woh toh hain hi... but I really want to thank you for showing trust in me, having faith in me, and giving something so precious to me."

"Stupid... Don't expect any thanks from me, haan... Tumne bhi toh diya... something precious to me... So... it's same same..." she said in a very low voice.

"Hmm... I love you, Sana," he said, picking her up from under her arms like she was a feather, weightless, and kissed her again, bringing her to his left side, clasping her under him. "I can't wait to get married to you... Kaise rahunga main yeh 3 hafte..." he said restlessly, moving her hair away from her face.

She touched the edges of his face, grazing his jaw and lip lines, calming him, turning him to lay on his back while she laid her head on his arm, facing him. "Mat socho... Think of it as just three weeks... It will pass in the blink of an eye. Let's plan what we will do further... Hum, honeymoon mein kahan jaaye?" she asked, trying to change his worried mood and compose him. She couldn't see him sulking when she knew she would be there with him all the time.

"I didn't think about that! Kahan jaana hain tujhe? Bol, we will go there!" he said, thrilled.

"I love to travel. I want to visit all the places in the world with you. Appa used to take us to many places every summer vacation and other holidays. Chennai toh jaate hi the, but besides that, we used to go to Mussoorie, Dehradun, Haridwar, Rishikesh, Nainital... You know, I realized traveling makes our feet learn how to form their own paths, and our hearts begin to beat to a different rhythm. The more time we spend away from familiar routines, the more we learn to embrace the unknown and abandon ourselves into the great vastness of the universe," she reflected, sharing her abstract thoughts with him.

"Wow, I love what you just said... Tu toh badi philosophical baatein bhi karti hain, meri Chamak Challo," he said, smiling and feeling proud of her.

"Abhi tumne mujhe jaana hi kahan hai... Aage aage dekho, bahut saare rang dikhenge..." she said, playing with his chest hair again.

"Waise, I love mountains. I wish to see snow-clad mountains sometime in my life… Just watch them and admire them," she said feebly, tired and exhausted after two hours of a soul-consuming act.

He patted her head and dozed off with her, his heart and mind content and satisfied.

Chapter Forty-Eight:
A Tapestry of Love

Three days were left for the marriage, and guests at Sana's place had already arrived from various states and countries. Appa had arranged for their stay in a few apartments within the community itself. Cooks were arranged, and the preparations were in full swing. The pre-wedding rituals began today at Sana's place.

Today was Sumangali Prarthanai (Suhagan Pooja or seeking blessings from married women), the first ritual before a wedding in a Tamil Brahmin home.

It is a ritual where brides seek the blessings of the Suhagans to enjoy a long-lasting marriage. The female ancestors who have passed away as Sumangalis (Suhagans) are remembered and their blessings are sought. Five or seven women, along with two kanyas (girls who have not attained puberty), are called for the pooja, and they are offered oil, herbal powder shampoo for hair, turmeric, and vermillion. Nine-yard silk sarees are gifted to them, and they are requested to be seated for the pooja. To make the event more lively, they even sing songs. They are treated to a feast. All the gathered ladies of the family, along with the bride, perform a Namaskaram (a gesture of greeting and seeking goodwill) to all the Suhagans and Kanyas, who, in turn, bless the family and the bride.

The evening was Mehendi, and Sana was the most excited about this. She dressed herself in a light green sleeveless Kurti and capris—she looked gorgeous. Everyone complimented her, and Kajal also joined in to participate in the sangeet for some time. Payal Di, as she was training in a beautician course, tried her makeup skills on her. Sana's friends and cousins applied mehendi, dancing around to Hindi and Tamil beats. The atmosphere was filled with fun and enjoyment. Guru was busy managing chores and last-minute financial transactions. Appa and Amma were occupied with taking care of guests and hospitality. Sana applied mehendi fully on both her hands and legs with the latest designs. Sid loves Mehendi, and she made sure to fill every part of her hands and legs with it.

The next day was Mangala Snaanam (auspicious/purifying bath). Turmeric and sandalwood paste ubtan were applied to both Sana and Sid in their respective homes. After this application, they were made to take a bath in holy water and get ready for the wedding rituals. Turmeric is a disinfectant as well as a natural beautifier. The holy water is said to cleanse the body and soul, making the bride and groom ready for a new life together.

The house was decorated beautifully with fresh flowers, adding grandeur to the ritual. Vedic mantras were recited in Sana's house as per Tamil Brahmin marriage rituals to sanctify the bride and prepare her for the upcoming challenges of married life. Surya (Sun God) and Varuna (Water God) were invoked to purify the bride and make her 'spiritually ready' for the wedding.

That day, by afternoon, everyone in Sana and Sid's house traveled to the temple where the marriage venue was. The night was the engagement ceremony (Nichayathartham, also known as Roka or Tilak in Hindi), in which all the elders from both sides performed the same engagement ceremony they had 3 months back. Sana was dressed in a purple silk saree, and Sid in a cream silk kurta. Both of them couldn't take their eyes off each other. Sana sneaked in and showed him her Mehendi, and Sid gestured his compliment with his eyebrow, admiring it. Surrounded by the crowd, they hardly got any moments to talk to each other. Though they were frustrated, they were happy from the heart to finally see the day they had dreamed about.

It was followed by Jaanavasam (Baarat), the grand procession of the groom's party when they arrived at the marriage venue for the wedding. Traditionally, the instrument of nadaswaram (similar to Shehnai) is played. Kajal, Sid's friends, and family danced and had a lot of fun as they added a Dhol to the music. The wedding party was welcomed by Sana's family, and gifts were exchanged. Later on, everyone visited the temple to seek blessings.

All the rituals for that day were completed with a grand dinner. Finally, at night, when the elders settled in their rooms to sleep, Sana and Sid's cousins and friends planned a surprise for them. Sana's parents and Sid's mom knew about it and gave them the green signal to go with the plan. Payal Di and Neelima (Sana's friend) were sharing a room with Sana, and they made her wear a light blue lehenga while Payal Di did light makeup on her.

"I am tired, Di. Tomorrow, I have to wake up at 4 AM. It's my wedding day, Di. Why are you doing a makeup trial on me now?" Sana asked, exhausted from the day-long rituals.

"Chal... mere saath," Di said, pulling her hand and walking toward the exit.

"Kahan? It's already 11 PM! Are you crazy? If Appa finds out, I'll be dead. I can't die unmarried before my wedding!" Sana replied.

"Surprise hai, baby... Chal, time ho raha hai," Di said. "Neelima, go and check if everyone has come," Di instructed.

Perplexed, Sana just walked behind Di, who was pulling her by the wrist. They reached the main hall, where the place was decorated with a Mandap for the next day's big day, looking outstanding. She saw a musical orchestra set up, and her cousins and Sid's friends were surrounding it. Kajal Di was bringing Sid, who was dressed in the same light blue kurta, looking dashing. They both just stood still, looking at each other, forgetting the crowd around them. They were in the middle of the hall when suddenly the lights went off. Sana unconsciously went toward Sid and grabbed his arm.

"Hayee, kya hua?" she asked.

"Acha hua, chal bhag te hain... tere se baat karne ke liye tadap raha hoon... Teen din ho gaye, sahi se dekha bhi nahi tujhe..." Sid said, moving backward with her.

Suddenly, they heard music from the orchestra, and the focus light was on Rahul and his wife. They both were dressed exactly like Sid and Sana, portraying them. They danced and acted out all the incidents from the start—how they met, how they proposed, their car rides, family meet, terrace meet... All the secrets known to Payal Di, Rahul, Kajal, and Sumit were disclosed to everyone, surprising Sid and Sana. They were seated in chairs together, watching the show, blushing and smiling. Everyone participated in their characters, including Guru Anna, to Sana's surprise!

"Aaj toh hamarey sare poll khul gaye yahan!" Sana said, embarrassed. Then she saw Sid being pulled towards the middle of the stage. Her eyes grew wide, anticipating something like this to her; she was not prepared to take center stage with all eyes on her. She was nervous, and then she heard his voice that calmed her nervous, edgy heart—the voice that made her smile, blush, and skip a beat...

"I still remember the day I saw you for the first time... you looked like an angel in that pink suit. I was astounded by your beauty, my heartbeat was pounding like never before, giving me signs that you are the one. I never believed in love at first sight, but seeing you changed that. I am the luckiest person in this world, Ms. Sanaya Iyer, to call you by that name, as today is the last day you will carry that surname. From tomorrow, you are Mrs. Sanaya Sidesh Sharma... mine, mine to love, mine to cherish. You are the love of my life, Sana..." He said with a grin, walking towards her. He then asked, "Will I have the honor of dancing with you?" with a grin and a twinkle in his eyes, extending his palm.

She didn't even think twice; she just placed her palms in his. Everyone around them was arrested by the scene they were witnessing, a pure bliss. The song played...

Pehli Nazar Mein

Kaise Jaado Kar Diya

Tera Ban Baita Hai Mera Jiya

Jaane Kya Hoga Kya Hoga Kya Pata

Is Pal Ko Milke Aa Jee Le Zara

Mein Hoon Yahan Tu Hai Yahan

Meri Bahon Mein Aa

Aa Bhi Ja O Jaan-E-Jaan

Dono Jahan Meri Bahon Mein Aa

Bhool Ja Aa

They swayed together to this song when Sana took the mic from him...

"I was, nonetheless, Sid. I had butterflies in my stomach the first time I saw you, and I was mesmerized by your personality. When you said my name for the first time with your sweet, heavy voice, my heart skipped a beat. At this young age, you achieved such a great position. How beautifully you handled your family and responsibility, sacrificing your dreams and passion. I had immense respect and admiration for you. I had always been reluctant towards the concept of love, due to our culture and beliefs. But my heart couldn't stop loving you, falling for you... it was instant... just like you. I am delighted to be named Mrs. Sanaya Sidesh Sharma; just like I am yours, you are mine. When I follow my heart, it leads to you... You are that person who entered my life out of nowhere, and suddenly, you are my world."

She held his hand and asked Payal Di to play the song...

Preet ki lath mohe aaisi laagi

Ho gayi main matwaali

Bal bal jaaun apane piya ko

He main jaaun vaari vaari

Mohe sudh budh naa rahi tan mann ki

Yeh toh jaane duniya saari

Bebas aur laachar phiru main

Haari main dil haari tere naam se jee loon

Tere naam se marr jaaun

Teri jaan ke sadke mein kuchh aaisa kar jaaun

Tune kya kar dala marr gayi main mitt gayi main

Ho ri ha ri ho gayi main

Teri deewani deewani

Tune kya kar dala marr gayi main mitt gayi main

Ho gee ha gee ho gayi main

Teri deewani deewani

Both of them swayed to the number in each other's arms, making everyone enchanted...

The next day morning, rituals started in Tamil tradition early at 5 AM... The muhurat time for their wedding was at 10:00-11:30 AM. So, they had to start everything early, as the Vedic customs in Tamil tradition are elaborate with a lot of rituals. Sid was ready to face the day, though he was uncomfortable with the attire he was wearing for the wedding. It was the traditional costume that a groom had to wear, and Appa came to help him wear it.

Sana was not spared either... she was uncomfortable wearing the 9-yard saree. She looked like a beautiful bride, and when both of them stood together after various rituals like Vratham (Fasting) and Unjal (Swing ritual), changing numerous attires, everyone was stunned by how beautiful a couple they made.

A professional photographer was taking pictures of them with all the attires and rituals. Sid and Sana were both avid and enthusiastic, but nothing was registering in their minds. They just followed what was told, like robots, as everything was new to them. Especially for Sid, who kept Guru with him all the time, translating and helping him follow what the priest was asking him to do.

Finally, it was muhurat time, and the proper wedding started. Soon, Sana was asked to sit in her father's lap for Kanyadhan, and he gave her hand to Sid, who tied the Mangal Sutra (or Thali in Tamil). After that, Sid was asked to hold Sana's hand for the seven pheras around the fire. With Vedic mantras being chanted, both of them had tears welling up as they performed the rituals. They were finally tied in a holy marriage according to Tamil tradition.

It was just half the day completed, but everyone was tired... still, a long day was left to complete their bond. The North-style marriage was waiting for them, arranged by Sid in Ghaziabad at a banquet hall. After lunch and changing into comfortable clothes, everyone headed toward that. Sana was with Sid in his car, with a driver driving this time. They both, holding hands, slept on each other's shoulders harmoniously, taking whatever rest they could before another eventful evening.

Chapter Forty-Nine:
From Slumber To Celebration

Sana and Sid were in deep slumber in the car when they reached his house. The driver called them thrice, but both of them didn't move a limb to his calls. He even honked the car to catch their attention, but they just flinched, moved closer to each other, and dozed off again. He finally walked out to call the crowd who was waiting at the entrance for the Griha Pravesh (Homecoming ceremony) of the newly married couple.

Maa opened the door and had a smile on her face when she saw the adorable, sleeping son and daughter-in-law. She called Kajal and asked her to click a photo of them in that posture to show them later what they did on their Griha Pravesh day. Kajal did as told, laughing, and shook Sana and Sid, calling them as loudly as she could, "Sid... Sana... Utooo..." They finally woke up. Sana, embarrassed, parted from Sid instantly when she saw a crowd of his relatives laughing and making fun of them.

"Aaoo tum dono bahar... andar jaa ke so jana thodi der," Maa said, smiling and giggling.

Sid looked like a South Indian groom, dashing like a hero, with a traditional Vesthi (Lungi) and Silk shirt, and Sana was wearing a cream-colored Kerala silk saree with a gold border, gifted by her eldest Mama and Mami who had come from Kerala to attend the marriage. Sana looked gorgeous, with Vermillion and maang tikka in her parted braided hair, Jasmine flowers around it, a red bindi, and her yellow Tamil-style Mangalsutra thread (called Thali) visible outside with her other jewelry. She was looking magnificently gorgeous even with sleepy, smudged kohl eyes and frazzled hair.

At the threshold, Maa took their aarthi and applied tikka, and both of them stood with big smiles and water-filled eyes. Sana and

Sid bent down to take her blessings. "Khush raho dono... Sana, you have been in this house before, but today, with this Griha Pravesh, we welcome you from the bottom of our hearts and accept you as an integral part of our family."

Sana hugged her tightly and said, "Thank you, Maa."

"Aaja bacha, you have to push this Kalash now; it is filled with rice from your right leg. This symbolizes you are letting in prosperity, wealth, and good luck within the household. Tu ab hamare ghar ki Lakshmi hain," Maa said, to which Sana looked at Sid, who was so proud of his mom and Sana. She toppled it with her right foot while entering the home. She was also asked to enter the home using her right leg first, as it is considered propitious. Both Sana and Sid entered together, holding hands. Then Maa asked her to dip her feet in water containing vermillion powder. This way, she would leave behind auspicious red footprints across the home as she walked, signifying the Goddess of Wealth and Prosperity. Sid held her hand, gripping it tightly all the while.

"Sana, the beautician will come to dress you up around 4pm, and you will go to the banquet hall with her. You have 1 hour for that. If you want, you can sleep for a while in Kajal's room," Maa said, seeing how tired she looked when everyone surrounded her in the living room, chit-chatting with her.

"Kajal ke room main kyun? Mere kamare main soyegi na!" Sid voiced out loud to bring laughter around the room, making Sana blush shyly.

"Abhi nahi aa sakthi tere kamre main.. Aaj raat ho jaane de.. there are some norms we have to follow, beta," Mom said, taking him with her to his room, so as not to create more embarrassment for Sana.

"Ab kya norms hain. Shaadi toh ho gayi na.. haan, I know one more shaadi is there.. but even then.. yeh kya baat huyi. Not done, Maa.." Sid complained, sitting down on his bed where all the kids of the family were also sitting and messing up the room, jumping on the bed, making him lose his patience. "All of you out.. now. I want this room empty in 5 minutes," he yelled at the naughty kids.

"Ab gussa mat kar Sid.. bache hain.. tu thodi der let ja.. you look tired too.. I will get you chai and something to eat after a while.. Bachoo.. chalo, bhaiya ko thodi der rest karne do.." Mom instructed all the kids and closed his room door for some privacy.

**

Sana had already reached the banquet hall where the beauticians were making her get ready for the night ceremony. Sid's friends and cousins were on their toes, making sure everything was taken care of, and they went back to get ready for the Baarat. The hall was huge and decorated beautifully, making the ambiance rich and elegant.

Sana's parents and their relatives were in awe seeing the arrangements. The difference was quite evident to all of them, from their simple arrangement at the temple in the morning compared to the grandeur of the arrangements here. He felt a little subdued and asked his wife, "Seetha, humne koi kami toh nahi ki, This looks so grand! Humara arrangement comparatively bahut simple tha na.." he said with a sullen face.

Amma agreed, but she did not want to say that aloud to her husband's already low self-esteem mind, "Humara arrangement was very good, Guru ke appa. Compare ki toh baat hi nahi hain.. this is a reception-type function na, so grand-type feel dene ke liye Sid ne kiya hain, and also uske clients and office colleagues aa rahe hain.. don't forget he is a VP of the company, he has a status and reputation. Aap beekar hi soch rahe hain.. Just be happy that hamari beti kitne ache family mein shaadi kar ke jaa rahi hain. She will live like a queen with him.."

"Haan toh, she lived like a princess with us as well.." he snapped back. "I still cannot believe my small little daughter is married! Abhi bhi woh bachi hi toh hain! Kaise handle karegi family and its responsibilities?" he asked.

"Kar legi.. sab seekh jaate hain.. Meri shaadi 18 saal main hui thi aap ke saath.. Kara na achhe se manage sab.. ho jaata hain.. we women naturally hone those skills.. and thank God, she is so close to us.. I will guide her in each step, and Priya behen is like her second mother.. she is so lucky.. warna aap kahan usse Dubai bhej rahe the, imagine!" she said, instantly regretting what she had said in the end.

His face dropped listening to her words; it pinched his heart. It was not a Herculean task for him to convince his mother and his brother. Though they were against it, with his conviction, he was able to change their thoughts. A limiting belief is a state of mind, conviction, or belief that you think to be true that limits you in some way. This limiting belief could be about you, your interactions with other people, or with the world and how it works, the culture, the religion. Those beliefs can have a number of negative effects on oneself, and he very well understood that now, experiencing it firsthand. They could keep you from making good choices. When he thought about Sana and the choice of the boy she made, his heart crippled with fear. Ultimately, limiting beliefs can keep you stuck in a negative state of mind and hinder you from living the life you truly desire.

He looked at his mother and brother and his family, everyone mingling with Sid's family, relatives, and friends, talking and sharing food. He felt as if he had instilled some positive affirmations in them. The world is full of beliefs, and as long as there are different kinds of people, this won't change. However, you've got to figure out which beliefs help you live the life you've always dreamed of. All of the beliefs that keep you from living that life are limiting and ones that you should get rid of. By doing so, you give yourself a chance to create a life that supersedes your expectations.

Growing up as parents, they likely had morals and values instilled in them. He tried to do the same with his kids. These often stemmed from their own familial beliefs and ideas about how both you and your own family should be. It could be things such as what career paths you should take, how to behave, and how to engage with others, whom to choose as a life partner. You can end up forming your own limiting beliefs based on the beliefs they instilled in you. He felt proud of his daughter at that time, the part of his heart that was able to break his limiting belief of religion, culture, and societal norms and embrace looking at the person instead.

He was proud that Sana had chosen a better half like Sid, who treated his family like his own, adapted to the rituals and procedures so gracefully, without cribbing or showing any tantrums, no demand, no hesitation from him. The respect he had for Sid grew tenfold, and the way he adjusted to Vedas, attire, rituals, and food... not only him but his entire family just adopted and accepted their culture without any distortions or prejudice.

He decided not to get any complex, instead demonstrating his respect and happiness for the rest of the day for his daughter and his son Sid... yes, son... not son-in-law... he had taken that place in his heart for the last 3 months. They could hear the Baarat music, and everyone got ready for the welcome. Everyone came in, dancing to the rhythm of the music. Abhi was sitting with Sid on the horse, whose face was covered with the Shehra, a flower blanket. Sid lifted it up from his face and waved at Appa from there, somehow sensing that he was looking at him. They completed the entrance ritual, all of them enjoying it. It was something new for Sana's parents, but they were having so much fun with jokes and teasing. Completely different from the morning atmosphere, which was more serious with Vedic rituals. Again, no comparison, but it felt different and nice to Sana's parents. It was an experience they would cherish for a lifetime and talk about every time.

It was time for the Varmala ceremony; Sid was waiting on the wedding stage, looking dapper, in cream golden shimmery wedding Sherwani and Shehra in his head, cleanly shaved and standing stately for his bride. She came in dazzling, exquisite in her maroon authentic lehenga, which Maa and Kajal chose from Lucknow when she went for her Kanpur visit (See the title Photo for an idea). Sid gave his hand to her, and she immediately held it to step up on the stage, with a smiling face when she saw his eyes giving her an impressive look.

Pandit asked them to exchange Jai Mala (flower garland) over each other's necks. This exchange depicts that they have both accepted each other as partners and are joined together for the wedding. Apart from being a traditionally significant ritual, Jai Mala is that zealous moment when even the shyest of brides burst into laughter. The families, too, joined to make it merrier. They lifted Sid and Sana high in the air so that one could prolong and beat the other in their attempts to put Jai Mala in each other's neck. Sure, hearty moments that made each and every guest in awe! They did very similar to this morning as well in *Unjal* (Swing ceremony) Tamil tradition way, even in that they were lifted by their respective Mama's or uncles.

After the Varmala session, both Sid and Sana were given photographs of all the guests and families. Sid introduced Sana as his wife to all his office clients, his colleagues, and friends. After that, they were asked to take a seat at the mandap to commence the wedding ceremony. The mandap space was filled with their immediate family members, Sid and Sana, who were holding each other's hands, and sat with the priest next to them near Agni Kund (Sacred fire), conducting the marriage ceremony. Both Amma and Appa, with Sid's mom, sat next to them.

All the rituals were done in front of the sacred fire Vedic hymns recited by the priest. The main wedding rituals performed at the mandap include Kanyadaan, Saat Phere, Maang Bharai, and Mangalsutra.

Everyone who was there for both the morning Tamil tradition marriage and North Hindu marriage was astonished to see how familiar both traditions matched in terms of basic rules. Overall, the culture of a Hindu wedding is not only beautiful and lively but also exhilarating. It's wonderful that so much time and detail go into making a couple of such a wedding feel supported and loved every step of the way. While the support and love for the couple during their special day can be seen across multiple cultures - there is just something about the way families come together.

Everyone had tears in the end; Amma went and hugged Maa, overwhelmed with happiness and emotions. **13th December** is a date to remember for everyone who attended Sid and Sana's wedding and experienced something so beautiful and special, a day that will not be easily forgotten...

Chapter Fifty:
Serenade of Souls

All tired and exhausted, they reached home by 4 a.m. in the morning. Sana and Sid were sent to their room, and Mom asked them to take a rest. When they entered the room, they were mesmerized to see the decorations around their bed. Roses and jasmines surrounded it, making the place aromatic and beautiful. Both of them smiled upon seeing the room and sat on the bed.

"It's so pretty..." Sana said, taking the rose petals and smelling them.

"Not more than you..." Sid said, kissing her alluring lips. After a while, Sana parted and said, "I am tired... let's sleep for a while!"

"Me too, yaar... you change and sleep for some time. Chai peeyegi?" Sid asked.

"Nahi... I am feeling heavy! I will first change this lehenga. Can you please help me bring that red suitcase? I have my clothes in that, and I'll change into them first," she requested.

"Hmm..." Sid went and got her red suitcase, laid it on the floor, and opened it for her. "Kya pehenegi?"

"Let me see..." She came and took out her pink kurta, white pajama, and dupatta from the lot. It was her favorite comfortable dress.

"Wear a night dress, na," Sid said, looking at the dress she took out from the suitcase.

"Yeh ghar ke kapde hi hain, Sid. Abhi yeh pehen leti huin. We still have your relatives and guests at home, so it wouldn't look good... at least yeh Indian wear hain and you know how comfortable

I am in these... so don't worry. Now please help me with removing these clips from my hair... if you don't mind... nahin toh Kajal di ko bula do, please," she asked him, getting irritated with the heavy makeup, lchcnga, and hairstyle.

"Kajal kyun be... Tera pati karega na tera saara kaam... chal bhet." He gestured for her to sit in the chair near the mirror dresser and took out the hair clips from her bun and the dupatta covering her head.

"You are looking so beautiful, Sana..." Sid said in a husky tone, looking at her in the mirror. Sana smiled, blushing, and bent her head down. He took out her maang tikka, opened her hair straight down, and helped her take the jewelry off—her necklace, earrings, nose ring, and bracelets—leaving just her two mangalsutras: one Tamil Nadu style in a yellow thread and one in black beads. Both were entangled together in her deep neck, showing most of her upper body. She did not feel any hesitation when he was staring at her bare parts. She knew how appreciative he was, his eyes displaying admiration, not judging her clothes or her nakedness.

"You know how captivating you look with this Mangalsutra, sindoor, bindi... I can't even put it into words, Sana... you are making me crazy for you." Sid, sitting on the floor on his knees, cupped her face and kissed her again. Kissing her forehead, eyes, nose, jawline, neck, and cleavage, he said, "I want to worship you with my love. I still can't believe we are married, and you are in my arms, all decked up like a bride—enchanting!"

Sana, closing her eyes, was just absorbing all the love Sid was giving her. Her eyes welled up with gratitude and happiness, and tears rolled down her cheeks. "I love you, Sid. Sachi, main humesha school mein ya college mein ya kahin par bhi ladko se dur rehti thi. Appa used to say that I am his pride and prestige. I never wanted to break his trust, but pata nahi kahan se tum aa gaye ek din aur mera saara control chala gaya. As if my soul recognized you, and like a magnet, I was falling for you. Bahut kam logo ko naseeb hota hai yeh fulfillment. I am so thankful that I got my soulmate, who adores me and wants to worship me... I don't know if I even deserve that admiration, but I promise you, till my last breath, I will love you and care for you. I will make myself worthy for you!" she hugged him tight, still sitting in the chair, with her hands full of dark henna, open hair, and lehenga.

Sid got up and took her in his arms bridal-style and went toward the bed. The room was dim, with very low morning light coming from the window curtains and a low-watt yellow dresser lamp. They consummated their marriage; though it was not the first, it was the second time they were this close, and it was nothing but blissful—a euphoric dance of souls. Bodies guiding them toward freedom, the brightness, the stars—both experiencing a trance, lost in a conscious state but like meditation, bringing them back to the now and heightening their inner and outer senses.

Her changing dress lay on the dresser, with her jewelry and other clothes on the floor. His clothes, which covered his body a while ago, lay on the floor, too, mixed with hers. The open suitcase, flowers scattered all over the place... both of them slept peacefully in each other's arms, exhausted physically.

When one has a soulmate as a partner, you see yourself as a source of love and therefore don't need to extract love from your beloved. They realized that love is not an emotion but a state of vibrational harmonization. They consciously embodied a state of love and projected these frequencies toward each other. Sana had transcended the belief that she lacked love and that she needed Sid to love her in order to feel worthy. She was already in a blissful state, a partner worshipping her mind and body.

Sid, on the other hand, realized that as a co-creator of reality, he also got to co-create his relationship. His projections, beliefs, and expectations toward her could have a profound influence on both his and her state of being. For this reason, Sana constantly envisioned him in his highest state of being.

As their journey went through the inevitable challenges—beliefs, customs, traditions, religion, caste—they always reminded each other of their essence. They didn't confuse each other's personalities, archetypes, or identities with who they were. This relationship was not based on personality compatibility but rather on soul compatibility. They were ONE, soulmates, interdependent, and connected to each other.

They found the love of their life. No matter what time they are together, with ups and downs, they will embrace them, fulfilling each other's needs for self-growth and contribution. Thankful and grateful for evolving as individuals, healing the pain, and enjoying the happiness together, they would embody a state of vibrational harmonization where they continued to accrete more light into their lives. Being on the same journey, they get to share all realizations and insights with each other.

Epilogue

"Sid, I think we should buy a house here... we can settle here after our retirement! What say?" Sana said, all excited, lying on the bed, actually more on Sid's chest, looking out from the window and admiring the Himalayan ranges in Jammu and Kashmir.

"Don't you think you're obsessed with this place? I mean, in our 15 years of marriage, we've come to this place at least 15 times, like every year tere ko yahan ke darshan karne hain!! Honeymoon destination, hamara family destination place bann gaya hain. Ab bacho ko bhi yahan ka chaska lag gaya hain!" Sid frowned, saying it, knitting his eyebrows. It was not that he did not like it; any place with his Sana was heaven, but her love for the mountains was too much for him to take.

"Haan toh acha hain na, our family getaway place... agar koi hum main se kumbh ke mele main gum gaya toh we will say that meet in our getaway location and will unite with the family... wah, kya baat boli tune Sana... you are a genius!!" patting her shoulders, she said to herself with an animated, proud face and smile.

"Wah, kya baat boli... Kumbh ke mele mein gum jaye toh Kashmir mein milo... wah... tere jaise toh smart koi paida hi nahi hua!" Sid said sarcastically, mocking her idea.

"Kya hain Sid... ab tum majak mat banao na... I am serious... we should get a nice home here and live here when Anjali and Aditya are on their own in life. Maa ko bhi yahan kitna acha lagta hain... it will be our old age resort! Please, na baba!" she pleaded, pulling his cheeks and shaking his head left to right, holding it.

"Aaahhh... chhod... gal kyun keech rahi hain re be!! Dard ho raha hain... Haan haan, we will buy it... ab madam ne bola hain aur wish pura na kare, itni himmat nahi hain mujhe!" he said, hugging her tight and rolling her over for a scorching kiss.

They parted when they heard a knock on their bedroom door. They made themselves presentable in a hurry.

"Papa... Mumma... open the door..." Anjali, their 14-year-old, was shouting at the top of her voice. She was an unplanned and surprised child. Sana got pregnant in February, just after 2 months of their marriage, and before their first wedding anniversary, Anjali was in their arms in November. Everyone calls her a Valentine's baby! The best gift Sana had from Sid is what she said to him, a part of their love in living form in their arms. Though they never planned for the second one, Aditya, immediately after 2 years, Sid and Sana welcomed them with open hearts and love.

They were actually thankful that they had kids in the early part of their age and marriage. It made their bond so strong, and now, at 50 years old and her 37 years old, they are almost free of early childhood responsibilities. Anjali, the name given by Seetha Amma, and Aditya, the name given by Priya Maa, were the apple of their eyes, not only for them but for the whole family.

"Kya hua mere Bebu ko, itna kyun chilla rahi hain?" Sana asked, opening the door and rolling her long mane into a bun.

Anjali hugged her and said, "Mumma... bhook lagi hain... and I am also getting bored... Papa, yaar, aap yahan bhi sone aaye ho? Get up, and let's go hiking, na.." She walked towards Sid, who was lazing in the bed, diagonally face down on the pillow.

"Best of luck to you, main ek gante se try kar rahi huin. Let's see if you are able to pull him out of this bed. I am going to take a bath," with this, Sana went towards the restroom with a towel and clothes for taking a shower.

"Upar chal na... Bebu.." Sid requested Anjali with her nickname, and she immediately stood on his back and started to walk above him, giving him a back massage, chatting non-stop just like her mother. She looked exactly like a replica of Sana, and Aditya was a twin copy of Sid!

"Papa, aap ne aisa kya kiya hain jo aapko jab dekho body pain hota hain? Chalo uttho, we will go down for breakfast... I hope aaj Aunty ne kuch yummy banaya ho." Anjali got down from Sid's back and pulled him up. Now, only he knew why he was having that pain! All night burning the calories copulating with never-ending desires... Like Sana says, "40 is naughty, but 50 is nasty,"... and he actually was able to relate to that!

"Teri Amma ko aa jane de bathroom se, meri Mata... I will take a shower and come down. Jaa Adi ko le jaa na, I will call Dadi till then," Sid said, picking up his phone and dialing his mom's number.

"Mereko bhi baat karni hain Dadi se, video call karo," Anjali said, sitting down on her knees on the bed behind Sid, hugging him over his shoulder.

"Maa, how are you? Enjoying with Kajal?" Sid asked as his mom, who was in Kanpur with Kajal.

"Haan bilkul, I am having a fun time with her, but I am missing Kashmir so much! I wish I was also there with you guys," smiling with glorified wrinkles and pure white hair, she said, looking so beautiful.

"Hooo Dadi, missing Kashmir? What about me? You are not missing me? Your partner?" frowning, Anjali asked. She was Dadi's pet, her spoiled brat!

"Obviously! I am missing everyone, Baba! Tum log wahan ho isiliye woh jagah itni khaas hain! Hiking nahi gaye abhi tak?" she asked.

"Maa, ab aap mat shuru ho jaana... Kal hi toh aaye hain yaar... We will be here for a week! Subah se pareshan kar diya hain sabne... Vacation hain, we need to rest, sleep, eat, and then rest again..." Before he could complete it, Anjali interrupted...

"Haan jo aap har roj Ghaziabad mein apne ghar mein karte ho... Kya hain Pa? This is not done... We just have 6 days and so many places to cover..." Before she could complete it, now Sid interrupted... "Which you have been and seen so many times!! Aaj rest karte hain Bebu... We will go tomorrow for hiking, I promise..." He literally pleaded with his daughter, lying down again in bed.

Sana came out of the bathroom with a hair towel tied into a bun and wearing gray joggers and a pink hoodie. "Anjali, we will go tomorrow, let Papa rest today. He is very tired, understand... Zidd nahi karte na... We will make some plans... Let's go to the local market, do some shopping, and buy some souvenirs and gifts for everyone... What say?"

"Okay!" Shrugging her shoulders and a bit disappointed, Anjali gave the phone to Sid and went towards the door to go out when Sana stopped her, holding her hand. "Adi ko bhi utha de Bebu... I will go down and see what Aunty has made for breakfast... Okay... Aur aise udaas nahi hote... especially when you are in Paradise on Earth... Aaja, ek huggy aur kissy de apni Mumma ko..." she asked, kissing her daughter in return for her kiss. "Love you, Bebu..."

"Love you too, Mumma," happy and jumping, Anjali left towards Aditya's room to wake him up.

They were in a guest house, which was their permanent place to stay since they visited Kashmir for their honeymoon, and they would almost come every year during Christmas time, in the snow, go hiking, make snowman, camp, and watch stars, and the Northern lights. It had become their family tradition. Though they had been to several places to tour and visit, this place held a special part in their heart. A spot that gives them solace!

All four seated at the dining table were having breakfast made by Aunty, who was the caretaker of the beautiful single-family guesthouse. Her family lived there, taking care of visitors who visited the place year-round.

"Adi, beta, khana khao na bache... give that phone to me!" Sana said, snatching the phone from her son's hand, who was a car game addict.

"Kya hain Mumma? I was about to finish that lap! Papa, ask her to give me the phone... I am not gonna eat without finishing that lap," Aditya cribbed. He was still a 12-year-old child, crazy for cars, and wanted to be a Formula 1 player.

"Give it back, Sana, let him complete, and then he can enjoy the food... You know one doesn't get peace when you stop the game in between. Right, champ!" Sid, who looked like Hulk, had a melting heart towards his kids. He was the most lenient, funny, understanding, and pampering father any kid could have. He would spoil them to the next level, and Sana was totally different, just his opposite, balancing parenthood. She was strict and would discipline them all the time, which Sid once said she got from her father... her Appa, who did the same with her in her early days and still does with his grandchildren. He appreciated that in her and was thankful that she took that control, which he never could do! But she had the heart of a mother and had her limitations; she would understand what Sid wanted to make her understand and would always melt when she saw both her kids' faces.

She gave the phone back to Adi and asked Sid, "Maa kya keh rahi thi? She is good, na? Enjoying with Di?"

"Ya, she is good... Appa Amma ko call karna..." Sid suggested.

"Hmm... after this... Bebu, you get dressed, we will go out in an hour," Sana said.

"Where are you guys going without me? I will also come..." Adi said in between his games.

"Maa ka chamcha... No, you will stay here with Papa and your game... it's just a girls' day out... no boys allowed," Anjali said, gulping down her food.

"Aise nahi bolte, Bebu... you also come with us, my Shona baby..." Sana said, kissing Aditya's cheek and hugging him, feeding him the food while he happily ate it, playing the game on his mobile.

It was almost dusk to dawn and bedtime for the kids. Sana was on her laptop, busy completing some office work. She was the HR head of a big hospital in Noida. She completed her MBA in HR and worked hard in her career, handling kids and home, managing work-life balance, of course, with the help of Maa and Sid, who supported her in all walks of life.

Sid had his own consulting firm now, and he was the most content he had ever been in any other work! He had his office set up in Ghaziabad itself and was king of his own company. He was very successful in a few years, and his company received a lot of accolades.

They sometimes missed their car drives, but whenever they got time, they sneaked in to go for a long drive. Though Sana drove the car to her workplace, most of the time, Sid was the one who would still do the driving and had their car time like they used to in the past.

"Moti, Appa se baat kari? Phone de, let me talk to him and ask about IPL," with that, he got busy talking to Appa. He was retired and enjoyed his retirement life with Amma. He loved to travel and had almost visited all temples around India, and would take Sid's mom as well with them. Guru was also settled in an arranged marriage with Devi, a simple girl from Tamil Nadu, who was a teacher by profession and lived in Ghaziabad with Appa & Amma. They also had cute 8-year-old twin daughters who kept everyone on their toes.

Aditya and Anjali came in with their usual banter, "Papa dekho na yeh Stupid Anjali ko!" Adi complained about his sister.

"Adi... what is this? Why are you saying bad words?" Appa yelled from the phone. He was on a video call with Sid and Sana.

"Nana Thatha (Tamil word for grandfather), see na, Anjali is not allowing me to play the game," pouting, he complained to his grandfather.

"So what? Will you use bad words? Say sorry to her, and dare you say any abusive words like this; I will not tolerate it," Appa said in a very strict, heavily accented voice.

Anjali, showing her tongue out and giving a thumbs up, teased Aditya to get scolding from their Nana Thatha, who was rigid, while Nani Pati (Tamil word for grandmother) was just the opposite, pampering them to no end and always feeding them with authentic sweets and food items.

After the phone call, all four of them were lying in bed. Anjali was in Sid's arm, and Aditya was in Sana's arm, discussing tomorrow's plan for hiking and camping—when they should start and what all to pack. It was snowing hard outside, and both kids were ready to make a snowman while in camp. They loved to ski in the snow and were planning to do that as well.

As a family, they may be loud, sometimes crazy, big and introspective, totally conventional and completely unorthodox, but their family was the one that made up a huge part of who they were. With family playing such a major role in their identities, it's no wonder that Sid and Sana celebrated their life and were observant luminaries who had such amazing insights into what it means to be a family. Family is a blessing, and the love they had for each other gave them strength. They accepted each other's customs and beliefs. Religion almost invariably teaches acceptance and loving-kindness towards others.

Appa wished to have the sacred thread Janeu function for Aditya when he turned 11, and Sid happily agreed to it, understanding his wants and accepting his beliefs. In the same way, Sana adjusted to all the North Indian customs and traditions which were new to her, very gracefully. Love, just as religion, asks us to accept each person's choice and to resist the notion of imposing our view on others. Since both religious and secular paths can lead to a respectful, loving attitude toward others, the purpose of peaceful coexistence can be served through either approach—as long as we truly apply it.

The End

Acknowledgment

The following songs are mentioned in the book:

Pal Pal dil ke paas -Blackmail (1973)

Ban ke titli – Chennai Express (2013)

Roop Ye tera – Sanjog (1971)

O Hansini – Zehreela Insaan (1974)

Pehli nazar main – Race (2008)

Bade ache lagte hain – Balika Badhu (1976)

Teri Deewani – Kailasha (album 2006)

Instagram.com/vstarlove7

Printed in Great Britain
by Amazon